IF I LOSE HER

BRIANNE SOMMERVILLE

Text copyright © 2023 by **Brianne Sommerville**

All rights reserved. For information regarding reproduction in total or in part, contact Rising Action Publishing Co. at http://www.risingactionpublishingco.com
Cover Illustration © **Nat Mack**
Distributed by **Blackstone Publishing**

ISBN: 978-1-990253-69-0
Ebook: 978-1-990253-65-2

FIC031080   FICTION / Thrillers / Psychological
FIC031100   FICTION / Thrillers / Domestic

#IfiLoseHer
Follow Rising Action on our socials!
Twitter: @RAPubCollective
Instagram: @risingactionpublishingco
Tiktok: @risingactionpublishingco

To my babies, Hannah, Ellie, and Calvin with all my heart

IF I LOSE HER

CHAPTER ONE

He's already made up his mind about me. The crisis counsellor scribbles his diagnosis at the top of his notebook, which he leaves open on the table for my eyes. *Postpartum depression,* the only explanation for a first-time mom leaving her four-month-old unattended in the backyard.

"I'm not convinced," I say. I fight the urge to correct his typo; he's split the word *postpartum* in two. "It doesn't make any sense. We didn't go outside all day—they issued a heat warning."

He says nothing.

"It's like someone is ... gaslighting me, or something," I mutter under my breath.

I imagine the neighborhood moms laughing over glasses of Cabernet, their sick way of welcoming me to the neighborhood.

The tapping of his pen brings me back to reality. There is still no response from the thirty-something glorified counsellor who has the task of analyzing my psychological state. He can't even prescribe me medication for his diagnosis.

Looking down at his notebook, he finally says, "I saw that play, *Gas Light*, when it came to Toronto. The husband tries to make his wife think she's crazy. Wants to send her away to an asylum instead of divorcing her."

This is the most he's said since I entered his "office" that doubles as a staff lunchroom during work hours. The fluorescent lighting is garish. I sit directly across from him at a round table trying to avoid touching the remnants of someone's salad. I adjust myself in the hard plastic chair, the kind that outnumbers students at every high school in North America. The late summer heat makes my legs stick to the bright orange seat every time I move, which I'm discovering is a lot.

He scratches his pen on the page until blue ink appears in an angry scribble. "*Gas Light*." He makes a note. It is unclear whether he plans to include this in his report or if he wants to see the revival.

I know his type. I've dealt with more than a few of these crisis counsellors before. Most of the time they just listen to you. Get you to resolve your issues on your own.

When I first arrived, he asked me if I wanted tea or coffee. I told him that as a nursing mom, I needed to avoid caffeine, and his beady eyes shot me a look of skepticism. Was I the nurturing mother who cut out caffeine, alcohol, and junk food to purify her milk, or rather, the woman who slept through her baby's cries all morning? The anonymous tip claimed Addison wailed for hours, but I can't believe that I slept that long.

He sips his coffee and I imagine the liquid mingling with his over-grown moustache hairs. "Why don't we start with your pregnancy, Mrs. Girard. Was it difficult?"

I consider correcting him—my name is still Joanna Baker. I haven't gotten around to changing my surname yet. I'm a feminist, yes, but I also have debilitating laziness when it comes to personal administrative tasks.

"Has any woman ever had an *easy* pregnancy?" I chuckle. It's a momentary lapse of judgement. I straighten in my chair. This is no laughing matter. "As far as pregnancies go, mine was relatively easy."

Sure, I'd felt nauseous throughout the first trimester, and my feet swelled during the third, but these are ailments one expects to endure while pregnant. I handled my emotions too, for the most part. A pleasant wife and mom-to-be. JP would agree on that, too.

"Has someone talked to my husband? I'm just not sure what usually happens when someone calls Child Services on one parent." I couldn't get a hold of JP before coming here. He had been in meetings all afternoon.

"He's up to speed on the situation. We'll talk about next steps once we wrap up our chat," he says. *Chat,* as though he's been equally contributing to the conversation. I am starting to feel like this man has lost his passion for this job.

"I had a fairly smooth pregnancy. No concerns; JP can attest," I say.

"Your husband mentioned an upcoming work trip. Does he travel a lot?"

"He's the vice president at an advertising agency. He visits the Montréal office frequently. His family is from there, so it's really his second home." I'm not sure if I'm trying to justify his travel to this counsellor or myself.

"Have you been having regular appointments with your doctor?" he asks. He checks number four off his list of questions. I narrow my eyes and silently count ten more until he interrupts me by clearing his throat.

"I had my six-week postpartum check-up a couple of months ago and everything was fine. Physically and mentally. You can call my OB-GYN to confirm." His silence pressures me to continue. "I'm in the process of finding a new doctor, though, because of the move." *The move*, a key event for his notes. A young couple packs up their glamorous lives in the city for the suburban high life filled with playdates and Costco shopping trips. The wife, abandoned with her newborn and her thoughts.

"And what about with your other doctor?" He checks his notes. "Doctor Lui, your therapist?"

"I haven't gone to Dr. Lui since college," I say. JP must have mentioned her when they called him. He's been trying to get me to see her since I got the baby blues after Addison's birth.

"Okay, so nothing that stood out in your pregnancy, then?"

"Nothing."

The light flickers above us, and I squint, adjusting my eyes. My only negative feeling during the pregnancy happened early on, but I refuse to mention it to this counsellor. I had been reading a novel about a high school shooting and had to put it away by the second trimester, not because I was afraid my baby might be a victim in a school shooting, but because I was worried that my baby would grow up to be the shooter, that I could have a negative impact so profound on my child.

"Why don't you tell me about your birth experience," he says, still focusing his eyes on his notebook.

I'd rather not go into detail about my birth experience with a man. Would he like me to begin with my second-degree perineal laceration? I pick at the side of my thumb and scan the room for something familiar, comforting, but all I see is a sad plant that hasn't been watered in days and a faded fire evacuation plan. Looks like my nearest exit is the window behind me.

I tell him about the code pink—baby in distress—and that Addison spent her first days on Earth in the neonatal intensive care unit due to a slow heart rate. I don't tell him about my fears during our separation. While Addison tackled those early days on her own, anxiety was my constant companion. I worried she would find it hard to trust me after her abandonment. As a woman who never got along with her own mother, my concern for my future relationship with my daughter had been almost as worrisome to me as her health.

"You all right, there?" he asks, referring to my thumb, which I've picked raw and is now bleeding.

"I'm fine." I wipe my thumb on my maternity jean shorts that I thought would be packed up in a box by four months postpartum.

"We're almost done here." He licks the tip of his ballpoint pen and doodles some more in his notebook. "It sounds like the last few months have been quite eventful. Moving cities, a new baby. How do you normally respond to change?"

If I'm honest, we could be here for a while. I chew on the inside of my lip. This sounds like a job interview. I answer correctly and I get to be Addison's mother. I'm not sure I want to know what answering wrong will mean.

"How have you responded to change in the past?" he presses.

"Listen, Mr. ...." I have completely forgotten his name.

"Just call me Herb," he says.

"Herb, right. Mommy brain." It makes me physically cringe. I told myself I would never be one of those women who become flighty after they have a baby, and who use that horrible phrase. "I'm as confused as much as anyone about this. Would you mind bringing me up to speed on the complaint? Who called it in? What exactly do you mean by next steps?" My left breast throbs as it swells. "I have to get home to feed Addison." I adjust my bra strap to drill in my point.

Herb presents a flow chart; a masochistic choose-your-own-adventure. It begins with a complaint. Likely from one of my neighbors who heard Addy crying outside. Then the organization decides whether the complaint warrants an investigation. In my case, it does.

I bury my face in my hands. I'm running on four hours of sleep and my breast has started to leak, my milk pooling in my bra. Herb wraps up his list of questions, avoiding eye contact, and advises that someone will be stopping by the house unannounced in the upcoming week.

I will have to start changing out of my pajamas.

Rain cascades down the windshield, offering hope that the sticky heat we've experienced throughout September will make way for autumn. I let the heavy drops fill the entire windshield before turning the wipers on.

After about ten minutes of stop-and-go driving, I turn right onto the rural road that takes me along the Oak Ridges Moraine—nearly one hundred miles of protected green that spans from the Niagara escarpment east to Trent River. Its rolling hills and forests are being suffocated on the north and south by expanding urban development.

This untouched green drew me to our town, but the urban amenities convinced JP to move here. Best of both worlds, really. Our house is a five-minute walk from a plaza with a grocery store, hair salon, and doctor's office. It's also down the street from a dairy farm. We've only had buyer's remorse on sweltering days when the smell of manure from the farm fills the air.

The road is empty, so I increase my speed to twenty over the maximum. I've yet to see a traffic cop doing radar on this stretch of the highway and can't wait any longer to see Addison. When I arrive, I'll need to feed her and put her to bed. I'm trying to stick to a consistent sleep schedule.

I'll also have to face JP and explain that I have no idea how Addy ended up outside. I have no recollection of the time after I put her in her bassinet for her nap and decided to take one myself. If it wasn't for my sister Amy's phone call, I might not have woken up when I did.

I turn up the radio in hopes that Michael Bublé's crooning will drown out my thoughts, but the song ends, and "Hungry like the Wolf" takes over. My wiper blades match the tempo of the bass, and my mind goes to a dark place. I think of Diane Downs, the mother who shot and killed her daughter and left her other two kids in critical condition, all while the Duran Duran song played on her car radio. I guess I can thank my college intro-to-psychology course for that mental image.

This is ridiculous. I love Addison. I would never do anything to hurt her. Logistically, it makes no sense—how could I even move her bassinet while I was asleep? More importantly, why would I do something like that? The whole thing is absurd. When Addison cries, I'm the first to run to her side. That's how it's always been.

The first couple of months were hard. I barely felt like a human. Every mother must feel overwhelmed in the beginning. That experience was not unique to me, and I'm doing so much better now. There are times when I might do something without remembering—forget a load of laundry in the washer, leave the milk out on the counter—but I've never put Addison at risk. I grip the wheel harder and press down on the pedal, the speedometer rising along with my heart rate.

Of course, I found those early days on our own an adjustment: getting into the rhythm of the new sleep schedule, stressing about my milk coming in, worrying about Addison's weight gain. Bath time was my Everest. How would I get everything ready for the bath while also looking after her? I had to balance the changing pad on the bathroom counter so that it wouldn't fall into the sink. Then I would sponge bathe her with my free hand, all the while avoiding her umbilical cord stump, which couldn't get wet, which is precisely why I had to sponge bathe her instead of running a real bath—which, oh my god, was going to be even harder to do on my own.

Then there were the hallucinations that happened for the first few weeks after Addy's birth. But they were just dreams, weren't they? They only happened during the night between bursts of sleep. Every night I would dream I was nursing Addy in bed. I was sitting up, leaning back on my pillow, which was propped up against the headboard. She was in my arms, suckling, half-asleep. It all felt very real. Then I would wake up, and she wasn't in my arms. I had dropped her. She was suffocating under the duvet. I would wake JP in a panic, frantically feeling around us in bed, crying out, "I can't find her—she's somewhere under the covers!" He had to grab me by the shoulders, shake me back to reality, convince me that she was perfectly fine beside me in the bassinet. I moved into the guest room with Addy, so we wouldn't disturb JP, and we've been sleeping there ever since. The nightmares stopped shortly after—as soon as I got my sleep under control. Nothing too concerning. Sleep deprivation is real.

A train's whistle screams, overpowering the song that still mocks me on the radio and I realize how close I am to the tracks. I slam on the brakes and squeeze my eyes shut. The ground rumbles beneath me as the train races past. I open my eyes.

Oh, dear God, how could I have ignored the crossing sign screaming at me? How did I not notice its flashing red lights?

CHAPTER TWO

T he house in front of me is unrecognizable. I sit in the driveway, waiting for my heart rate to slow. I am still shaken up from my encounter with the train—what if I stopped two seconds too late? What if Addison had been in the car with me?

The rain continues to pelt against the windshield, streams of water distorting my view. Every light is on in the home, and it glows against the leaden sky.

Our house stands on the corner of a street of identical houses, new builds made to look like modern Italian villas with stone bases, tan stucco finishes, and wrought iron accents. In the spring, we leaned into the design by planting a slew of magenta and orange geraniums around the property. We'd even draped some along the Juliet balcony railing outside of Addy's window. I can't remember the last time I watered them, and it shows. Their petals are muted and shriveled. At least tonight they are getting a good soaking.

I check my reflection in the sun visor mirror, hoping to see a woman who is put together—like one of the momma influencers who appear in my social feed. Instead, my mascara is smudged, and my eyes are puffy and bloodshot. The humidity has frizzed out my dark bob. I make a run for the porch, not bothering to shield myself from the storm.

When I enter the house, Addy's beautiful belly laugh erupts from down the hall. I remove my sandals and wipe my damp feet on the shoe mat before stepping onto the marble floor. I approach the open-concept kitchen with caution. JP is making faces as Addison swings in her chair in a pendulum motion; she reaches for his face every time she gets close.

I'm startled that my visceral reaction is jealousy. I'm *jealous* that my husband is making our daughter laugh. I think I'm just defeated and embarrassed that he had to clean up the mess from today's incident.

I hover beside the island as if this isn't my house or my family, then I clear my throat to announce my presence. "I'm so sorry. I have no clue what happened."

JP ignores my apology and unbuckles Addison from her seat. He approaches me with her held tight in his arms. "There's Mummy—I think she's ready for dinner." He doesn't meet my eyes.

"Yes. I'll go feed her right away." The tears flow freely now. "JP, I'm really sorry about everything."

JP hands Addison over, and in an over-the-top baby voice says, "That's okay, Mummy." Switching to his regular tenor he adds, "Let's not cry in front of Addy. We'll talk it out once she's asleep."

As I head upstairs with my daughter, JP's cell phone rings. It's likely my mother-in-law, Margot, calling to check in. JP would have told her by now, the doting son he is. I wonder how many people are privy to our situation. Margot has never been one to keep things to herself.

I feel complete holding Addison close as we rock slowly in the nursing chair. She is starving and tries to latch a few times before I have a chance to expose my nipple. I admire her delicate features, the peach fuzz on the top of her round head. Her blue eyes meet mine occasionally before darting back down to concentrate on suckling.

She strokes my breast affectionately with her top hand. With the bottom hand, she continues with a less endearing habit she recently acquired. She grabs the back of my arms, scratching and pinching with all her might, frustrated by her hunger. She has no clue that she is hurting me and when I let out a whimper, she pulls off the breast, surprised. Normally I would loosen her grip, but tonight I don't. Tonight, I deserve it.

I close my eyes and let the pain in my arm take over, thinking about the high school habit that I carried throughout college. Dragging tweezers, scissors, or any sharp object nearby in a downward motion on my inner thigh, retracing until I finally drew blood. Whenever I lost control of my relationships or my weight, I would take pleasure in marking my perfect skin. It's been a while since these thoughts made their way to the front of my mind.

After about twenty minutes on the right breast, Addison is satisfied and flashes me a smile. It's amazing how children can forgive so easily. I wipe my tears with the back of my hand and return her smile.

"I love you, baby girl. You are my everything. How could they think I would do that to you?"

After five minutes of rocking, she falls asleep in my arms, something my eldest sister Meg always advised against. *Don't rock your baby to sleep, trust me.* She swears that it's the reason her son Coltrane wet the bed until the age of eight. I hardly see how they are related, but there's no point in arguing with her. Meg is the epitome of Super Mom, and she doesn't let anyone forget that.

I sway in the chair for another twenty minutes watching Addison sleep, partly because I love the little expressions she makes as she dreams—eyelids fluttering, brows furrowing, and an occasional smile. I can't bear to face JP downstairs.

The rain continues to fall, and a rush of water escapes the eavestrough. Addison's room grows darker, reminding me of my own fatigue. I rise slowly with her nestled in my arms, careful not to wake her. I creep across the room and notice her teddy bear—my old bear—in the crib. He looks like a baby with a blanket placed over him. He wasn't there earlier today. I've always kept him on the bookshelf.

JP must have been playing a game with Addison.

JOANNA'S BIRD

Seven years old

Jo didn't want to believe that a mother could abandon her baby. Then she found the stranded bird under the tree in their backyard.

The bird craned its neck, pink and wrinkled, and opened its beak wide so Jo could see deep down its throat. She wanted to scoop the bird up and whisper that everything was going to be okay, but it kept screeching. Jo didn't want to lie. The bird had only a few wet feathers covering its small body, making it a few days old. Its mother was nowhere in sight.

Amy dragged over a cinderblock and sat down to get a closer look. Their eldest sister Meg stood frozen by the swing set, grasping the candy-cane-striped pole.

Jo fled to get a snack for the bird. When she returned with a soda cracker, her sisters, in their matching corduroy dresses, had moved closer and were now huddled around the spot where it lay.

"It's hungry," Meg said, averting her eyes.

Jo approached with a small piece of cracker. She would be the hero. She tossed it towards the baby, but the cracker got caught in the bird's wing. Amy shrieked, which added to the frequency of the bird's cries.

The screen door swung open, and Mother plodded across the uncut lawn in her slippers. She was still dressed in her Sunday's best—other than her feet.

"Lunch is soon." She sighed. "What were you doing in the pantry?" Her blue eyes met Jo's with a look of irritation the girl recognized well.

Jo crouched towards the bird, hoping one of her older sisters would come to her defense. The snack wasn't for her. She was only trying to feed the hungry bird.

Mother hovered above them, her shadow looming larger than her small frame.

Jo reached towards the bird. She could fix this.

"Joanna, leave it alone." Mother grabbed Jo's arm. When Jo pulled away, tiny crescent moons fell in a pattern down her forearm where Mother's nails had dug in deep.

Jo wasn't going to hurt the bird.

The maple's leaves were just starting to bud, making it easy for Mother to spot the nest in the tree. "I think the mom knows the baby is here."

"Can we get a ladder and put it back?" Jo asked, rising on her tiptoes to get a view of the nest. Her arm was still throbbing, but she put on a brave face.

"Haven't you done enough? You probably broke its wing."

Jo's stomach twisted into familiar knots. Why did she keep making mistakes?

"I'm putting a can of soup on." Mother turned back to the house.

Jo wouldn't give up on the bird. She reached once more toward the bird and as if Mother had eyes in the back of her head, she said, "We don't even know that the mother wants it. The baby could be sick. Or weak. Just leave it."

Later that day, when the bird still lay crumpled in the long grass, Jo finally accepted its mother wasn't coming back. The baby bird's whimpers had subsided, and it barely had the energy to lift its head when Jo approached. It gave one last plea for food, opening its beak as wide as it could.

That's when Jo picked up the cinderblock.

CHAPTER THREE

Addy lies on her change table waiting for me to finish fastening her diaper. I kiss her tummy and guide her limbs into her sleeper. She refuses to bend her left knee, making it impossible to complete the task.

"Come on, sweetie, you gotta bend your knee."

It always amazes me how I can feel so much better after a good night's sleep. This is relative; in my current situation, six hours is a win.

I adopt a funny face to make her giggle. After a few fruitless attempts, she flashes me a gummy smile. This is enough of a distraction to get her to bend her leg. At last, I can zip her up.

The sun is shining through the French windows, making a crisscross pattern on the wall next to her change table. She reaches for the shadow. I consider snapping a picture with my phone, but I stop myself. I need to be in the moment, more present. It's better witnessed alone. This is, quite literally, the calm after the storm.

Noise travels from the kitchen as JP makes breakfast—the clinking of glassware, the banging of pots. It sounds as if he is using every dish and cooking utensil we own; he insists on creating a *mise en place* even for simple dishes like boxed mac and cheese. Cooking has always been his stress reliever and since we barely spoke last night, I imagine he needed a distraction this morning. When Addison and I arrive at the stairs, I can smell my favorite: blueberry pancakes. Today is a new day. I'm not going to let my negative thoughts taint it.

I skip down the stairs snuggling Addison and singing one of my many made-up songs about the mundane tasks of motherhood. This one is about diaper changing and is my attempt to make the task more tolerable.

Addy has the cutest baby butt,
even when it's a stinky butt,
now it's all cleaned up but,
it's still the cutest butt.

"Morning, Daddy. I just had a big poopy. Too many nachos last night," I say in a high-pitched voice while waving Addy's right hand in front of her nose.

JP turns to face me and brushes his brown hair out of his eyes, leaving a trail of flour on his forehead. "Sleep okay? I was hoping you'd come back down last night."

"I know, I'm sorry. I was so tired. I fell asleep after feeding Addy."

He wears a look of genuine concern but shows his discomfort, shifting his weight from side to side. "I'm making pancakes. Wanted to use up the buttermilk." He turns back to the stove and flips the pancake with one swift lift of the pan. It lands perfectly.

The kitchen is a mess—ingredients clutter the marble countertop, dishes flood our stylish apron sink, and the dark, floor-to-ceiling wood cabinets have flour smeared all over them. I wish we would have chosen white cabinets, but JP thought dark wood was timeless. I think they show grease more.

I lean against the island counter and allow Addy to sit on the counter-top. "Pancakes sound perfect. I slept okay. She was up at midnight and then four, but she let Mommy sleep in until eight today."

When did I start referring to myself in the third person? Sadly, I think it's been going on for a while. Perhaps it's my way to separate Jo the person from Jo, Addison's mom.

JP eyes the torn skin on my thumb and lets out a disapproving sigh. "You're doing that again?"

I pull my hand away. "It's nothing." I clasp my hand to hide the wound.

"How many do you want?" JP dishes pancakes onto two plates that sit across from each other on the counter. All he needs to do is turn on the overhead light and he'll have himself an interrogation room.

"Three's good. Thanks."

He stops at three and passes over a bottle of maple syrup from his uncle's farm. There's nothing quite like Québec maple syrup, and we get this stuff by the case.

I place Addison in her swing then climb onto my usual seat at the counter. My mouth waters in anticipation. The pancakes are exactly what I need after skipping dinner last night. I worry about the conversation that's coming, so in between mouthfuls, I do my best to fill the silence. I animate Addison's favorite toy—a zebra stuffy named ZuZu—with a shoddy South African accent. "Howzit, Addy? It's me ZuZu, the South African zebra. How do you like my stripes?"

"Listen, about yesterday," JP starts.

I jump in. "I have no idea what happened. I wish I did. I put her in her bassinet down here just after ten. I know it was ten because I heard the train go by. Then I lay down beside her on the couch. The next thing I know, I wake up to Amy's call and realize that Addy's crying but it's coming from outside. The bassinet was on the patio table, under the umbrella." I notice I have been using the stuffy as a prop to set the scene and drop it to the floor. "Thank God she was in the shade."

JP sits quietly, looking at me intently and coaxing me to continue.

"I'm guessing it was Marjorie who called it in. She has nothing better to do than watch us from her back window."

JP stands abruptly from his seat at the island, and his hands escape the confines of his pockets. "Who cares who called it in? You left Addison outside by herself." He motions to the back door. "In that heat!"

"It's just—I don't understand why I would have done that. I mean, I was exhausted yesterday because she was fussy the night before. I think she's teething."

"Do you think you might have done it in your sleep?" JP paces around the kitchen putting ingredients back in the cupboards even though he still has pancakes on his plate to eat.

"I don't think so. I've never sleepwalked before."

"I know, but Jo, come on. You have to admit that you've adopted some weird sleep habits since Addy was born."

I freaked him out too much with the hallucinations early on after Addy's birth. Now I'm a sleepwalker who lugs around a twenty-pound portable crib while unconscious. Makes complete sense.

"Okay. But having bad dreams about Addy is different from sleep-walking," I say.

20

"Well, I think it's worth you getting checked out." He stops his make-busy tasks and returns to his seat at the counter. "If it's not with Dr. Lui, then maybe a sleep specialist or something." He shovels a few bites of soggy pancake into his mouth.

"Yeah. You're probably right."

"For your and Addy's safety." The worry in his eyes cuts into my heart.

"I think maybe it's time Addy has naps in the nursery. I've been wanting to set up the video monitor on her crib," I say.

JP moves the pancake around his plate like a toddler stalling so he doesn't have to eat his vegetables. The sullen look he wears tells me he's lost faith in me as a mother.

"I can set up the monitor for you today," he finally says.

"Thank you. I think this is a good move. Gives me a bit of separation from her, and then we have the camera in case anything weird happens again."

He looks up abruptly with furrowed brows. "Let's hope it doesn't come to that."

Addy fusses, so I move to the floor, zebra in hand, to score more smiles. "Top of the morning to you, Addy," I say as cheerfully as I can muster.

I glance at the sliding glass doors that overlook our back porch. The sheer curtains rustle in Marjorie's window. She's spying on us. It has to be our 75-year-old widowed neighbor who made the anonymous complaint.

CHAPTER FOUR

JP left for Montréal this morning—a trip he nearly cancelled—and I can finally breathe. He isn't here to follow my every move and ask me when I'll be making an appointment with a therapist. With Addison in her bassinet, I finally have some time for myself.

Bathing was once a necessity but now it's a luxury. I turn the tap all the way to the right to fill our en suite Jacuzzi with the hottest water possible. I usually leave my baths as red as a tomato and as shriveled as a prune. Facing the mirror, I slowly strip down layer by layer, until my clothes collect in a pile next to me like I'm a snake that's shed its skin.

I tilt my head to one side and my reflection follows. I blink three times, each one pronounced. Every time I reopen my eyes, my reflection is there staring back at me, as it should be. When I was a kid, I used to be terrified of mirrors. I was convinced that the *me* I saw in the mirror was a separate entity, tricking me into believing I was the one in control. I would try to catch my reflection in a lie, a delayed movement, an angle slightly off.

I look at myself and wonder if the body that stands before me is playing a trick on me. I don't recognize it in its postpartum state. I give myself a once-over from head to toe; the white lighting I chose, which I thought would make the room brighter, only serves to accentuate every flaw. My eyes are glazed and heavy, the bags beneath them pronounced. What I wouldn't give for a full night's sleep, and the chance to get my eyelashes filled again. I developed a bad case of eczema during pregnancy, and the red blemishes still hover around my jawline. My nose and mouth are unchanged and I'm thankful for that.

This time of year, my skin is usually an olive tone from basking in the sun on weekends. This summer we had a record heat wave—not the best conditions for a newborn who can't regulate her body temperature—so, we spent it mostly indoors. My current pigment is a sickly yellow-green that will remain this way until the spring.

I've noticed that my hair has been falling out lately; it's especially thinning near my left temple. Another fun postpartum side effect. I've been parting my hair in the middle so it's less noticeable, but it reminds me of the haircut I reluctantly sported from ages five to seven.

Fifteen pounds of extra weight still hovers around my stomach and hips. The skin is loose surrounding my navel and the linea nigra cuts through it vertically, dividing my torso in half. Presently, my breasts are asymmetrical since Addison passed out before I could switch sides; blue veins pulsate through the right breast, which swells by the minute, and the left hangs like a deflated water balloon, with no purpose after Addison's last feeding. The horizontal stretch marks lining the outside of both breasts look almost iridescent, like the markings of an albino tiger. Both nipples are raw pink, in contrast to the dull areolas, which have faded in color from excessive sucking.

I stand there, in front of the mirror in both awe and shame of my post-partum body. Why is it that female body is celebrated during pregnancy? *You're glowing. Being pregnant suits you. You have the perfect bump.* A month after you've given birth, society can't accept what it's become. I get whiplash just thinking about it.

My eyes are drawn to the overgrown black tuft between my legs. It was once kept as smooth as a baby's bum when I had the time, energy, and money to invest in myself. It isn't sexy like a 1970s porno bush, more of a frightening, thick forest. I won't let JP near that region. I tell myself I'll tend to it once I decide to reopen for business.

I almost let myself stop there but force myself to look at the self-inflicted scars on my inner thighs. The cluster of thin, raised marks run in no evident pattern or cohesive direction, insecure thoughts from fifteen years ago that will stay with me for life. I trace one of the longer incisions that spans two inches long. I remember this one clearly. It was my first, executed with Mother's metal nail file I had watched her using on her nails earlier that day. Maybe I wanted to feel close to her and thought that would connect us by intimately sharing the object.

That was the day Mother said she didn't love me the same way she loved Meg and Amy.

It was also the day that she died.

I conceal my scars by clasping my hands in front of me. This is the position I stand in whenever I'm exposed. Even when I'm intimate with JP, I start out in this awkward pose, like a nervous sixteen-year-old about to lose her virginity.

I retreat from the mirror and proceed to the bath, which is full of foamy bubbles that smell of lavender. I light a candle with a matching scent and turn off the lights. Stepping into the bath, I pause to let my body adapt to the temperature. After a few minutes I'm satisfied and I sink to the bottom of the tub, inviting the bubbles to engulf me.

I close my eyes and allow the warm water to rise to my chin. I stretch my legs out, grazing the other side of the tub with my big toes. My sisters and I grew up with one bathroom that we had to share among the four of us. The door was never locked, and it was rare to find a moment alone. The tub in the washroom was small, not large enough to stretch out in. We had to sit upright in order to stretch our legs out or lie down with our knees bent.

I hold my breath and sink beneath the surface. Slowly, I float back to the top. When I resurface, my ears pop, but I swear I hear the front door shut. I pause, slowing my breath so not to make a sound, and remain absolutely still. *Am I hearing things?* No, it had been distinct, the front door had definitely shut. I grab my phone and blow out the candle. The lavender mingles with the smell of burned wick. I wait. The house is silent.

I'm almost positive I locked the door after I took the recycling to the garage. There's no way someone could have opened it. Maybe JP flew home early. I send him a text and wait, hoping to hear the ding of his phone from downstairs as he receives it. Nothing.

I know what JP would say, *You're being silly. You listen to too many true crime podcasts. No one is in the house. We live in the safest neighborhood.* But JP isn't here. I'm alone with my thoughts, and I've never been as logical as JP.

I'm naked and wet in the dark. The closest weapon is my hairdryer. If I make my way into the hall, I could grab a Maglite flashlight from the linen closet. One swift hit and I could surely knock out an intruder.

I hold onto my knees and pray that my mind is playing tricks on me. It's because I'm alone in the house. It's because of the week I've had. If it wasn't for Addy, I might wait it out in the cooling bath, but I must check on her. Then I can face the rest of the house.

I don't dare drain the water. That would give me away. Instead, I carefully step out of the tub and pat my body dry with the towel I'd laid out. I wrap myself in my robe but skip the slippers which make a scuffing sound when I walk. Using the flashlight on my phone, I guide myself out of the bedroom. Moonlight spills into the hallway from the windows above the staircase.

Standing on the upstairs landing, I spend a moment allowing my eyes adjust, and when they do, I realize I am far too close to the edge. I stumble backward, clutching the handrail. I can't decipher whether the door is locked from where I stand. I creep down the hallway toward the guest room where Addy is nestled in her bassinet. I open the door a crack, but it's difficult to get a visual. I tiptoe towards the bassinet and breathe a sigh of relief. There she lies on her back, snuggled in her sleep sack, her arms outstretched above her.

Now that I know Addy is safe, I cautiously approach the hallway and proceed to the linen closet. I carefully open the door, pausing briefly when it creaks, and reach for the flashlight on the top shelf. Once I return to the top of the stairs, I shine the light towards the front door. It appears to be locked but I must check to know for sure. I'll never fall asleep if I don't. I ease down the cool marble stairs one step at a time, my hand gliding along the brass railing. When I arrive at the bottom, the brass ball on the newel post shifts beneath my hand, and I almost miss my step.

I look towards the front door, and I can finally breathe—it's locked. It was in my head. It had to be in my head. Maybe a neighbor's car door.

Maybe my imagination. So much for my relaxing bath. How will I ever fall asleep tonight? One thing is for certain—I'm sleeping with the steel flashlight.

Good Luck Chewing Your Hair

Five years old

Jo dug her bare feet farther into the sandbox and watched her dad's truck pull out of the driveway. She didn't know that it would be the last time she would see him. If she did, she might have tried to stop him. A sand drift of tiny crystals fell from her legs, leaving behind a faint dust. She licked her finger and ran it down her shin bone, which was speckled with tiny golden bruises that matched the setting sun. Her long hair covered her face—the wind daring the left side to reach for the right.

Mother called her by her full name, "Joanna Louise Baker!" and scared the wind away.

Jo chewed on the ends of her hair, which tasted faintly of salt from the sweat that glistened the back of her neck. She made her way to the screen door and stepped inside. Mother's ice-blue eyes were surrounded by red puffy skin, but any tears had been wiped dry.

"Stop chewing on your hair, it's rude." Mother released the screen door, and it grazed the back of Jo's heel. Jo winced.

"Why aren't you wearing any shoes? Honestly, you make no sense sometimes."

"I like the way the sand feels."

"You should always wear shoes outside. A school friend of mine once stepped on a stick and it went straight through her foot. It got infected and the doctor had to cut it off."

"Where'd Dad go?" Jo asked and then shoved the hair back in her mouth.

"Stop chewing your hair, Joanna," Mother ordered.

Jo spit out the soggy strand and let it fall to her shoulder. She wanted to ask where Amy and Meg were, but Mother was getting increasingly annoyed.

Mother tilted her head to the side. "It's too hot for long hair." She raised her eyebrows like she had an idea.

Mother dragged the stool from the wall, into the middle of the kitchen. Then, she hurried off down the hallway and Jo could hear the linen closet open and close. Mother returned with a beach towel in her arms and a half smile on her face. She covered the peach linoleum with the rainbow terrycloth.

"I'm going to give you a trim."

"Why?" Jo asked. Jo liked her hair. She liked when Meg braided it in pigtails after her bath.

"You're going to need one for school."

Jo climbed onto the tall stool and adjusted in the brown leather seat. The rip where the foam spilled out scratched the back of her thigh.

Mother yanked a wet comb through her hair. She worked efficiently like she was on some sort of deadline.

She jerked Jo's head every time she released a knot, but Jo didn't want to protest. They were spending time together.

Jo yelped when Mother scraped her daughter's left ear with the comb. It grew hot with pain. "Your hair is tangled."

Mother went to the drawer and presented the scissors, still stained from the orange freezies she had cut open for Jo's snack. She gathered Jo's hair and snipped with the sticky blade—short enough to expose Jo's neck.

"Time for bangs?" With a lift of Jo's chin, Mother positioned Jo's head towards the ceiling. "Stay still."

A brown coffee-like stain near the ceiling light kept Jo's mind off the clumps of hair that fell to the floor until bits of hair got caught in her eyelashes.

When Mother finished, she said, "Bangs are a bit short, but they'll grow back."

Jo's bangs were barely a fringe, exposing three inches of her forehead. Jo tugged at the sides of her hair, which fell just above her chin.

It was more than a trim.

CHAPTER FIVE

Addison lies on her back on her activity mat in the nursery, excitedly kicking and grabbing onto the colorful animals that hang above her. Meanwhile, I scroll through my social feeds, living vicariously through my single friends who are soaking up the last days of summer cottaging or patio hopping.

Out the window, the sun invites me to take Addison for a walk. We could stop in at Steeped, a trendy café on our main street that I frequent on good days. The staff has grown accustomed to my neurotic drink order.

"What do you think, Addy? Should we stay inside today or go out on the town?" I tickle her belly, and she giggles. "I dunno, it's tempting. But we should really keep a low profile today. Don't want Marjorie to complain about something else."

Addy reaches for an elephant just out of her range, almost rolling to her stomach. I sit on my knees, hunched down at her level, like I'm her own personal cheerleader.

"Yes, yes Addy. You're so close, babe. You can do it."

She surrenders and starts to fuss. I nudge the toy closer so it's within reach. "Oh, fine. Here you go, but next time you have to roll and get it, okay?"

Halfway through Raffi's song "Baby Beluga," the doorbell rings. Would Child Services stop by on a Sunday? I'm decently dressed but my hair almost looks wet by how greasy it is. The bob cut was an attempt to discourage Addy's hair pulling, but it's more noticeable now when I decide to skip four days of shampoo. I run down the stairs, Addison on my hip, to answer the door.

Meg and Amy greet me, and although I'm relieved it isn't Child Services, I'm nervous to face my sisters.

"Surprise, it's us." Amy smiles awkwardly, holding a couple of shopping bags and a takeout coffee tray.

I narrow my eyes. Amy has clearly told our eldest sister about the incident. I'd rather Meg be ignorant to the fact that, unlike her, I'm failing at this motherhood thing.

Meg purses her lips. She carries a casserole dish that could feed a family of eight. Her two youngest boys hide behind her, each clinging to a leg.

"Addy, look it's your cousins." I bring her down to their level. The seven-year-old twins, no longer shy, approach.

"We just wanted to check in," Amy says, with an apologetic smile. "We come bearing gifts."

Meg shrugs. She probably thinks I'm depressed again. She witnessed me at my worst. My depression—inherited from Mother—peaked when I was a junior in high school. It was a rough year; one I try not to think about much.

"It's just a few things," Meg says shifting her weight. "I made you a lasagna, too."

I lead them inside, through the kitchen to the living room. Amy drops the bags on the counter and follows me to our large sectional couch. She places the coffee tray on the ottoman and steals Addison from me.

"Did you miss your Auntie Amy?" she asks, bouncing Addison lightly on her knee.

My arms enjoy the break from the usual twelve-pound weight. The boys sit at the other end of the couch playing with their portable video games.

"So, Davis, Parker—how's grade two going?" I ask.

They mutter a *fine* and continue with their games. Every so often one yells in frustration when their character dies, or cheers when they beat a level. Davis seems to be better at the game and cheers more often.

Meg makes herself at home, putting various items into our cupboards and fridge, including her homemade lasagna. She pauses for a moment to present a pill bottle. I get a glimpse of how her patients view her, dressed in her nursing scrubs with her mousy blonde hair pulled back.

"Jo, I brought the magnesium pills. Take one before bed to help with your restlessness. Where do you want them?"

"The cabinet above the fridge is good."

She continues to maneuver around the kitchen, reorganizing our shelves.

Amy blends into the grey couch with her monochrome tunic and leggings. She lights up as she plays with Addison, mimicking various cartoon characters to encourage laughter from Addy.

"Who should I do now? Elmo?" She immediately adopts a spot-on Elmo impression. "Elmo thinks Addy's the best. Elmo loves Addy so much."

"Did they teach you that in theatre school?" Meg calls from the kitchen.

"Aunty Meg's just jealous she can't make you laugh like I can." Amy kisses Addison and continues to bounce her on her knee.

"When did you dye your hair?" I ask Amy, who is rocking a deep auburn color that I don't recall her having three days ago.

"Last week. I'm not loving it though."

"Is it for your next role?" I try to remember who she was just cast as in her amateur Shakespeare company. Last month, we saw her as the vengeful Tamora in *Titus Andronicus.* She plays the femme fatale well. "Lady Macbeth, right?"

"Goneril, from *King Lear.*" The way she cocks her head tells me she's already described this role to me in detail. "And no, the director is making me wear a wig for it. Maybe I'll go as dark as you next time," she teases.

"So, where's JP?" Meg asks, joining us in the living room.

"Business trip. Montréal," I reply.

Meg raises her eyebrows, her not-so-subtle way to express her disapproval of him abandoning me after a traumatic experience. Meg has never been his biggest fan since I started dating him two years ago. Not everyone can marry their high school sweetheart.

Amy changes the subject. "We got you your fancy drink. Decaf Earl Grey with non-fat, steamed milk, steeped for half a minute, with a splash of *agave.*" She overpronounces agave to emphasize how pretentious my drink order is.

"It's the little pleasures in life," I say, searching for the cup with my name on it.

Meg moves to the other side of the couch where her twin boys sit. She proceeds to force-feed Davis and Parker bran muffins, then falls to her knees to clean up the pieces they've dropped. I worry she'll find crumbs that don't belong to the muffins.

"Meg, no one likes bran muffins." Amy reaches for one anyway. "Next time, buy chocolate chip, alright?"

The boys smile in agreement.

Meg squeezes her way in between Amy and me and puts a hand on my leg. "How are you doing? Why don't I trade my day shifts next week and come by? Help out a bit?"

"Oh no, that's not necessary at all. We're fine."

Neither of my sisters asks the question, but their restlessness shows me they're dying to know what happened yesterday. Luckily, Addy breaks the silence with a rumbling number two, and Amy erupts in laughter.

"Why don't I take care of that?" Meg volunteers. "It's been a while since I've changed a diaper." She scoops up Addy and heads upstairs.

This gives Amy and me some time alone. My back sinks into the couch.

"Okay, let's hear it," she says as she shuffles closer to me.

I glance at the boys to see if they're listening, but they're staring intently at the compact screens in their laps.

I set the scene for Amy, this time without help from Addison's stuffed animal. She nods as though she can relate but looks just as confused as I am. Recounting an event I don't understand myself has left me exhausted, and I lean my head on the armrest.

"Still having trouble sleeping?" she asks.

"Yeah, Addy's still waking up during the night. It's not horrible, but it takes me so long to fall back asleep."

"What about exercise? That might help."

I roll my eyes. "Because I have so much free time for exercise."

"You getting laid?"

A laugh gets caught in my throat. Then, I realize she meant it as a serious question.

"You've got needs, woman. Is JP taking care of that?" she probes.

"No. But that's on me. I haven't felt much like—I'm not really in the mood, I guess."

"How long's it been? Don't say before the birth."

"Second trimester?" I wince as I say it.

"Good God, woman."

"It was a mess down there. I had, like, seven stitches."

"Okay, but that was four months ago," she says.

"Alright, you got me. Guess we're just in a bit of a rut." I gulp my drink and rub my thumb over the pencil crayon attempt of my name, *Joe*.

Amy continues. "Rich and I have sex every day. If we miss a day, it feels weird. Like we've gone to bed angry."

Meg returns at the tail end of the conversation, holding Addison. "Just wait until you have kids. That all goes out the window." Amy's smile drops, and Meg realizes what she's done. "Sorry, Ames. That was a stupid thing to say. It *is* gonna happen for you guys."

"I know. We haven't given up yet." Her forced smile conveys her pain.

It's my turn to change the subject. "I'd say let's sit out back, but I'm avoiding my neighbor."

Amy perks up. "Which one? Nosey Widow or Nosey Mom-of-Two?"

"Who are these people?" Meg asks, her eyebrows raising an inch.

"Two neighbors who are incapable of minding their own business. Marjorie's the one whose yard backs onto ours. The widow. She likes to watch us."

Amy jumps in with her impersonation of Marjorie and a flawless Scottish accent, "Is that baby warm enough? There's a bit of a chill today."

I attempt the accent, doing my best impression of the seventy-five-year-old. "You know, Joanna, if you trim your old hydrangea shoots, new flowers will bloom."

"Stick to public relations, Jo. That sounded Australian," Amy says between laughs.

"Okay, and who's the nosey mom?" Meg asks with urgency, presumably wanting to be filled in.

"Claire. She lives beside us." I motion to the window above our kitchen sink that faces their breakfast nook. "She's around our age, a stay-at-home mom. We're fake friends."

"You don't like her?"

Amy chimes in. "She sells candles through one of those pyramid schemes and won't take no for an answer."

"Gotcha," says Meg.

"She's just kind of annoying. We went to a mommy-and-me yoga class together last month, and I decided one was enough." Addy wasn't a fan of watching me struggle with my tree pose—in fact, she let out piercing screams for the entire hour-long class.

Addison squirms in Meg's grasp, so I welcome her back in my arms. I hold my daughter over my shoulder and rub her back in a circular motion. "It's okay, Addy babe. Mama's here." I continue in my regular voice, "Today, it's Marjorie I'm avoiding. She's the one who complained."

Meg tosses a rattle from the couch into Addison's toy bin. "Are we going to talk about what happened at Child Services?"

I guess there's no way of avoiding her question.

"What is that?" Parker asks. His game lets out a descending tune, suggesting he's lost.

"What is what?" Meg returns the question.

"Child's surfaces?"

"Child Services." She brushes his curly locks out of his face. "It's an organization that looks out for kids."

"Like a charity?" He looks rather impressed with himself that he knows the word charity.

"Not exactly. The people who work there help make sure that kids are treated well by their families. They protect kids and keep them safe."

Her definition makes my stomach sink. Does she think I'm not treating Addy well?

"Like superheroes?" Parker guesses.

I answer before Meg can respond to her son. "They just asked a few questions. Said they would be sending someone by this week to see how Addison and I spend our day."

Meg puts her hand on my lap. "This is a big deal, Jo. You get that, right?"

Amy jumps in. "I'm sure it will all blow over. Once they see you with Addy, they'll see you're a great mom."

"Did they tell you what day they're coming?" asks Meg.

I can't bring myself to meet her gaze. "Some time in the next week."

Meg looks around the kitchen. She's eying my breakfast dishes, still on the counter.

"Those are from this morning, Meg. Haven't had a chance to clean yet."

"I didn't say anything," she says. Then she brushes a few bran muffin crumbs off the ottoman into her hand. "Oh, I hope you don't mind, but I put a bit of diaper cream on Addy. She looked sore."

I stand abruptly. I've had enough visiting today. "I should go feed Addy."

"You can do it here. It's nothing the boys haven't seen before," Meg says.

Amy gets the hint and rises. "We'll get out of your hair. We just wanted to stop by and see you both."

They agree to let themselves out as I run Addison upstairs to feed. Later, when we come back down, I see that the dishes have been cleaned up.

CHAPTER SIX

I wear Addison in a baby wrap and unload the dishwasher, antici-pating Amy's arrival following her drama workshop at the children's hospital.

For the past two days, I've kept the house spotless—vigorously clean-ing during Addy's naps instead of catching up on my sleep. I need to ensure the house is at its best when the service worker drops by. I've also been hunting for Addison's diaper bag, which has disappeared on me, along with her zebra stuffie.

Amy is fifteen minutes late, having to rely on the train's schedule. She stands at the door, her eyes red and puffy. Has she been fired? If there are hospital budget cuts, it's safe to assume her drama workshop will be the first thing to go.

"Oh no Ames, what's wrong?"

"Bad day at work. Can we sit?"

"Of course." I lead her to the living room, still wearing Addy. "I'll grab you water."

"Got any wine?"

"In the wine fridge," I offer. "But I'll need your help choosing a bottle. JP has a couple of reserves in there that he'd be heartbroken if we casually drank."

"I'm only kidding; water is good. Can I hold Addy?"

"Sure," I say, unwrapping my daughter from the stretchy polka dot fabric.

Amy takes her from my arms. "Hey, baby girl. Come cheer your Aunt Amy up." She kisses Addison on the cheek and brings her to the couch where she props her up against the inside of her bent knee.

"So, what's going on?" I ask, bringing her a glass of water.

"I had my drama workshop at the hospital today and was making the rounds to the different floors." She takes a big gulp of her drink and I wait in anticipation. "I was about to go to this little girl Katya's room to check in. She's the one who's really into the improv games I do. She has natural comedic timing and she's only eleven. I knew she had been preparing for her third open-heart surgery. On my way to her room, one of the nurses tells me she passed away yesterday."

"Oh my God. That's horrible," I say and have the urge to take Addison back and hold her close.

My mind goes to Katya's mother. I think of the moment when she knew. Perhaps it was the somber look on the doctor's face. I picture her sitting on the floor of Katya's room later that day, holding Katya's favorite stuffed animal she still slept with even though she would be a teenager soon. I wonder how long they will keep her room just as it is. Whether they'll skip the vacuuming and dusting to preserve her smell. Maybe it's the scent of fresh laundry. A floral body spray she liked. I wonder if there are more children in the family. Will her mom have the

41

strength to get them breakfast tomorrow? If Katya was an only child, what will her mom do now? What will keep her going?

"It's just the first time a child I've known has died. I didn't think it would be this hard."

"I couldn't do what you do. I can't imagine how hard that must be." I rip the raw skin on my thumb, which still hasn't healed from last week. "But just think about your visits and how they would have brightened up her days."

"Yeah. It's just—there's no closure, you know? Like, I didn't know that last week was the last time I'd see her. And now, I can't even go to her funeral and say bye."

"That's okay. A lot of people don't do well with funerals. I haven't been to one since ..." I trail off.

We were young when we buried Mother. Amy had just started college. Meg had to organize the funeral, choosing a headstone and coffin between menu tastings for her wedding. At the service, we each read something instead of pursuing a traditional eulogy, mostly because we didn't know enough about her life before we were born. Mother was an only child whose parents had passed away before sharing stories with their grandkids. We also couldn't agree on what to say. Meg wanted to recite a passage from the Bible, an ode to Mother's vocation; she taught Sunday school at our local church for twenty years. Amy preferred to tell childhood stories. I opted for a poem because saying nothing wasn't an option. I landed on "Warm Summer Sun" by Mark Twain; it was the shortest one I found in my quick internet search for popular funeral poems.

"No, it's not that. I'd like to go but we aren't allowed to. It was in my contract."

"Oh ... well, maybe that's for the best."

Amy doesn't look satisfied with my answer, her lips parted in antic-ipation of what I'll say next. I don't have the energy for much more. Whenever I think of Mother and that day, it sucks the life out of me.

"How about that wine?" I suggest.

She nods and I retreat to the wine fridge to grab a bottle. I decide on a red from Ontario, assuming JP won't miss it. I pour her a hefty glass; it only makes sense since it will go bad before JP gets back from his trip.

I take a turn holding Addison and let Amy drink her wine. After a few sips, she stares at me inquisitively, like she is observing a piece of art, trying to find meaning in it.

"What?" I giggle out of discomfort.

"You're getting along better than you were at the beginning?"

I'm taken aback and readjust Addison in my lap. "What do you mean?"

"No, I just mean—you're getting more comfortable with mother-hood? With Addy?"

"Oh, yeah. I think it's like anything. The more you do something, the more comfortable you get. I can change diapers in under a minute now." Once again, I chuckle, making light of the conversation as I fear where she is going with this.

"And you feel more of a connection with her now?"

I furrow my brows. "I always felt a connection. She was in my womb for nine months."

"I just meant, now that she is older, you feel like you've got everything under control." She fiddles with her wedding ring, the opal stone catch-ing the light above her. "... forget I said anything."

I look down at Addison and fight the urge to cry. I'm used to this judgement from Meg, but not Amy. My tears fill my bottom lid, getting dangerously close to spilling over. *Don't cry, don't cry, don't cry.* Amy remains quiet, and I distract myself by bouncing Addison on my lap. My mind goes to Katya and her mother again, and the waterfall of emotion streams down my face.

"Oh Jo, I'm sorry. I just thought I remembered you saying something during the early days about ... it's not important. I can only imagine what was going through your head the first month. The hormones. The lack of sleep."

"I might have. I don't remember. Those first few weeks were a whirl-wind."

"Of course, they were," she says, and she slides closer to me on the couch.

I step out of my body for a moment, looking down at myself. I feel like I'm dreaming. I rack my brain for clarity. Amy wouldn't make this up, but I don't remember saying anything like that. How could I say that I didn't have a connection with my daughter?

"You know you can always tell me what you're feeling. I'll never judge you. Please, forgive me. I'm just in a mood," she says, putting her hand on my knee.

"It's fine. I'm okay. I'm just tired. Another rough night of no sleep." I wipe away the tears with my sleeve.

I excuse myself to the washroom, leaving Addison with her aunt. There are red splotches surrounding my eyes, and once again I'm left staring at my reflection, disappointed by what it reveals. I sit for a few moments on the toilet seat, allowing my breath to calm. When I return to the living room, Amy has finished her wine.

"Why don't we take Addy for a walk?" I say. I haven't left the house since JP went on his trip. Some fresh air might help us both.

The temperature has dropped since last weekend. Jackets aren't needed, but I bundle Addy up in a blanket in the stroller that cost more than her entire bedroom set. We walk around the block so I can check the mail before we make our way to the café to indulge in sweets.

We cross the street to the sidewalk, pushing Addison's stroller over a brown patch of grass where the sod didn't take. Apparently, everyone got the memo to go outside today, and it's a reminder of how I barely know my neighbors, despite having lived here for six months. Perhaps I've been a tad reclusive.

Amy starts to sound like herself again, poking fun at a neighbor who looks like the dog he walks. Wrinkles look cute on a Shar-Pei, but not so much on a middle-aged, bald man.

As we approach the mailbox, I notice Marjorie painting on her front veranda. She closes her paint tray and shuffles down the driveway to meet us, instead of retreating to the house, which I would have expected.

I mutter, "That's her," under my breath so only Amy can hear.

She returns with, "Don't say anything, Jo. It's not worth it."

Marjorie is dressed for the weather in wool pants and a heavy cable knit turtleneck that matches her golden hair—an obvious dye-job. No seventy-five-year-old has tresses that color. She likely gets a perm too because, from the roots, there is an inch and a half of straight hair before it springs into bouncy curls that hover above her jawline.

Marjorie bends over so she can see under the stroller shade. "If it isn't Miss Addy," she says, her Scottish accent strong. "Oh, look at the wee thing. She looks so cozy in there." She straightens and smiles at Amy. "I don't think we've met. I'm Marjorie."

"I'm Amy. Jo's sister." Amy returns her handshake.

"Jo's sister? I hope you don't mind me saying, but you don't look much alike."

"We get that a lot." Amy smiles politely.

"And how are you, Miss Jo? Addison keeping you busy?"

"Yep."

"Looks like autumn is finally here. Our hydrangeas should be turning a nice pink soon."

I offer a slight smile, but Amy clearly can't stand my silence. "What are you painting?" she asks.

"Oh, I do a bit of daily watercolor. Mostly still life. Decided to get out of the house today. The subject was my bird feeder. Do you paint?"

"No, but I appreciate a good painting."

I picture the art in Amy's apartment. She doesn't own any paintings. Her walls are filled with photo collages and a few unique pieces from her travels—a tapestry from Australia, a golden Buddha from Thailand, but no paintings. She is being gracious, but Marjorie will end up giving her an original watercolor of her China set if she doesn't stop.

"Miss Jo, you don't seem like yourself today." I'm surprised she doesn't realize why.

"Just busy. Expecting a visitor sometime this week and need to make sure the house is in order."

"Oh, visitors are always nice. A good excuse for a clean. Or to make bread," she offers.

"It's more of a nuisance, really."

"Oh? Is it too late to un-invite them?" She chuckles at her joke.

I offer her nothing, barely even a smile.

"You seem upset, Jo. Did I do something to offend you?"

Amy decides to cut in. "Oh no, Jo's just a little tired today. We'll let you get back to your painting. Enjoy your day."

"Amy's right. I am tired. But it's because one of my neighbors felt the need to call Child Services on me. Apparently, I'm not fit to be a mother." I can't help myself. It must be the lack of sleep.

"You're joking! Who would do such a thing?" She rubs my forearm, offering comfort. "You are a great mother to little Addy."

"I don't know who it was. It was an anonymous complaint," I say, softening my tone.

"Well, I just can't imagine that. I'm very sorry, Joanna. I'd love to be a character witness if that's something they do."

My stomach sinks. I've just spent five minutes being rude to an old woman—a widow—who has been nothing but nice to Addison and me.

"Thank you, Marjorie. That's a very nice offer. And sorry if I came off short before. This whole thing has taken a lot out of me."

"Well, of course, it has. I can't even imagine."

"I'll let you know if there's anything you can do. I'm hoping it all blows over."

"I'm sure it will."

We say our goodbyes and cross the street to collect the mail. There's an inordinate amount of pizza flyers today. I decide I'll splurge on a large Hawaiian to myself for dinner. JP hates pineapple on pizza and I'm tired of eating Meg's lasagna. The noodles are starting to clump together.

"Do you still think it was her?" Amy asks.

"No. I think it's pretty clear it wasn't."

"Nosey Mom of Two then?"

"Maybe," I say.

I had been convinced it was Marjorie; I'd have bet on it. Now I'm not sure I trust my own gut.

CHAPTER SEVEN

The café is packed with high school students wearing sweaters and ordering autumn-themed lattes, which are advertised with clever chalkboard illustrations near the register. My favorite is a sketch of Linus with a speech bubble that reads, *it's the great pumpkin spice latte, Charlie Brown.*

We should have avoided the lunch hour rush. By the time we arrive at the front of the line, Addy is awake from her stroller snooze and wailing at the top of her lungs. This is precisely why I don't leave the house.

Amy comes to Addy's aid, releasing her from the stroller and escaping the standstill line. "Get me a chocolate chip muffin and a medium dark roast," she says, before pushing past a sea of teens who don't bother to step aside. I treat myself to two brownies; one for now and one for post-pizza. I know I'll feel guilty about this later, but I need the rush of endorphins to get through the rest of this week on my own.

I exit the line with our goodies, maneuvering the stroller past customers still waiting for their orders. Amy chats with a brunette sitting at a four-top by the bookshelf. The woman holds her toddler in her lap and a little girl sits beside them on a booster seat. The double stroller is wedged between her table and another table filled with teen girls wearing matching top knots and scowls on their faces. Once I get a view of the woman's profile, I realize it's Claire from next door. Fate really wants me to tackle my neighborhood drama today.

"Jo! Over here!" Claire waves her arms.

I move through the obstacle course of tables and chairs and make my way to Amy.

Claire speaks a mile a minute like she has just inhaled five shots of espresso, but there's only one cup on the table. "Your sis tells me that you guys are out for a stroll. I was just telling her that I never see you guys around. I come here pretty much every day, after the park. I meet some of the neighborhood moms on Thursdays. You should join us tomorrow. What did you get?"

It is hard to keep up with Claire. I've already forgotten a few of the questions she asked.

"Uh, yeah. Out for a walk. Just went with a brownie and latte," I say.

"What have you been up to? Addison is getting so big!"

"She'll be five months in a couple of weeks."

"We just got back from vacation. Paul's parents have a timeshare in Florida—Key West. The kids swim, and Mommy drinks daiquiris." She laughs so loud that the girls' scowls grow bigger.

"Oh yeah? You just got back?"

"Can't you tell by my tan?" She strikes a pose and then breaks into another jarring laugh. "We were gone for two weeks. I had Lisa down the street pick up our newspapers while we were gone. You can never be too careful. I avoid putting any pictures up on social media until we're back. People can be *cray cray*."

If Claire was on vacation for the last two weeks, then it wasn't her who called in the complaint, either. I've already zoned out her next question, and Amy is forced to jump in on my behalf.

"Oh, we were just going to head back now actually. Jo, you wanted to feed Addy?"

"Yes, gotta head back. We'll have to catch up another time."

Amy and I are quiet on the walk home. I think she senses that I'm deep in thought. I devour brownie number one by the time we get back to my driveway.

For the rest of the afternoon, I can't focus. If it wasn't Marjorie or Claire, then who called in the complaint? I think about Claire's standing park date offer. Hanging with her and the neighborhood moms could help me figure out who called Child Services. I'm not even sure what good knowing would do, but there's a chance that it could get me one step closer to finding out exactly what happened last week. Thankfully, I have Claire's number from yoga.

After what feels like an hour-long conversation while bouncing Addy on my lap, we make plans to meet out front the next day at eleven and walk to the park together. Claire can barely control her excitement and is harder to get off the phone than a telemarketer. After I hang up, I realize that she was just breaking into another story.

Tomorrow, I will find out who was behind the complaint.

CHAPTER EIGHT

The sun sets, leaving behind colors that inspire hope. I lean forward, my forearms resting on the railing of our back deck, and I watch the pinks and rusts that peek above Marjorie's roof slowly fade to dusk.

In the summer, the neighborhood was buzzing until at least nine at night. Claire would always have her kids out in the backyard much later than I thought a preschooler and toddler should be. They would be in their bathing suits playing in the kiddie pool and Claire would sit at the patio table chatting with a friend she'd invited over. She always seemed to have a friend over. A man a few houses down would be mowing the lawn, his wife yelling at him over the machine's roar to watch out for her rose bushes. The smell of backyard barbecue would waft in through our open windows. When I was pregnant with Addison, I got burger cravings and JP would offer to get me a cheeseburger from a nearby pub.

I scan the row of backyards, beginning with Marjorie's, that leads north to the park. They are all empty at this time of night. Kids have ditched their jump ropes and soccer balls to sit in front of their television screens, likely coaxing their parents to swap the news for their favorite cartoons. It looks like the parents next door to Marjorie gave in and the entire family has piled on the couch to sing along to an animated musical.

I look left past our wooden fence to the road, which wraps around our house and connects to Marjorie's street. We have the corner house, which means we have a slightly bigger backyard than our neighbors. It also means that people walking past our house on the sidewalk have a pretty good view of our porch. Anyone in the neighborhood could have seen or heard Addison last week.

As I turn to head back inside, I notice a woman walking briskly along the sidewalk beside my house. Her gaze is focused on her hurried steps, which make a scuffing sound on the asphalt. She looks familiar, so she must be one of the neighborhood moms. She glances my way, and I lift my hand to wave. She ignores me, refocusing on the sidewalk ahead. I let my hand drop, feeling a bit silly. I retreat inside and close the sliding glass door behind me.

I change into my pajamas and retire to our bedroom to watch television. An alert rings on my tablet, an incoming video call from JP. I haven't talked to him since he left for his trip three days ago. Just a few texts here and there, aside from his requests for photos of Addy.

I prop myself up against our headboard and answer it with an eager smile. "Hey! How's the trip going?"

"Pretty good." JP sits on a hotel bed decorated with turquoise and yellow satin pillows. The dim lamplight casts a shadow of his shirtless body on the oversized headboard behind him. He holds a glass of red wine.

"You look like you're in a music video," I say.

He lets out a laugh. "Yeah. It's a very modern room. Maybe I should try to snag some of these pillows for our house." He grabs a shaggy purple pillow which wasn't originally in view and pets it like a cat.

"I'd take a hotel robe and slippers."

"Noted." He rubs his eyes. "I'm ready to come home. This trip has felt long."

"Yeah, it's been a doozy. Two more days."

"Sorry I didn't call until tonight. We've had client dinners. I got out of tonight's, though. Doing some prep for an early meeting."

"Well, you missed Hawaiian pizza. Jealous?"

"You're gross. Who puts pineapple on pizza?"

I laugh and then let out a sigh. "I want you home. I'm starting to freak myself out."

"Why?" he asks with urgency.

"It's lonely. And quiet. The other night I had a bath—"

He cuts me off, "Ooh, sexy."

"Stop it. I'm trying to tell you a story."

"Sorry, I'm listening, go ahead."

"The other night—"

"In the bath," he says slyly.

I ignore his quip and drop my smile. "JP, I thought I heard something. I was convinced someone had broken into the house."

"Was the door not locked? Rule number one, if you're home alone at night and having a bath, lock the door. You've seen enough horror movies."

I frown as he makes light of the situation. "It was locked. Eventually, I went downstairs, and everything was fine. I'm just getting in my head, I guess."

He places the wine down on the glass night table and brings the laptop closer to him on his lap. "I'll be home soon and then I don't think I'll be doing a long trip like this for a while. Maybe one night here and there. How's Addison? You didn't send me any pics today."

"She's good. Eating, pooping, sleeping."

"Sounds like the dream."

"Doesn't it? To be four months old."

There's a pause that lingers a little too long. Conversations over video chat are always more forced than if we were together in the same room. "I might try her in the crib tomorrow night. She's been doing her naps in the nursery."

'That's good. Has anyone been by?"

"Amy came over today. We took Addy for a walk."

"Oh, that's nice." He crosses his arms. "But I meant from Child Services."

"Not yet."

He nods. "You're ready for it?"

I hold the tablet away from me and use it to scan the spotless room. "The entire house is just as clean."

"Wow, good for you. Well, text or call after they come."

"For sure, I will. Do you need to leave?" I can sense he's wrapping up our call and I'm not looking forward to being on my own again.

"Yeah, I should get back to this presentation I'm working on."

"Okay, love you. Talk soon."

"Love you, too. Give Addy kisses for me," he says and then the screen goes black.

I stretch out on the bed, the weight of my body sinking into the feather duvet. If I lie here much longer, I will fall asleep, and then Addison would be left alone for the first time overnight.

I roll out of bed and tiptoe to the guest room. Addison stirs as if she smelled me. She lets out a cry and my left breast throbs in response. It's amazing how we are tethered to one another. How she senses my presence. My body understands what she needs with the sound of one cry.

I rush to the bassinet. She is getting too big for it, her head two inches from the top. She should move to the crib, but it's bittersweet knowing that she'll have passed another milestone. I'll miss having her within arm's reach. The bassinet will get sent to our unfinished basement, along with the box of her newborn clothes. At least I know with Addison sleeping in her crib, there won't be any strange events, and if there are, I'll have the video monitor to consult.

Addison falls asleep on the breast, a regular occurrence. Using my index finger, I release the suction, allowing my nipple to escape. She stirs slightly and then nuzzles into me. I place her back in the bassinet, and to my relief, she remains still.

A scuffing sound from outside interrupts the silence. I make my way to the window to investigate. Peering through the blinds, I scan the road. It's the woman again, rewinding her steps from earlier in the night. She looks up towards my window, and I let go of the blinds, startled. When I reclaim my position at the window, she has already disappeared into the night.

A Bug Attracted to Light

Six years old

Strawberry was Jo's first teddy bear; she was his third child. By the time he found his way to her, his fur was matted, and he had lost one eye, but he smelled like Meg and Amy, and that was comforting to Jo.

Jo snuggled in bed with Strawberry, the covers pulled over her head because she had a habit of seeing things. Shapes that were harmless during the day took on new forms when Mother turned out the lights. Jo pulled the covers down to just above her nose and focused her eyes across the room. The white curtain that swayed in the open-window breeze resembled a woman in a nightgown. Jo pulled the covers up and turned onto her stomach.

The air became stale, but she was afraid of what she might see if she exposed her face. She brushed away sweaty bangs and talked herself down. It was just the curtain blowing in the wind. She counted backward from ten, not knowing what would happen when she got to one. Then, she removed the covers with force and ran into the dark hallway.

Mother's room was easy to spot, the lamp by her bed casting a warm glow through the crack beneath the door. Mother liked to read Ana Seymour romance novels at night. During the day she kept them tucked under her pillow, where she thought the girls couldn't find them. Even though Jo was just learning to read, she knew what they were about. The pictures on the front featured men with their shirts ripped open and women with their eyes closed, lips parted.

Like a bug attracted to the light, Jo glided towards Mother's door and pressed her ear to the rough grain of the wood. Was Mother reading aloud? Jo tried to make out Mother's words. She let out a sigh and asked for forgiveness. Mother was reciting her nightly prayers.

The floor creaked beneath Jo's feet, giving her away. She knocked quietly and the light vanished. Jo nudged the door.

"Mother," she called out. Mother did not answer. She must have fallen asleep.

CHAPTER NINE

I rush upstairs in search of Addison's hat for the park. If I don't hurry, Claire might arrive and ask to come inside. There's no sign of her when I peek out Addison's window that overlooks the garage. I hold up the yellow seersucker hat that JP's mom sent him home with the last time he was in Montréal. It matches the first outfit I picked out for Addy, the one that sits on the changing table, covered in regurgitated milk. She wears a burnt orange onesie. When I throw on her tan sweater, she looks like an autumn scene.

Getting myself ready for an outing with new friends was a daunting task this morning. *What are the other moms going to wear? Do people dress up for the park? Are leggings appropriate?* Throw a four-month-old baby into the mix, and it gets that much more daunting. *Is there a wind today? Does she need a hat?*

This morning she vomited on the both of us, so we are sporting backup outfits. I have limited attire options nowadays, as my clothes need to fit my postpartum body. I decided on an empire waist smock with buttons down the front. I bought it in Paris when I still had a social life. It was made to hang loose, but I fill it out in my current state. Paired with leggings and a cardigan, it's suitable for the breezy fall weather.

Just as I fasten the strap on Addy's hat, there's a knock at the door. When I open it, Claire stands in my doorway with her hair curled in loose waves and a full face of makeup. She wears skinny jeans tucked into suede boots and a stylish, oversized knit sweater with shoulder cutouts. I feel dowdy next to her but tell myself that she isn't the one who gave birth four months ago—her son is a year and a half. I'll get there in time.

"Hey lady! Ooh, cute dress. Where's it from?" she asks.

I slip on a pair of loafers and swing a beer company's branded backpack onto my shoulder—my makeshift diaper bag until I can find Addison's. I step onto the porch with Addison in my arms.

"Paris, actually." I'd normally feel pretentious saying that, but not to Claire who has kids' toys and snacks stuffed in her designer purse.

Her youngest, Charlie, squirms in the back of the double stroller, trying to escape, while Madeline sits in the front taunting him with the dinosaur that she stole from him.

"Do you mind?" I ask, motioning for Claire to hold Addison so I can unfold the stroller, which leans against the wall in the foyer.

"Not at all. Oh, my God. She's so tiny. I forgot how tiny they are at this age."

I lug the stroller down the steps and expand it on the driveway. I'm out of breath from this minor physical activity and take a moment before retrieving Addison.

"Who's going to be there today?" I ask as I buckle her in the seat.

"Right, so you'll know most of the girls, I think. You know Lisa at the end of the street? She hosts this great barbecue at the beginning of the summer."

"Yeah, JP and I stopped by this year."

"Yes! Exactly. I forgot you went to that. You were about to pop!" She grabs the dinosaur from Madeline, gives her a *don't you dare* mom-look, and returns it to Charlie. "It's always a good time but I swear, if she doesn't start serving veggie burgers, we're going to overthrow her as summer barbecue host."

"You're a vegetarian?" I ask.

"Yeah. I only eat fish and poultry."

So, not a vegetarian.

"Mind if we go the long way?" She veers her stroller south towards the street that connects with Marjorie's.

"Not at all," I say, catching up with her.

"I hate going near the construction down there." She motions to the end of the street where a row of ten half-finished townhomes stand. "Gets my boots all dusty."

We pass Marjorie's house, but she isn't on the veranda today. Too cold outside for painting.

"Let's see, who else will be there? Janine ..."

The name doesn't ring a bell.

Claire continues. "And her cousin, Angela, who you will love. She's hilarious. Big personality! And Serene from yoga usually joins."

Oh yes, Serene. She spoke about her waterbirth in great detail that yoga class.

We turn down the side street that leads to a park with a state-of-the-art playground. No longer do children scrape their knees on pavement or get sharp gravel imprints on their hands and legs after sitting on the ground for too long. Playgrounds in new suburban neighborhoods are built on rubber flooring made from recycled tires. Germ-infested sandboxes have been replaced with equally questionable splash pads. The familiar monkey bars, slides, and swings have been upgraded with sensory add-ons to aid in child development.

The trees in the park are still young, supported by ugly metal rods. Their small branches sway with the slightest wind. South of the park is a small swamp which was supposed to be the focal point of the neighborhood. An early concept sketch had promised a clean, blue pond with a fountain in its center, outlined by cobblestone and iron benches for reflection. In reality, it's an eyesore, and a hazard for kids—a murky green, knee-deep puddle, with overgrown grass surrounding it. Essentially, a breeding ground for mosquitoes.

As we near the park, we spot two toddlers fighting over a steering wheel in one area of the jungle gym designed to look like a school bus. Lisa shouts at her three-year-old daughter from a nearby picnic table that she *better share, or else*. The other toddler erupts into a tantrum and bolts towards the pond, forcing his mother to scramble up from her place at the table and chase after him.

Claire leads us to the picnic table where the rest of the women sit. I'm relieved to discover that the others aren't as dolled up as her. This is a casual play date at a park, after all.

Serene appears to have jogged here, sporting workout gear with her red curls pulled back into a ponytail. She sits at the end of the table breastfeeding her boy, who is not much older than Addison. When she notices us, she tilts her head to the side like a puppy and says, "I know you from somewhere."

"Yoga. I came with Claire to a class," I say.

She repeatedly nods as if she is trying to remember me in that context. She finally stops and smiles. "Yes, that's it."

Lisa stands up to welcome me. "Hey, glad you came. Getting any sleep?" she asks in a warm voice much different from the one she used on her daughter. She wears a cream, cowl-neck sweater and light jeans. Her dark hair is short like mine, but she's had more years of practice styling it.

"Not really, but we're doing alright." I look down at Addison who is fast asleep. Any movement—car ride, stroller, rocking—tends to knock her right out. I park her in the shaded area next to the table and take a seat beside Claire.

"She's much quieter than I remember her at yoga," says Serene, who now clearly remembers Addison and me.

After I nod, I survey the one woman I don't recognize. She has tanned skin and long, dark, wavy hair. Her V-neck sweater emphasizes her breasts. She's curvy in a sexy but wholesome kind of way.

She reaches her hand from across the table. "I'm Angela." She has an overly firm grip but a friendly smile. "Here, have a cookie." She slides over a box of store-bought chocolate chip cookies.

"Oh, thanks. I'm Jo. Nice to meet you."

I accept a cookie and notice Serene rolling her eyes.

"You're supposed to *make* the snack when it's your week," Serene says and then positions her baby at the other breast.

"Why?" asks Angela.

No one in the group responds.

"Seriously? Why are you supposed to make them? What does it matter?" Angela shoves two cookies in her mouth and says with a mumble, "These cookies are my crack."

"They aren't made in a peanut-free facility. It's a courtesy to make your snack and ask about dietary restrictions," says Serene.

"She has a point," says Claire. "You're Italian. Aren't you all good cooks?"

"I'm not even going to respond to that. I guess it's a good thing I'm going back to work in two weeks. You all won't have to suffer through my devil cookies anymore."

A familiar blonde woman joins us, holding her two-year-old, whose face is wet with tears. "Are you causing trouble, Angie?"

"Always," says Angela with a smirk.

I decide that Angela is my favorite. I snatch another cookie and chime in with, "I actually love these cookies. Haven't had them in so long."

"See! They're a hit!" She gets up from the table and goes to check on her daughter, who is playing with a few toys on a blanket nearby.

The blonde woman reaches for a handshake. "It's Joanna, right? I'm Janine. We met at Lisa's in the summer."

I recognize this woman, but not from the barbecue. It was Janine who was walking by my house last night. She doesn't seem to remember snubbing me. Maybe she didn't see me wave.

Janine is stunning—tiny and demure like Audrey Hepburn, with a golden blonde pixie cut. She and her cousin Angela couldn't be more opposite in both looks and demeanor.

"Yeah. Nice to see you again," I say, unsure whether I should mention her walk yesterday evening.

Claire interrupts to dish on a neighbor. "Okay, okay, did anyone notice the new car in the Marinos' driveway?"

I knew there would be gossip today, but I thought it would take a little longer to get to it.

"A Corvette, really? Mid-life crisis to a T," Lisa says.

"Is this the guy whose wife left him?" asks Angela, trying her best to follow the drama.

"Yeah, but he was having an affair," says Claire.

"We don't know that for sure," Janine says in a small voice.

It's my chance to find out if the girls know anything about the call. If they heard anything, they'll likely share. "Did anyone hear about a mom in the neighborhood getting a Child Services complaint?"

There are simultaneous gasps and shrieks.

"What? No way!" Claire is giddy. "What did you hear?"

I continue, a little uneasy. "Oh, well, um. I don't know much about it." I wonder if I've made a huge mistake bringing this up, but there's no turning back now. "I have a friend who works in administration at the Child Services office, and she mentioned that there was an anonymous complaint made on a mom in my neighborhood. She couldn't remember her name, though."

"Did she say what the complaint was for?" Lisa asks.

Serene has finished feeding her boy and now stands a few feet away from the picnic table, rocking him to sleep. "I bet it was related to nutrition."

Angela jumps in. "Oh, come on. Is this another shot at my damn cookies?"

"No, I'm being serious. At school, if a child repeatedly comes without lunch or an adequate meal, we've had to call Child Services. So, maybe it was something like that."

The women stare at me, waiting for me to continue. Claire has practically climbed on top of me.

"It wasn't food related. There was a baby or child—not exactly sure of the age—that was left outside on their own for a while." I try to act casual, but I'm not the actor in the family.

"Outside where? Like at the park? Or on the street?" Lisa asks.

"Maybe? I really don't know the details. Thought someone else might have heard something." I rock Addison's stroller back and forth. She doesn't need the soothing, but I'm worried the mothers will be on high alert for non-maternal behavior after my story.

They consult with each other, and Angela breaks the tension, "Well it's not me! I live a half-hour away!"

"Maybe it was that woman with the five kids. What's her name?" Claire asks.

"Sandra!" Lisa exclaims after a few moments.

They all giggle while guessing who the mystery woman could be, except for Janine, who is silent. She makes her way to the jungle gym and watches her son play. She fiddles with her necklace. If I were the other girls, I would have thought she was the mother in question. She's my number one suspect as to who called Child Services on me.

My cellphone rings and my stomach drops when I see the name displayed on the screen. *Child Services*. I can't answer the phone in front of everyone—they'll know I'm the mother being investigated. The service worker is probably at the house for our visit.

"Shoot. I have to go. JP locked himself out." I gather my things.

Claire's smile turns into a pout. "We just got here."

I say a quick goodbye and agree to join them next week for a girl's night at The Landing, a local pub famous for karaoke and cheap shooters. I push the stroller with one hand and dial the service worker's number with the other as I jog the route home. My cell phone dies before the service worker can answer. I quicken my pace even though I'm out of breath. I need to get to my house before they leave.

CHAPTER TEN

A silver Honda is parked behind our SUV when Addy and I get home and a thousand butterflies flutter in my stomach. A woman steps out of the car when I approach with the stroller, and I do my best to slow my breath. I give myself a silent pep talk, *this looks good, you are taking your baby for a walk, and she's dressed appropriately for the weather.*

"Ms. Baker?" calls the woman, who looks to be in her mid-twenties. She brushes tight curls that match her sepia skin out of her face. She tucks a file folder under her arm and straightens her fitted navy blazer.

"Joanna. Hi, nice to meet you," I greet her with a smile and handshake. "I hope you weren't waiting here long. I tried to ring you back but my battery died." I hope that doesn't put my responsibility into question.

"No worries." She bends down and gives Addy a wave. "Oh, she's gorgeous. I'm Monica from the Child Services office. I trust you were expecting me?"

"Yes, I was told you'd be dropping by this week. If you just give me one minute ..." I unbuckle Addison and realize my hands are shaking. *Get a hold of yourself, Jo.* I lift Addy out of the stroller and rest her on my hip, contemplating my next move.

"Can I give you a hand?" Monica sets her files down on the hood of her car to free her hands.

"Actually, yes, if you don't mind holding Addison for a second while I put the stroller away." I fold up the stroller and drag it up the stairs to the front door, very aware that my beer-branded backpack is on display.

This woman must be wondering how I'd planned to do this without her help. I normally lay Addison on the grass at the side of the porch. Then I quickly run the stroller into the house and leave the door open. She can't roll yet, and I'm so quick that it's never seemed like a bad idea. I'm wondering how that would be perceived by any neighbors walking by.

With the stroller safely positioned in the house, I return to the driveway. "Please come in," I say, and take Addison from her arms.

Monica is polite and warm during the appointment, which takes the pressure off only slightly. I'm still completely aware of the situation and how important it is that I make a good impression. I give her a tour of the house, highlighting safety features like the power outlet covers, and the non-slip baby bath. I show her the crib, free of blankets. Monica reaches over the side of the crib. "Missing a back to your earring?" She passes me a silver backing. "Gotta watch things like this."

"Oh, I don't wear earrings. One of my sisters', maybe." I think about her marking an x on the file. One strike.

As we walk down the stairs, she says, "You'll want to invest in a carpet runner for these stairs."

"Yes, that's on our list."

Strike two.

When we reach the living room, she asks if we can look outside. I knew this was coming but it doesn't make it any less humiliating. She wants to see where Addy was deserted. We step onto the back deck and make our way to the patio table. I take a seat, but Monica remains standing beside one of the chairs, resting the folder on the armrest.

"So, I understand you and your daughter were outside the day the complaint was made. According to the onlooker, she was crying quite a bit and it seemed as though she was left by herself."

Hearing the account brings me back to that night at the Child Services office. I imagine Monica has read Herb's report on me. His diagnosis. I realize it doesn't matter how put-together I look today or how comfortable I am with Addy; Monica has probably made up her mind about me, too. After a week of reflection, I decide the best course of action is to admit fault—say I was inside grabbing something momentarily and avoid the whole memory lapse, which didn't help me in the last interview.

I rise to set the scene, mainly because I need to move my hands to cover up the shaking. "Yes, Addison was in her bassinet on the table here in the shade, underneath the umbrella. She had been napping and woke up when I was inside."

"Were you inside long?" She looks at her notes. "It says here that your daughter was crying for a while."

"I was only gone a few minutes. Just had to run to the washroom and didn't want to move her bassinet and wake her."

"Okay, why don't we go back inside and have a seat?"

Strike three.

I've failed the test. She doesn't want to tell me outside in case I cause a scene. She is going to lead me inside, invite me to sit, and then inform me that I'm not fit to mother my daughter. There is nothing I can do about it.

Monica tucks the folder in her bag once we sit down on the couch. "Listen, you seem like a great mother, and your house is in perfect order."

"Thank you, I appreciate that." Here comes the *but*.

"We receive complaints like this more often than you'd think and they're usually nothing to be too concerned about. Neighbors tend to forget how much babies cry in the first six months."

I give a small chuckle and relax my stiffened posture.

"What worries me in your case is that you admitted you didn't remember bringing her outside in your initial interview. Is that true?" she asks.

I don't know what to say. I pull Addison in close, feeling her warmth against my chest. *Please don't take my daughter away.*

"Well, I'm not sure if that's the truth, or if what you told me today is accurate, but I do think it would be in your and your daughter's best interest if you could talk to someone regularly. Just to help with the stress. I can recommend someone, but if you have a therapist you used to see, that would be preferred, since they know your history."

Monica leaves me with a list of three therapists to consider who operate out of a hospital that is twenty minutes away. Once I've scheduled an appointment, I am supposed to call her.

I carry Addison in a seat-hold position to the front window and offer a wave to Monica as she gets in her car. I watch with bated breath as her car pulls out of the driveway. The knot in my chest that's been coiling like a strangling vine all week finally untangles. At last, I can breathe.

71

Monica appears to be on my side, and that's all I can hope for right now. I never did ask her if she has kids. I just assumed so because she seemed to understand what I was going through. Maybe she was just being polite.

I look up the number for Dr. Alice Lui—a woman who knows more about me than my own husband—and jot it on a notepad we keep at the front door. I'll call her tomorrow after I've had a chance to update JP. *Dr. Alice Lui*, I trace over her name a few times with the ballpoint pen that sits nearby. Alice was a sort of maternal figure for me and someone who could be worth reconnecting with. She helped me process everything the year of Mother's death and the horrible car accident with my ex-boyfriend Cody. But once I reach out, aren't I admitting there's something wrong? I run my finger along the raised pattern of scars on my inner thigh, barely tangible beneath my leggings. I don't want those dark feelings of my adolescence to return.

Addison squirms in my arms, protesting my stillness. "Okay, Addy girl. What would you like to do now?"

I sit down on the piano bench in the front room with Addison in my lap and play one of the few songs I remember Meg teaching me.

Dolly dear, sandman's near, soon you will be sleeping.

Addison grabs at the keys and a trail of slobber follows.

"Oh, look at you. You're ready for a duet. Should we play *Heart and Soul*?"

She pounds at the keys and lets out a high-pitched scream. I play the tune once more for her. I really should call Alice, book the appointment, and convince Child Services that I'm committed to this process, but I play another tune instead. Procrastination masked as playtime with my daughter.

Come on, Jo. Just call her.

Returning to the front hall with Addison on my hip, I consult the notepad before dialing Alice's phone number. I put the phone on speaker and get ready with my pen to write down the appointment details. After three rings, a young man spouts off a greeting for Dr. Alice Lui's office, prompting me to leave a message.

"Hi Alice, it's Joanna Baker calling. I used to be a patient of yours when I was a teenager—and in my early twenties, I guess. I was hoping you were accepting new patients. Or accepting patients you used to have? I wanted to chat about some things, including my recent motherhood. Um, yeah—I'm a mom now. So, there's that. I have a five-month-old baby girl. Well, she'll be five months on the twentieth. Anyway, we should catch up. I mean, we should schedule an appointment. To talk about some things, I have going on. You can reach me at—"

The voicemail cuts me off before I can leave the most important information, my phone number. Jesus, Jo, that was awkward. I remain on the line for my options to re-record the message and my second attempt isn't much better. Maybe I should have written the message down first. On my third message, I'm satisfied and return the pen to its home beside the notepad. My eyes fall to the page, and I realize I've retraced *Dr. Alice Lui* so much that it looks angry; thick black letters stare back at me and they're almost unreadable.

Alice returns my call later that evening when I'm bathing Addison. She sounds different than I remember. Older, more professional, maybe.

The same warmth is there, though, that made me so comfortable talking with her ten years ago.

She suggests that I come to her office this coming Tuesday. Maybe this won't be so bad after all. A rush of adrenaline takes over as I recognize I've completed one daunting task. The appointment has been scheduled.

"Okay, now that that's done, let's do your shampoo," I say to Addison.

I squirt a small amount of baby shampoo in my palm and gently rub it on Addison's nearly-bald head. She closes her eyes, smiling to herself.

"You love the free head massage, don't you? I expect to see that reflected in my tip." Using the wet washcloth, I wipe away the suds. "Almost done now. Let's get you out."

Organization and foresight are everything when you're a mom. Bath time on your own is very doable if you have everything you need at your fingertips. A hooded towel lies on top of the changing table next to the bath, ready to wrap around Addison. Her clean sleeper is folded within arm's reach and her diaper—*damnit*. I forgot the diaper.

"That's okay. I'll just get you out onto the towel and then run to your room for the diaper real quick."

I lift Addison from her bath seat, realizing how sore my knees are after kneeling for ten minutes. I place her on her towel and bundle her up so she's nice and cozy on the changing table.

"Okay sweetie, Mama will be right back."

I run into her room to grab a diaper, only to realize there are none in the top drawer of her dresser. *Shit*. I could have sworn I had just replenished them. I race back to the hallway to grab a new box from the closet. Unable to remove the tape that binds the cardboard together, I stab at the tape with her baby nail clippers, slicing through the narrow seam to open the box. Before I can free a diaper from the plastic insert, I hear every mom's worst nightmare, a small thud followed by wailing. And I know this isn't just a *where are you, mom?* cry. No, this is an *I'm in pain* cry.

When I return to the washroom, the scene before me sends my stomach into summersaults. I let out a horrified scream.

CHAPTER ELEVEN

Addison lies crumpled on the bathmat, her cries building in intensity. She must have rolled off the diaper pad, which explains the thud that sent shivers down my spine. At least she didn't land directly on the tile. I pray that the plush fabric has lessened the impact. I rush to pick her up and attempt to comfort her, hushing her and kissing her cheeks.

"You're okay, you're okay. Mama's back. You just scared yourself."

Of course, that's how she chooses to roll over for the first time. A search on my phone convinces me that crying is a completely normal reaction, even if the baby isn't hurt. I continue to console her, holding her close and whispering that I'm sorry. I carry her to the toilet where I take a seat on the lid. She calms down as I nurse her. Meanwhile, I inspect her all over, feeling her head for bumps.

Jo, you are such an idiot. Never again, never again will I leave her like that. What was I thinking?

I continue to cradle her, when a warm, wet stream runs down my arm and onto my pants. She's peeing.

"Okay, and you're covered in pee now, aren't you?"

I guess we start over, then. Bath number two.

My mind plays tricks on me as I lie in the guest bed. I wish JP was home. At first glance, his guitar case resting against the closet door looks like someone dressed in a black hoodie watching me.

The room is almost sterile because of how unlived in it is. We chose a white comforter and pillows because they looked clean and bright. There is no side table or dresser, so I sleep with my water glass on the floor. A 16- by 24-inch framed picture leans against the wall of JP and me outside the courthouse on our wedding day. We haven't gotten around to hanging it up yet. There had been a huge snowfall the night before and everything was covered in sparkling white crystals. I was just starting to show—Addison was the size of a bell pepper—and I wore an empire waist dress and matching shawl. JP and I were terrified, still questioning if we had made the right decision to get married, but we hid our fears behind beaming smiles.

I open the blinds to let the moonlight in. Light pours through the French pane window and projects a grid pattern on the opposite wall. Addison's bassinet looks lonely, the way it sits empty by the window.

Tonight is the first night that Addison will sleep alone. I'm hopeful our separation will help me sleep better. I send JP a text: *Video cam keeps buffering. How do I reset it?* It's nine o'clock, which means JP should be back at his hotel, but I don't want to call and disturb him in case he's at a late dinner.

Twenty minutes pass, and he still hasn't texted back. My many attempts to reset the camera are fruitless—maybe it's a problem with our router. The app blinks with light pink bars and an error message reads *trouble connecting to camera.* Occasional white noise breaks through the silence and Addison appears in a bird's eye view, the night vision making her look ghostly dressed in her white sleep sack. The phone goes silent, and she is replaced by the pink bars once again.

I'll leave it for tonight. I'll keep my door open so that I hear when she wakes. My phone makes an alert, and I grab it quickly, hoping it's JP with video instructions.

> How's it going? Did you and Addy have a good day?

I debate telling Amy about the change table fiasco. I'm not sure I want to get into this over text. The truth is, sometimes I don't know how to talk to Amy about my doubts as a mom. I feel guilty that it was so easy for me to get pregnant with Addison. I'm one of the lucky ones and it's not lost on me.

> Service worker stopped by today. It actually went okay. I think it's all going to work out. But I screwed up, Ames. Addy fell off the change table in bathroom. She's okay. I just feel like I keep messing up.

She replies with the shocked face emoji.

> You sure she's okay? Poor baby.

Oh, great. I shouldn't have said anything. She really did seem fine after we snuggled. I change the subject.

> She's good, don't worry. Fast asleep now. Sleeping in her crib tonight like a big girl! Which reminds me, do you know how to reset a router? The baby monitor is useless right now.

I close my eyes until I hear the alert.

> She's growing up so fast! Have you heard of this thing called Google?

She sends a wink face to drill in her point. I decide not to respond to her text message right away. I get the sense that she is annoyed at me. She has a point, I guess. It's just that JP has always set up anything technology related. I don't even know what brand of router we have. I'm about to open my browser to search when another alert goes off.

> So, what's the next step with Child Services?

> I'm going to see Dr. Lui on Tuesday. Now, I just have to get my sleep under control. But all in time.

I lie on my back, my phone held at eye level, and a red icon tempts me to check my social notifications. I ditch my router research to scroll through my feed. My college friend's baby who is a month younger than Addy is already rolling both ways, front to back and back to front. I check my baby app and click on the *milestones* button in the menu. Rolling over, *three to six months*. Always a range, so that the parents whose kids are late bloomers don't feel bad. Addison rolled from back to front tonight. I just missed it. I'm sure she'll be doing both by the end of the month.

Another alert comes through.

> Just don't overthink it. Why don't you do some reading? That always knocks me out. You can always take those vitamins Meg got you. She swears by them.

I forgot that Meg brought the magnesium over. I guess it's worth a shot. I head downstairs to the kitchen, which is in complete darkness until my hand finds the light switch. I read the back of the bottle that Meg placed in the cupboard above the fridge, to ensure they are safe for nursing moms. Once I'm convinced, I swallow one white pill with a gulp of stale water left on the counter.

My thoughts consume me as I test out various sleep positions back in my bed. First, I try the left side, but quickly adjust. After having to exclusively sleep on my left during pregnancy— better blood flow for baby—I can't anymore. Right side it is. Where do I usually put my arm? Under my head? Under my pillow? I stretch my arm out reaching under the second pillow on the other side of the bed and my hand grazes the Maglite.

I tell myself I have nothing to be afraid of. I locked the door.

YOUR NAME IS JOANNA

Eight years old

Mother was reading to Meg and Amy in the living room while Jo lay in bed very much awake. It was Amy's giggle that gave them away, reminding Jo that she was too young to be included. They had arrived at a comical scene in *Little Women*. Meg's whispers were just as loud. Mother didn't bother shushing either of them.

Jo sat up in bed and scratched her big toe through the hole in her quilt. It wasn't fair that they read chapters without her. Mother said it was Jo's bedtime but she was only two years younger than Amy, so why didn't she get to stay up past nine?

Jo kicked off her blanket and slid out of bed. She opened her bedroom door a crack, trying to place what was happening in the story.

More giggles that she wasn't a part of. She shuffled down the hallway and leaned against the wall that led to the small family room at the front of the house.

"Do the voice, Mom," Amy teased.

"What voice?" Mother was playing coy. She sat on the couch in the middle of her two daughters holding the paperback in one hand. The daughters who looked like her. Blonde, blue-eyed, and beautiful.

Amy's legs were outstretched on Mother's lap and Mother was rubbing them with her free hand.

Meg leaned her head on Mother's shoulder. "Do Marmee's other voice. You did it different last night."

Mother adopted a voice that sounded softer and sweeter than her own.

Jo interrupted with a whisper. "I'm thirsty."

Their heads turned her way in unison.

Amy burst into giggles again. "Where'd you come from?"

Meg sat up straight and leaned forward. "Another nightmare?"

"I want a cup of water, Mom."

The sweetness drained from Mother's voice like water through a sieve. "Joanna, you can't keep doing this. Why aren't you asleep yet?" She shoved Amy's legs with force, sending her toppling over. "We'll finish this another time."

"Oh, come on," Amy pleaded, composing herself. "Jo, why'd you have to ruin it?"

"I should get to listen, too. I'm named after Jo."

"Your name is Joanna, not Josephine," Mother corrected her.

She was in the kitchen now, filling up a cup with water from the tap.

Jo traced her name with a finger on the peach wall. "It's Jo," she whispered.

Mother passed Jo a green plastic cup with barely an inch of water and waited until Jo finished her sip. When Jo handed it back, Mother tossed it into the sink with a clatter. Amy laughed once more but this time, it was at a higher pitch, and she sounded nervous.

"Let's go to bed. Mom's tired." Meg guided her sisters down the hallway towards their rooms. "Next time, just ask for me, okay?" she whispered, nudging Jo through her doorway. Meg kissed Jo on the top of her head. Jo closed her eyes, imagining that the gesture was from Mother.

CHAPTER TWELVE

I jolt awake in the dark to the sound of sporadic chimes building to a crescendo, then silence. My phone is no longer where I left it on the floor beside the bed. It sounds like it's coming from Addison's room. She doesn't seem to be stirring.

I have trouble remembering if I've already woken up to feed her. Usually, I would have fed her around eleven, before bed, but I must have fallen asleep. I'm confused when I find that the blinds are closed. I swear I left them open. I wanted to brighten up the room that is normally pitch black.

When I step out of bed, I lose my balance and end up on the floor beside the bassinet. My head pounds. It feels like I drank a bottle of wine to myself and am paying for it. I use the bed to guide myself back to a standing position. As I make my way across the room, I notice something in the bassinet. It's Addy, fast asleep. I watch her chest carefully, holding my breath until I see it rise and fall. She is still wearing the sleep sack that I dressed her in at the beginning of the night.

Think, Jo, think. Did Addy already wake me for her night feed? Maybe I brought her in the room while half asleep? During the first few weeks, I'd nurse Addison in bed and would barely remember waking to do so. Why do I feel so delirious?

I tiptoe into Addison's room. The crib is empty, and the blinds are raised. There is no sign that she ever spent the night in the nursery, except the hum of the humidifier and my phone, which sits on the ledge of the crib. I retrieve it and discover it's six in the morning. As far as I can remember, Addison hasn't eaten since I put her to bed at seven last night. There are no messages from JP, just one missed call from an unknown number. I peek out the window and the world is silent.

I step back into the hallway.

Addy fusses and I run to the bassinet. After a little squirm, she starts to fall back asleep. I rouse her and bring her into the bed with me.

"You must be starving, little one," I say, offering my breast, but she doesn't try to latch. Normally, if we skipped a feed, she would drain one breast completely. She would grab it with her dimpled fingers and squeeze it like a juice box, suckling until there's nothing left. Today, she keeps her mouth closed. She cuddles in close and drifts off to sleep as if she had just finished a meal.

I must have woken up at some point in the night to get her. It would be very strange for her to sleep for ten hours straight. I must have fed her and brought her in the guest room. Forgot my phone on the ledge. That's logical. But why would I have opened her blinds? Why don't I have the faintest memory of this?

Chapter Thirteen

I try calling JP, but it goes straight to voicemail. I am unsure what time he'll be coming home today. We never talked about whether he would go into the office after his flight.

"Oh, Addison. Now would be a great time for you to say your first words. Was it Mama who came in and got you last night?"

She blows bubbles in between coos.

"I'll take that as a yes."

We make our way downstairs and when we arrive at the foyer, I confirm the door is locked. *Jo, you're starting to lose it.*

I pour myself a bowl of cereal and eat it at the counter while Addison rocks in her swing.

Thoughts of last night consume me. I keep telling myself that I must have fed Addison while I was half asleep at some point, then brought her into the guest room with me. That's the only explanation. She couldn't move from the crib to the bassinet by herself.

I try JP's phone again, but nothing. Hopefully, he'll realize the battery died and charge it. I notice a notification from Addison's baby monitor app that reads, *your night summary is available.* These are the features you get when you splurge for the premium subscription, and they advertise it to worried moms as a must-have.

I click on the video and the time stamp reads 6:50 p.m. I watch myself tiptoe towards the crib, holding a sleeping Addison in my arms. I rock her over the crib and place her on her back on the mattress. And with one steady motion, I release my hand from under her back. It reminds me of Indiana Jones from *Raiders of the Lost Ark* when he tries to stealthily remove the golden idol. I am successful and she remains asleep as I leave the frame. The light turns off and the night vision kicks in.

At 8:08 p.m., Addison stirs, but falls asleep in less than one minute. The camera goes black and the video reads, *connection issues.* Just as expected. That's around the time I noticed the app stop working last night. I'm about to exit the app when the video resumes. I have a sinking feeling in the pit of my stomach, as if I've been pushed off the ledge of a building.

A close-up of a hand enters the frame and I clasp my mouth in fear.

The arm falls to rest on the ledge of the crib momentarily, right next to my phone. The figure appears to be a man's body from the neck down. He turns away and presumably exits the room.

I watch the video another five times. It looks like the person was touching the camera. Perhaps pressing one of the buttons that sit on top of the head, likely the reset button. It would make sense, since the video resumed at the very moment I saw the hand. The man is slight in stature. He's wearing a hoodie and jeans. It's quick, and in night vision, but the figure resembles JP. The timestamp reads 5:00 a.m., and Addison is no longer in the crib.

I haven't heard from JP since I texted him last night asking how to reset the camera. Did he come home early, move Addison to the bassinet, and then reset it? If so, where is he now? I dial his number again and then send him a text to call me right away.

It has to be JP. I watch the video another time, studying the man's movements. That's how JP moves his hand, right? Does he own a hoodie like that? Yes, I think I've seen it before.

I check the back door and it's locked. No one could have gotten in last night unless they had a key. It must have been JP.

Addison and I head upstairs, and I put away a load of laundry to distract myself. I manage to fold three sleepers before the pit in my stomach grows and I'm tempted to try his phone again. Then another time. And another. Each time, it connects me straight to his voicemail. If I hear, *JP Girard, you know what to do,* one more time, I may throw his PlayStation into the recycling bin.

A car door slams outside, and I rush to the window. A taxi pulls away as JP saunters up our driveway, cell phone and briefcase in hand, but no luggage. Addison continues playing on her piano mat. Beethoven's *Ode to Joy* tinkles behind me.

The front door closes and JP calls out, "Hey, where are you guys?"

"Up here," I yell.

JP runs straight to Addison when he enters the nursery. "Addy, I missed you. How's Daddy's girl?" He picks her up from where she lies on her mat and kisses her on both cheeks.

JP is dressed in business casual—a cotton button-down shirt and dark jeans. He looks like he could have just stepped off a plane, but I'm questioning whether that's the case.

"I think she got even cuter since I left."

"Did you lose your cell?" I ask.

JP lies beside Addy, blowing on her belly and making her shriek with laughter. "No, but I have to charge it. Why?"

"I've been calling you all morning. Texted you last night, too."

"Shoot, sorry about that." He blows again on her navel, and she grabs at his face. "Everything okay?"

I can't wait any longer. I need to find out if someone was in our house last night or if JP came home early. I place my phone on the floor beside him and play the video. He props himself up on one elbow. He must know what's coming. When the unidentified hand appears on the screen, he shrugs.

"Please tell me this is you," I say.

"It's me. Who else would it be?"

I exhale the breath I've been unconsciously holding—no one broke into our house. But that feeling of relief is quickly replaced by confusion.

"So, you came home last night? What time did you get in? Where did you sleep? Where were you coming from just now? Why not take the car?" The questions pour out of me like a magician's infinite silk trick, and he looks taken aback.

"What do you mean? I came home last night. I saw you this morning. I came into the guest room and gave you a kiss before I left for my meeting. I told you I'd take a cab to my meeting and let you have the car."

"What time was this at?"

"I dunno, 5:30?"

"I don't remember that at all." I join him and Addison on the floor. "The video freaked me out so much when I watched it this morning. I thought someone might have broken in. What were you doing in her room?"

"I'm sorry, Jo. I really didn't mean to freak you out. I was just resetting the monitor. You texted that it wasn't working."

"I thought you said that your phone was dead."

He pushes himself to a seated position so that we are now at eye level. "I forgot to charge it last night, so I plugged it in this morning for a few minutes when I was getting ready to go. When I got your text, I reset the monitor."

I guess I was just so tired that I don't remember our conversation this morning or feeding Addison and moving her to the bassinet. I stand up to resume the laundry, then turn to face him again. "So, you didn't move Addison?"

"Move Addison? What do you mean?"

"You didn't see Addison in the crib and move her into the bassinet in the guest room?"

"Jo, what are you talking about? Did something happen last night?"

"It's nothing. I must have fed her in the middle of the night half asleep, that's all."

I continue to fold sleepers, bibs, and burp cloths. Mothers nurse their babies half asleep all the time. This doesn't mean anything. I was just half asleep. That's why I don't remember.

I move efficiently between the dresser, Addison's walk-in closet, and the linen closet in the hallway, busying myself with chores, so I don't have the capacity to think about last night.

"Are you okay? How was the week?" he asks.

"Child Services came by yesterday."

JP stumbles to his feet and joins me at the dresser. "What did they say?" He rests his forearm on my pile of burp rags.

I move his arm off, adding another folded cloth to the pile. "That I seem like a good mother."

Those words came out of Monica's mouth. She seemed satisfied with my tour, my answers. I'm sure it will blow over. It has to—I can't let myself think of the alternative.

"So, that's it? They're gonna close the case?"

I can't decipher whether JP's tone is hopeful or surprised.

"No. They want me to go see someone. A therapist."

JP inches closer, but I dare not look up from the piles of tiny outfits. Talking about going to a therapist feels humiliating. JP doesn't know all the details of that side of me, and I'd like to keep it that way.

"You okay with that?" he asks.

"I guess I have to be."

"I think it's going to be really good for you, Jo." It must put his mind at ease knowing I will be speaking to a professional about my doubts.

He continues, "I think that you can admit that the first few months have been hard for you."

"Hard for me?" Everyone seems to expect women to just adapt instantly to having a baby. Isn't there a learning curve like everything else in life?

"Come on, Jo. You know what I mean." He tilts his head to the side. JP has always had the quintessential example of motherhood in his mom. I must look like a monster compared to her.

"I'm sorry if I'm not living up to how you'd hoped I'd be as a mom," I say.

"Hey, that's not what I meant." He pats me on the back and we both seem to notice how platonic it feels. "It's been an adjustment for you, that's all." His face lights up suddenly like he's remembered something. "Be right back." He races down the hallway to our bedroom and returns holding a paper shopping bag. "I got you both a present," he says, smiling ear to ear.

"Oh yeah?" *Ah, the pity present.*

"Well, it's not exactly a present. I picked up something I think you'll like."

JP retrieves a storybook he bought for Addison and then passes the bag my way. He joins Addison on the floor and reads her the board book about a mouse and a strawberry and a hungry bear. I pause my laundry to open the bag. Inside are the hotel robe and slippers I asked for. He's also included a box of decaf Earl Grey tea.

"Oh, thanks." I smile and then place the bag down, resuming my folding.

"What?" He props himself up on his side.

"It's nice, thank you. I'll definitely use the robe and slippers. It's just ... I haven't been drinking tea lately."

"I know. It's decaf."

"No, I've cut out all tea since the kettle has been waking Addison up. I'm just drinking water ... or sometimes cranberry juice, but it's all good. Thank you, I appreciate it." I smile again, this time bigger, so not to offend him.

When Addison was still having portable naps in the bassinet, I noticed she would wake up shortly after the kettle would make itself known with the three high-pitched beeps. I have yet to test out this theory now that she is napping in the nursery.

He grabs the bag from where I've left it on the floor. "I'm sorry, but that's fucked."

"Hey, watch the language."

"You can't just cut out tea because you think the kettle is waking her up. How loud is this kettle?"

"It's not even that loud, but without fail, every time I make tea she wakes up. So, I only drink tea from the café now."

"Alright." He removes the box of tea from the bag and makes his way to the door.

"Where are you going?" I ask.

"To have a shower. I still smell like plane."

Addy and I are left alone again.

CHAPTER FOURTEEN

JP spent most of Saturday in line for a new cowboy video game at the store across town. He spent the rest of the weekend playing it, while I tended to Addy and then flipped through photos of her on my phone as she napped. He even took yesterday off work because he swore that he was coming down with something, but I think that was a lie, since I cleared an empty bottle of wine from the coffee table this morning. I'm pushing JP away, but he's not trying very hard to reconnect, either. I think he feels like he's walking on eggshells when he's around me, so his solution is to just stay away.

Today is my first appointment with Alice. Well, technically, it's more than that—I saw her once a week for my last two years of high school and then occasionally when I was home for the weekend from college. It has been a decade since our last appointment.

Ten years ago, I didn't know it was going to be the last one. I didn't send her flowers or a thank you card. I just never re-booked after college graduation. I was like the set-up who didn't call after the third date even though they said they'd had a great time.

Meg has agreed to watch Addy since JP is at work and her house is on the way. She and Derek live in a split-level in an older neighborhood about fifteen minutes away from us. I've always loved Meg's winding road and the pine trees that surround each house. The houses were built around the landscape, instead of today's method of clear-cutting and bulldozing everything in sight before breaking ground.

With three bedrooms, the house is small for four boys, but it has a large backyard for burning off energy. I spot the treehouse that Derek built as we approach the house, its yellow slide protruding from the green pines. I'm forced to park at the foot of the driveway to avoid running over a bike that's been left haphazardly on the asphalt.

Meg greets me at the door with a hug and then scoops Addy up in her arms, kissing her numerous times on the cheek. I don't think her boys let her cuddle them like that anymore. Meg has done a nice job updating the 1970s home with modern fixtures and chic décor. She's always had a flair for interior decorating. There is still proof that this is a house full of kids; hockey equipment clutters the front landing and there are action figures strewn across the basement floor.

I drop my backpack at the front door and pass her a separate lunch bag with my liquid gold—a bottle of five ounces of breast milk that took me an hour to pump last night.

"Thanks again for looking after Addy," I say.

"It's no trouble at all. I'm always happy to spend time with my niece." She goes in for another snuggle. "Are you sleeping any better?"

"A little."

"Did you try the magnesium? It's really the most natural thing you can take while nursing."

"Yeah, I'll give it some time. Thanks for the advice."

I kiss Addison goodbye and turn to leave but Meg calls me back. "Jo? I'm really glad you're doing this."

"Yeah, well ... I have to. It was mandated."

"I know. But I'm happy you're going back to Dr. Lui. She was good for you."

I soften my gaze. I feel slightly guilty for getting so frustrated with Meg. I know she's trying to be supportive, just like she was when Mother died. She is only six years older than me, but when it happened she was forced to take on my baggage. She delayed moving in with Derek until I went to college, even though they were newlyweds. She stayed with me at the hospital after the accident with Cody, sleeping on an uncomfortable chair while I recovered. It was her who urged me to go to therapy after discovering the marks on my thighs.

I give her a hug, then kiss Addison once more.

"Thanks, sis. I won't be long."

Alice's office has moved to the newer part of town in an updated commercial unit sandwiched between a Whole Foods and Pottery Barn. When I open the frosted glass door, it elicits the tinkle of chimes, and I step onto a tan doormat with the word *hello* written in a white cursive font. If it weren't for the sign—*Alice Lui, Clinical Psychologist, PsyD*—I would have thought I'd entered a spa by mistake.

Tranquil music plays at a low volume so that guests can hear the gentle rush of the stone waterfall feature. Copper-potted succulents sit on the window ledge, and I can't tell whether they are real or fake. The seating area looks comfortable, with beige lounge chairs carefully positioned in a horseshoe around the room, facing the front desk, which is far too trendy for a therapist's reception.

A young man who looks to be in his mid-twenties sits behind the semi-circular desk, which is equipped with unnecessary upward lighting. He sports a military haircut and no evidence that he can grow facial hair. He is dressed in a tight-fitting olive-green dress shirt and a black wool tie. A woman, whose hair matches the ash wood desk, stands at the printer tapping the toe of her patent leather Oxford shoe behind her. I didn't think I would feel underdressed at the shrink's office. Alas; here I am in khakis and a baggy V-neck sweater looking down at my loafers while this woman struts about in a black dress with a white, rounded collar.

The man and woman smile and say in unison, "Welcome to Dr. Lui's," and then giggle as if they didn't mean to say it simultaneously. I feel like I've stepped into a suburban horror movie and I'm about to be hypnotized by the sinister therapist. The woman continues to fiddle with the printer as the guy signs me in and tells me to have a seat. I recognize his voice from Alice's voicemail greeting.

The waiting room remains empty, and I'm extremely thankful. I choose the seat closest to the door that I am assuming leads to Alice's office, and leaf through a lifestyle magazine with tips and tricks on how to have a *spooktacular* Halloween. A few moments later, a teenage boy hurries through the office door and says a quick goodbye to the style twins before exiting to the street. I watch through the window as he breaks into a swift jog.

When I turn away from the window, Alice stands before me. She greets me with a smile. "Joanna, it is so nice to see you again." She holds the door open for me and ushers me into her office, which looks like it has been furnished by the Pottery Barn next door.

I sit on a brown leather couch, across from her matching armchair. A blue Persian rug covers most of the hardwood floor. Her wooden desk, which is made to look weathered, is positioned near the window at the back of the room. A few of the same succulent pots from the reception add some green to the room. I conclude that they are fake. They aren't near the window, and I'm pretty sure succulents need sunshine to survive. The only thing in her office that doesn't look like it has been curated from a style guide is the bookshelf, which has paperbacks squeezed into every available inch with little apparent order.

The last ten years have been kind to Alice, both in looks and prosperity, judging by her office. Alice, who must have been about forty-five when we last met, has aged gracefully. Her hair, which was once kept short, hovers just above her shoulders, with streaks of grey framing her face. She has more wrinkles around her eyes and forehead, but she has the same warm smile.

My worries about rehashing my past fade.

She moves forward in her chair and leans in. "You're all grown up, and a mother now?"

"Yes, as of four months ago. Her name is Addison."

"Beautiful name. Do you have photos?"

What mom doesn't? I scroll through my camera roll to find a photo of Addy when she turned four months old. I had dressed her in a jean dress and yellow headband and positioned a mini chalkboard beside her with her likes: Zebra stuffy, car rides, Mom and Dad—and her dislikes: hiccups and being wet.

"This is her from a few weeks ago." I pass Alice the phone.

"Wow, she's so fair."

"Yeah, that's the Baker side coming through. She looks more like Amy and Meg."

I don't need to explain to Alice who Amy and Meg are. Alice has heard me speak of them in almost every therapy session and they even came in once for a group session at her request.

"She's precious, really. And how are you adapting to motherhood?"

"Well, that's sort of why I called you. Overall, it's going okay. I love her so intensely in a way I never imagined I could. But my anxiety sometimes takes over. Especially lately."

"What is it that you are worried about?"

"Everything. Is she nursing enough, gaining weight, does she have a fever, is the bath too hot, is she warm enough outside, is she developing at the right rate—"

"Take a breath," she says.

I close my eyes and breathe in through my nose for a few seconds, hold for a couple more, and then slowly exhale through my mouth. I repeat this a few times until she says, "That's good. Just like that."

I'm surprised that I remember the technique she taught me after I had my first panic attack in high school. I wanted drugs to make the anxiety go away. She wanted to teach me breathing exercises first.

"I think I'm mostly worried about being a good mother."

"That's a completely natural thing to worry about. Many moms do."

I fiddle with my thumb but catch myself before I pick too deep.

After a few moments of quiet, she leans in closer. "Are you worried about the kind of relationship that you might have with Addison?"

I bite the inside of my lip.

"Your relationship doesn't have to be like yours and your mother's."

"But what if it is? What if Addy and I don't get along?"

"Joanna, it is not your fault that your relationship with your mother was the way that it was. You were a child. She was the adult."

I stare down at my lap, telling myself not to cry, to at least wait until our second session.

"You were the victim in an emotionally abusive relationship. That doesn't define you, or how you form relationships with other people."

She's said this many times before, but it feels like the first time someone has acknowledged it in ten years. Amy and Meg never talk about it. I think they've convinced themselves that it wasn't true, just ghost stories we made up to frighten each other, or nightmares blending with memories. I sometimes wonder whether they don't want to admit that their youngest sister had a very different childhood than them. Perhaps they ignored it at the time because they were scared that if they tried to stop it, they'd be the new targets. "I would never hurt Addison like that."

"You have a kind heart, Joanna. I think you are going to make a great mother."

That's when I burst into tears, relieving the ache that was trapped in my throat. Finally, I explain the real reason for my call, in between sobs. I don't hold back, assuming the Child Services office will get in touch with her anyway. I tell her that I left Addy outside. That I don't remember it at all. That I've possibly been blacking out, sleepwalking, or who knows what, and I'm terrified of what I might do next.

She lets me cry, waiting patiently until my sobs transition to shallow breaths. She gives me advice to help with my insomnia—developing a proper sleep routine, putting my phone away for the night, taking a break from screen time an hour before bed. I was hoping for a quick fix—a prescription for a pill that would make me normal.

"Joanna, call me if you experience additional memory lapses. We'll want to keep a close eye on those, with your history."

I nod. She doesn't say the words *postpartum depression, anxiety,* or *psychosis,* but she must be considering the possibility, just like the others.

A question gnaws at me: what if they're right?

CHAPTER FIFTEEN

I watch from my car as the six o'clock train pulls into the station. The doors open and commuters run to their vehicles in a race to get out of the parking lot. Grown men aggressively push past neighbors, one accidentally whacking another with his briefcase. Women practically sprint in heels and leap over chain dividers in the parking lot like they are hurdles.

I start the car and scan the passengers for JP and Amy. JP will blend in with the other men rushing home from work, dressed in a suit, but he will at least know where to find our car. I stand halfway out my door and keep an eye out for Amy, searching for her latest hair color.

September left with its warm nights last week, making room for October's damp cold to rush in. My leather jacket doesn't do much to stop the wind and I regret my choice to forego tights.

"Oh hey, stranger," Amy says as she approaches the car. "Wow, that's some dress."

"Oh good, you found me." I tug on the material. It suddenly seems too short for a mom having a date night with her husband. "It's too much, isn't it?"

"No way. You look hot, Mama. How'd today go with Dr. Lui?" she asks.

"Fine."

"Sounds riveting," she jokes. "Come on, you can talk to me."

"I just told her what I'm stressing about. How I want to be the perfect mom."

"That's good. You need to open up about your anxiety. You don't want to

bottle that up."

"Well, I'll have lots of time to talk about it. It's going to be a weekly thing."

She makes her way to the other side of the car to claim the seat next to Addison. "That's good, Jo. It will help."

JP jogs towards us, clutching his briefcase. He kisses me on the cheek and then eyes my dress and Amy in the car. "What's going on? Girls' night tonight?"

"Hurry, get in. We'll be stuck here for hours if we don't get moving."

Once out of the parking spot, I begin the game of maneuvering past pedestrians and cars all trying to find their way to the exit.

JP twists in his seat to greet Addy and her aunt. "I didn't know you were coming over tonight, Amy." He turns back to me. "What's the plan for dinner? Do we want to order something?"

Amy chimes in. "I'm letting you cash in one of your babysitter coupons. I thought you two were owed a night out."

"Yeah, I honestly don't remember the last time we went out to dinner!" He sounds genuinely excited.

I turn right like most of the cars ahead of us, heading on Main Street where we have our pick of restaurants. "Where do you feel like going?" I ask, even though my heart is set on pasta.

"Lady's choice," he says.

"Italian?" We pass my favorite restaurant, Barolo—a family-owned Italian joint that doesn't take itself too seriously.

"Works for me."

His phone beeps, indicating a new text message.

We make the left turn onto our residential street, still following a few cars from the train station. One by one, the cars peel off into neighboring driveways. When I pull into ours, I help Amy bring in Addison's carrier. After a rundown of my far-too-detailed babysitter notes and a tutorial on how to download the monitor application onto her phone, I head back out to the car for date night.

Tuesday evenings in the suburbs are quiet. The restaurant is empty, and we have our pick of tables. Once again, it's *lady's choice* and I tell myself this is an act of chivalry as opposed to indifference. I decide on a two-seater booth next to a window that overlooks the town's main street, which gives me something to do while JP finishes up on his phone.

Our view is of the tallest building on the street—an Anglican church with stained glass windows and a steeple that looks down on the town. Next to it is a block of connected two-story brick buildings with shops on the main level and apartments on the second. Steeped Café appears busy for a Tuesday evening—there must be an open mic night underway.

The streetlights that line the sidewalk are designed to look historic, with black, wrought iron lanterns, outfitted with LED lights. Banners hang from them and rotate with every season. For October, they are a deep red with an illustrated cornucopia stuffed with corn, squash, and other harvest foods. The words *Fall into Courtfield* are written in a flowery script along the top.

I text Amy, reminding her to lock the front door. It's unnerving being away from Addison. I've forgotten how to act or what to talk about.

My gaze returns to JP, who is still glued to his phone. I have yet to hear a compliment on how I look, which is strange since I haven't made an effort like this since before Addy's birth. I decided on a black, off-the-shoulder pencil dress, with a coordinated choker necklace. I even straightened my bob and put on maroon lip stain. What's even stranger is he hasn't asked how my appointment with Alice went. I don't really want to get into it, but it's odd he hasn't asked. I peer out the window, scanning the passersby below. What would I even say? I broke down in tears and she hinted I'm likely suffering from postpartum depression? That's a great topic for date night. Very romantic.

I clear my throat to catch JP's attention.

He looks up. Stares at me blankly. Finally, his eyes focus like he's just remembered where he is: on a date with his wife, not at the office. "Oh, sorry, just finishing up a couple of emails." His lips mouth the words as he types. "Done." He returns his gaze to me and sets the phone face down. "I'm all yours."

Finally. It's only been five months since we've had a date.

"You look beautiful, by the way," he says, reaching for my hand across the table.

I meet him halfway and graze his fingers with mine. With my other hand, I tuck my hair behind my ear. "I'm still not loving my haircut."

A server wearing a black dress shirt and matching bistro apron saunters over to our table. He gives us a spiel about the specials, but I only half listen because it is my usual, the spaghetti Carbonara, that I'm after. We start with a bottle of Grignolino—JP's order. I'm not sure what this is, only that it's an Italian red wine that costs more than our entrées combined. JP says I will love it, that he tried it recently at a client dinner in the city and it has notes of cinnamon—whatever that means.

As we sip our wine and stab at our calamari, JP shares news of Deary Pharma, the new client his company landed.

"We've doubled our new business from last year with this account alone," he boasts.

"That's great. Really, you should be proud."

"It wasn't me actually—for once. Lauren, one of our senior graphic designers landed it. She went to high school with the VP. I think he has a bit of a crush on her."

"Well, I doubt they chose the agency because the VP has a crush on your graphic designer."

I've met Lauren before and she's gorgeous and confident. I wouldn't be surprised that someone would have a crush on her. I'll admit it's crossed my mind that JP might be attracted to her.

"We're the best in the biz, but Lauren got us in the door."

I gulp my wine, not noticing any cinnamon.

All this talk is making me miss work. All I can brag about is the fact that I got two loads of laundry folded this afternoon while Addy napped, my audio book playing in the background. I miss the adrenaline of accomplishing something—the celebrity dinners, cramming the night before a press day, celebratory drinks when a film had a decent opening. JP and I had our share of celebratory drinks before we had Addison and before he got promoted to vice president and work started to consume him.

It feels like a century ago since we met at a film premiere, but it's only been two years. An independent distributor had chosen both JP's advertising agency and my PR firm to work on an art-house horror flick about the Salem witch trials that fall. JP, a creative director at the time, was invited to the premiere as a thank you after his team edited the film's trailers; I was working the red carpet.

At the end of the film, I had to clean up the props and take down the photo backdrop. Most of my team had left and I was stuck trying to disassemble it by myself, all while wearing a tight dress and high heels. JP gave me a hand with the backdrop and after everything was packed up and a courier was scheduled for the next morning, he suggested we go for a nightcap. We stayed at the bar until closing time.

It was JP's crooked smile that invited me in, and the way he brushed his hair off his face, revealing a chickenpox scar above his eyebrow. I intently watched his animated hands as he talked. His fingers had been calloused from playing guitar without a pick. I've always been a sucker for musicians.

I kept hiccupping that night—I was a few drinks in—and he would let out a laugh every time. I apologized after each spasm. *Sorry, this is so embarrassing.* He laughed. *I actually think it's cute.*

We sat close in the cab home, JP in the middle seat, and when the car got to my place he jumped out and opened the door for me. I turned towards him before making my way to my apartment. I was hesitating, unsure if I wanted to invite him in. He peered at me as if he was studying me and then that crooked smile stretched across his face. I was so self-conscious. *What are you looking at? Oh God, am I swaying?* He laughed. *No, you're not swaying. I'm just smitten.* I made fun of him for using the word and then he kissed me—a peck on the cheek that made me feel like I was seventeen again. Nothing further happened that first night, but after a few more of these film premiere nightcaps, I didn't get out of the cab at my stop.

Now, JP finishes his glass of wine and motions the server over to pour him another one, even though the bottle is sitting at our table well within reach.

Noticing my look, he says, "What? It's his job."

I try not to roll my eyes. The server obliges and tops up my glass even though I've barely had any. I smile and thank him, still embarrassed that JP called him over.

JP holds up his glass to toast. "To Deary Pharma, who is paying for this dinner," he laughs.

I hold up my glass to meet his. "To Amy, for giving us the night out."

"To Amy." He clinks his glass to mine, then takes a big swig. He leans forward with his elbows on the table. "That reminds me, I'm out tomorrow night. A few of us are going to dinner and drinks to celebrate."

Why am I not surprised? His company finds any reason to celebrate.

I nod. "Are you home Friday night?"

"Yeah. It's just tomorrow. We're going to this expensive sushi place. It's aburi-style—you know, when they flame-sear the fish?"

I purse my lips. JP can be pretentious when it comes to food. It's not that he's particularly knowledgeable about food and wine; he just has the authority to expense work dinners, so likes to test out trendy restaurants and talk about them to people who weren't there.

I continue my thought, "I was invited out to a girls' night on Friday. Claire, from next door."

"Claire? Really? I thought you hated her."

"I don't *hate* her. I don't even know her, really. I thought it would be good to get to know some other moms in the neighborhood."

"I'm all for it. Go, have fun. Who's all going?" he asks.

"The only people you would know are Claire and Lisa who hosted us for that barbecue in the summer. Oh, and Janine? She was at the barbecue as well."

JP nods. "What are you girls doing? I can drive you if you want to drink. Pick you up at the end of the night?"

"No, you can't." I laugh. "You'll be at home watching Addison."

"Right, right." He looks embarrassed that he forgot about our daughter.

"It's fine, I wasn't planning on drinking anyway. We are just going out for dinner and karaoke."

"And you're not planning on drinking? Sober karaoke sounds terrible."

"Well, I'll drink something. We'll probably just cab together."

"I'm glad you're getting a night out. Plus, it's a chance for Addy and me to hang on our own."

"It'll just be bedtime routine, then she'll be asleep, and you can game, or whatever," I say and then watch as JP's gaze falls to his hands.

"I do enjoy spending time with Addy, you know," he says and his voice is the softest it's been since we arrived.

"You're right. It will be nice for you both."

JP's eyes widen. "Oh, so my parents are going to be flying in on Saturday afternoon."

I have a hard time matching his excitement. "Right."

How did I forget his parents were coming this weekend? I'll need to make up the guest room for them and join JP in our bedroom.

"I figured that way they can spend some time with Addison, and we can make a nice dinner."

"Are they flying home right after the baptism?" Please say yes. I'm still mad at myself for agreeing to do it in the first place—it's an unnecessary stress. Anything to do with religion reminds me of Mother, and thinking about Mother makes it hard to breathe.

"No, that would be a lot of travel for just two days. They'll stay until Tuesday."

I get along with my in-laws just fine, but I've never been a fan of hosting people for more than a night. I always find it awkward in the mornings—guests in their robes making breakfast in my kitchen. I don't have much of a relationship with my father-in-law, Louis. He is the kind of person who starts every conversation addressing only his son, making me feel like it isn't meant for my ears. Margot, my mother-in-law, is pleasant. She's never been anything but nice to me, but she asks far too many personal questions. A few weeks ago on the phone, she had the audacity to ask me if my menses had returned, then went on to tell a story about a friend of hers whose daughter got pregnant with her second when her firstborn was five months old. I wish I had the nerve to tell her I haven't slept with her son in almost six months.

A rustling sound from my phone interrupts my thoughts. I have Addison's video monitor on loud and we hear her stir momentarily before she settles and falls back asleep.

"Do I need to take away your phone?" JP asks with a smirk.

"Why?"

"You're becoming obsessed with that monitor."

"What? No." I flip my phone over, so it is face down.

"I think Amy can handle it," he says.

"You've also been on your phone a lot tonight," I retort, my tone sharper than I planned. I check the app once and I'm obsessed, yet he's been on his phone all night and that's completely reasonable.

"It's just because of this new account. There's some stuff we need to get sorted this week."

The server arrives with our entrées and the savory smell of garlic is a welcome distraction. After we take a few bites, he returns for a quality check and JP and I both hesitate, our mouths stuffed with pasta.

I swallow and dab my lips with my napkin. "It's delicious, thank you."

Addison's cries reverberate from my phone. JP and I both reach for it but he wins the race.

"Give her a chance to settle. Amy will go to her if she keeps it up." He turns the volume down on the phone and shoves it into his pocket.

"Give me the phone. I'm serious, this isn't funny." I reach across the table, but he ignores my request.

"Jo, relax. She's fine." He doesn't bother to check, the phone still wedged in his pocket.

"Let me just see her. What if Amy doesn't have the monitor on loud? What if she fell asleep?" My face flushes and the pasta in my stomach feels like it's expanding. I need air.

"It's eight o'clock. I doubt Amy's asleep."

"Give me the phone!" I shout.

A couple at a nearby table looks our way. We are now their dinner entertainment. JP slides the phone over and sinks into his chair. "God, Jo. You need to calm

down."

I consult the phone immediately. Amy sways from side to side, holding Addison in her arms next to the crib. She rubs Addy's back, which seems to have lulled her back to sleep.

"Where was this concern for Addy when you left her outside?"

His comment hits me like a punch in the gut and I nearly choke on my spaghetti. "That's not fair. It wasn't—"

"It wasn't you? Come on, Jo. Take some responsibility."

I can feel my pulse quicken. I dig my nails into my palms and invite the sting to deepen. *Just breathe*.

We eat the rest of our meal in silence. JP responds to emails and texts on his phone in between bites of Spaghetti Bolognese. I wait until Addison is safe in the crib, and only then do I let myself eat my noodles, which are now room temperature.

When the server returns to collect our plates and offers dessert, I decline, despite my sweet tooth.

Chapter Sixteen

After twenty minutes of aggressive rocking, Addison is finally asleep. I tiptoe out of the nursery and down the stairs to the kitchen. My sushi sits in takeout containers on the kitchen counter, the miso soup getting cold.

JP will be out late—*they have so much to celebrate*—so my plan is to stuff my face with spicy salmon and binge-watch home renovation shows. I lay out my sushi on the coffee table and begin shoveling maki into my mouth with my fingers. I disregard the cheap wooden chopsticks and try not to let the fact that they sent four sets make me feel like I ordered too much.

On the television, a couple is flipping a Nashville bungalow. Its chipped, powder-blue siding and rusty, wrought-iron veranda remind me of my childhood home. It even has a similar white screen door.

We didn't get a lot for the house—it was a 1950s bungalow with wood siding, a worn roof, and a separate single garage—but a friend of my mother's was a realtor, and she and her husband helped us with some much-needed renovations (like the removal of that screen door). They also waived the commission on the sale.

Each of us girls ended up with a decent amount of cash and once Mother's life insurance paid out. I was able to cover four years of college and a post-graduate degree in public relations—thanks to Amy and Meg who agreed it was unfair that Mother left me a fraction of what she'd left them. Meg used some of her share for her wedding and put the rest in a savings account. Amy finished her last two years of theatre school and then travelled on Mother's dime.

I didn't have much left over after school, but thankfully JP has always been good at saving. That, and he is an only child whose father comes from old money. Louis has already set up an education savings account for Addison.

In two days, JP's parents will arrive at the airport and JP will pick them up, helping them with the numerous bags they undoubtedly packed for a casual weekend. Louis will watch hockey with JP and then they'll hit the green for a final game before they put their clubs away for the season. Margot will cuddle with Addison as often as she can, and take her shopping, spoiling her with toys and outfits that she will outgrow in a month. They will join us for Addison's baptism, that Margot insisted on. They will then stay an extra two nights, and fly home on Tuesday. Should be easy. That's what I keep telling myself.

I stuff the last roll in my mouth and lie back on the couch, letting my legs stretch out to reach the edge of the ottoman. I consult my phone. Nothing from JP. In the early days of us dating, he would send me funny pictures—a whole restaurant table of self-proclaimed foodies taking photos for social media, more concerned with the look than the taste. I rarely get those texts anymore. Maybe it's because he's one of the bosses now.

On the television show, the couple has decided to build a second-story addition and will be repainting the house white. I watch the rest of the episode while cleaning up the kitchen, then two more while lying on the couch. The renovations start to repeat themselves. Natural wood floors, rustic yet modern accents, grey and taupe with a pop of color here and there.

I fall asleep at the beginning of the third episode and wake to a black screen—the sleep timer in effect. The midnight train whistles in the distance. I imagine drunken teens returning home from a night in the city and am thankful I'm over that stage of life. I drift in and out of sleep, stirring at the noises of the suburbs.

The next time I wake, my eyes take a moment to adjust. A white figure stands before me. I must be dreaming.

I squeeze my eyes shut tight but when I open them, the figure is still there, hovering over me. My eyes focus.

It's Mother.

She's a vision in white, her blonde bob perfectly styled. I reach out to touch her face but she backs away from the couch. I push myself to a seated position and notice her silhouette escaping through the back door.

"Mother?" I call.

The motion light activates, illuminating the porch.

My heart beats fast like it is trying to escape my chest.

I feel around for my phone and find it wedged between two cushions. I shine its flashlight across the room to the back door. It is closed.

I make my way to the door and find it's unlocked. I slide the door open, inhaling as I do. I poke my head out cautiously, afraid of what might be waiting for me on the other side.

The night is still.

Whatever it was—*whoever* it was, has disappeared.

SHE'S GONE

Seventeen years old

The familiar tingles covered Jo's body—the half-sleep, half-awake feeling. She was completely conscious, but paralyzed, and the pressure on her chest was getting heavier. After willing herself awake, she felt a presence in the room with her.

Mother was there.

"Jo, honey. Are you okay?" Meg appeared in the doorway; her hair wrapped up in a towel.

Jo pushed herself to a seated position and scanned the room. No, of course, Mother wasn't actually here. It was just a bad dream.

"You were talking in your sleep again," Meg said.

Meg and Jo had had the house to themselves since Mother died. Amy was away at college.

Jo reached for Meg's hand. "I'm sorry. Was I being loud?"

The Strokes band T-shirt she wore clung to her back and chest from the damp sweat. She tugged on Julian Casablancas' face to free the fabric from her breasts.

"Water?" Meg passed her a glass from the side table.

Jo drank half the glass with wide eyes, still searching the room.

"No one's here, Jo. I can stay with you for a while. Until you fall asleep."

Jo lay back down on the bed, pulling the sheet up to her shoulders. It was hot but she wasn't willing to sleep with nothing protecting her. Meg lay down beside her. There wasn't enough room for both of them in the twin bed.

"I think she was here tonight."

"She's gone, Jo," Meg said, and petted Jo's head.

CHAPTER SEVENTEEN

When JP enters the bedroom, he looks surprised to see me. Before he can say anything about the time and why he's so late, I jump in with, "Thank God, you're home." I mean it. I am relieved to see him after the night I've had.

He rushes over to me, probably sensing something's not right. "What's going on? Is Addison okay?"

"Bad night." I rub my eyes.

He lets out a breath. "Shit. Can't sleep, eh?" He undresses methodically, starting with his belt. I think he's trying to appear sober but it's obvious he's had a few too many drinks tonight; I can smell the vodka from a few feet away.

"Come, sit." I need to confide in him. I need to talk to someone about what happened, and I don't think it's wise to call Alice at two in the morning. It can't be possible. I know how crazy it sounds. How do I explain that I saw my dead mother in the house?

JP loses his balance when stepping out of his jeans but catches himself, grabbing the dresser with a loud thud. He looks up at me with a childish grimace, as if to say *please don't kill me.*

I don't have time to get mad at him about noise. I need someone to tell me I'm not losing my mind. I pat the spot next to me on the bed. He stumbles over in his boxers while unbuttoning his dress shirt.

"Hello, wife," he says with a goofy smile, leaning in to kiss me on the cheek. He might not be in the best state to hear my story. He pulls away abruptly. "Want pizza?"

"What? No. Is anything even open right now?"

He gives me a sly grin and then runs out of the room. With heavy feet, he charges down the stairs. I glance at the baby monitor on my phone, but Addison doesn't stir.

JP returns shortly with a small pizza box. "You sure?" he asks, opening the box to reveal a mismatch of slices with a variety of toppings.

I laugh. "This is so random."

"It's the best. I just went to the pizza place in the plaza, and they gave me all the slices they were gonna toss for the price of one slice." He looks so proud of himself, wearing a boyish smirk.

My stomach answers for me with a loud grumble.

He climbs into bed and rests the open box between us. "Go ahead, take your pick."

I grab a slice of pepperoni and take a large bite. It tastes like cardboard. The pizzas were probably made early in the day. After a few bites, I refocus. "Something's going on with me."

"You're in your head too much. Just let your body fall asleep on its own. Stop stressing so much about how long it's going to take you." He dunks his crust into garlic sauce. The smell permeates the room.

"It's more than that. JP, I saw ... I think my mind is playing tricks on me."

JP folds a second slice in half and stuffs it into his mouth. Sauce drips down his chin, and he lets out an obnoxious belch. Maybe I should wait to talk to Alice at our next session.

I won't be able to sleep a wink if I keep this to myself. "I fell asleep watching TV downstairs and when I woke up, I thought I saw something."

JP sets down his slice and moves his hand to the small of my back, rubbing in a robotic, circular motion. "Okay, what do you think you saw?"

I suck in a deep breath before continuing. "I swear it was my mother. She was standing over me."

He drops his hand as if he can't focus on two things at once. "What are you talking about?"

"It felt so real. I woke up, and there she was." I close my eyes, allowing myself to revisit the image of Mother. She wasn't how I remembered her at the end. She looked younger, as if she were able to choose her age upon death.

"She was young. Like my age."

"Okay." JP resumes the circular rubbing, but his face has turned from sympathetic to skeptical.

"She was wearing a white dress, and her hair was styled as it always was—curled under."

JP sways for a moment and I realize that this must be an impossible thing to discuss when you've had too many shots. I continue because I've said this much. "It felt so real."

JP opens his mouth but quickly closes it and lowers his gaze.

"When I first woke up, it took me a minute to remember where I was, and when I finally realized I wasn't dreaming, she disappeared out the back door."

"And you're sure you were fully awake? It wasn't one of your weird dreams?"

"Positive. I was fully awake."

"Because this kind of sounds like those hallucinations you'd have about Addy getting trapped under the covers."

"I know this was real."

JP gets up and begins dressing again. He swaps a t-shirt for the dress shirt that is crumpled on the floor and skips the belt.

"Where are you going?" I ask, half expecting him to retrieve dessert following the pizza feast.

"To check the backyard," JP says and pulls on a sweatshirt.

"I'm coming with you."

Our movement triggers the backyard floodlights. I follow JP closely, shivering despite my many layers of clothing. He holds the Maglite above his head like a weapon, surveying the backyard. He searches under the table, behind the shed, and makes his way to the side gate, which he discovers is wide open.

"Jo, come here," he says, not realizing I've been following less than a foot behind him.

"The gate," I finish his thought.

"You didn't come out here at all today?"

"No. Too cold. What is that?" I ask, pointing to something in the grass.

JP bends over, nudging the item with his foot. I don't wait for him to make the discovery and grab Addy's zebra, inspecting it for clues.

"We didn't bring this out here," I answer JP's question before he has a chance to ask it.

We creep towards the open gate.

"What the fuck?" JP shines the light to reveal a teether, pacifier, and a package of baby wipes. Addison's items are strewn across the lawn and the missing diaper bag has been ditched at the side of the house.

"I've been looking for this."

"Did you leave the bag out here? Maybe a raccoon got into it?"

"No. I ... I don't think so."

JP grabs my arm at the elbow, pulling me towards him. "I need you to remember, Jo. Did you bring the bag outside? Did you leave the gate open?"

I can't say anything. I just stand there dumbfounded, like a child being scolded for something they didn't do. I slump down onto the dewy grass. "I don't know, JP. I don't fucking know."

CHAPTER EIGHTEEN

I settle into the guest bed after laying Addison down for her afternoon nap. Sunlight streams through a crack between the blind and the window ledge and I am thankful the room isn't dark enough for my mind to deceive me.

I've been on edge all day. Every time I turn a corner, I think I'll see *her* again. I nearly screamed this morning when out of the corner of my eye, I saw my robe hanging on the bathroom door. Tonight is supposed to be my girls' night out, but how can I go when I'm like this?

Just as I pick up my phone to cancel on Claire, I receive three incoming texts in a row. She has started a group chat for our outing.

> CLAIRE: Tonight's the night bitches! What are we thinking? Meet at eight?

> LISA: Yes! I seriously can't wait. I've been arguing with a toddler all day.

SERENE: Mine's teething and won't sleep. I may not have time to do my hair, but I WILL be there!

ANGELA: Can't wait to hear any song other than The Wiggles!

CLAIRE: Calling dibs on Feel like a Woman

JANINE: I'm there. Looking forward to it ladies.

LISA: Dibs on Wrecking Ball (but only if someone buys me enough shots)

SERENE: What is this dibs nonsense? LOL

ANGELA: I swear to God if anyone does Dolly's Jolene, I'll smack a bitch.

I'm compelled to chime in with my request even though I was fully planning to cancel. Every time I go to karaoke, I must sing Alanis Morrissette. I text before I can change my mind.

You Oughta Know is my go-to.

I put down the phone feeling strangely satisfied, and it isn't long before I hear another ding.

CLAIRE: Yay! Part of me thought you were gonna bail, Jo. So happy you're coming!

I send the coy smiley face before silencing my phone and burying it under the pillow. Maybe a night out is just what I need. A night away from this house and my thoughts.

I stand in our walk-in closet, admiring my work in the full-length mirror. JP arrived home promptly at six o'clock to relieve me of mom duties. It gave me forty-five minutes to perfect my transformation. I had time to use a curling iron to give my bob a sexy wave and to do my makeup, not shying away from eyeshadow, liner, and my favorite maroon lip stain.

My legs are exposed in my jean skirt, but the heel booties I chose make me feel more confident. My shirt hugs my body, accentuating my curves, but it covers up my arms, which I've despised lately. I landed on a black, V-neck long-sleeve, and my cleavage is on display. I almost consider changing when I realize it will only get more pronounced throughout the night as my breasts prepare for Addison's night feed.

JP opens the closet door holding Addison. He stares at me, his mouth slightly open. "Wow."

"Oh, stop," I say, adjusting my shirt.

"You look hot."

"Thanks. It's been a while since I've put this much effort into getting ready."

My cheeks grow warm as I start to blush, so I turn away to look for a clutch. But as much as I'm embarrassed, it feels good to be acknowledged. It reminds me of how JP used to act around me. Before I got pregnant, he couldn't keep his hands off me.

"You sure you feel up for tonight? You know, after ..." He trails off, forcing me to fill in the blanks.

"Maybe it will help me take my mind off of things."

He nods. "How late do you think you'll be?"

"Not too late. Depends how boring it is."

"Well, have fun. You don't get to do this often."

"Did you pick up the security camera?" I ask.

JP stares blankly at me. He's forgotten. "I'll do it Monday on my way home from work."

I need to know if what I saw last night was real, or if it's in my mind.

"Text if you need anything tonight," I say. I check my phone to make sure the volume is loud. "Just feed her the bottle when she wakes up, and I'll be home to give her the next one."

After a snuggle with Addison and a kiss on the cheek from JP, I head outside to meet Claire so we can await our cab. It all feels very high school: meeting up to compare outfits so you don't show up in something off base.

Claire stands at the foot of my driveway. She doesn't look different than usual because Claire is someone who always takes the time to do her makeup and hair. Tonight, she wears a rather skimpy off-the-shoulder dress that I imagine she bought in her twenties when she clubbed regularly.

When Claire notices me, she gives me a look similar to JP's. "Holy eff, Jo. You are a hot tamale."

"Me? Look at you!" I walk slowly down the driveway, getting used to my heels.

She runs up the driveway to meet me. "I'm always looking for an excuse to wear this dress. It's lucky, if you know what I mean." She tries to wink but ends up blinking both eyes.

A van cab pulls up at the side of the road, its side door rolling open before it comes to a complete stop.

"Girls' night out! Girls' night out!" chants Lisa in a rather demonic tone. She motions us to enter before crawling to the back to claim the seat next to Janine. As she struggles to climb over the middle bucket seat in her leather skirt, Claire and I get a view of her choice of undergarments for the evening—pink lace bootie shorts that clash with the red tank top she sports.

Once we are settled in the van, I turn around to greet Janine. She smiles at me shyly before saying, "You look really pretty, Jo. I love that lip color on you."

I return the compliments to both her and Lisa on the five-minute drive to dinner.

When we arrive at The Landing, Angela and Serene are waiting out front. I'd love to have witnessed the two of them having to make small talk as they awaited the rest of us. From their interactions at Mom Group, it's clear that they aren't each other's favorite people.

Angela looks beyond thrilled when we pile out of the van. "You're late!" she yells.

Claire checks her phone. "By like five minutes."

Angela saunters over to greet us. She teeters in the high stilettos she's chosen for the evening, which contrast with her casual jeans and leather jacket. Serene plays it cool and waits for us to make our way to her. Her red locks are perfectly coiffed, despite her texting about how she wouldn't have time to style her hair. Claire grabs for me, and we end up walking into the pub arm-in-arm. I think I am her new shiny toy, but I don't mind the attention.

Pub basements are always an enthralling scene no matter what town you're in. The Landing is housed in a historic building from the late 1800s. The imperfect grey stones that make up its foundation are exposed in the basement. Solid wood beams support the ceiling and intersect with floor-to-ceiling pillars. I count at least three guys who would fall over if they weren't leaning against the weathered posts. The floorboards are sticky from mixed drinks spilled nightly and are speckled with chewing gum residue that has turned black with dirt.

A small wooden stage makes up one corner of the bar where a single standing microphone is positioned. Opposite the stage is a projector screen displaying the lyrics in a turquoise serif font. Occasionally, an album cover will appear with a cheesy slide transition.

A man finishes his song with an off-key note before quite literally dropping the microphone with a loud thump.

The bartender yells over to him, "Watch it, would you?" The man is already schmoozing his next conquest.

Claire, Lisa, and Serene sit at a table near the stage, skimming through a binder of karaoke songs. Janine, Angela, and I join them.

"Ladies, what are we thinking? Group song to warm us up?" Claire asks.

"Anything but Spice Girls. Last time everyone knew the dance moves and I looked stupid standing still," says Angela.

"Fine, Destiny's Child then," Claire announces and closes the binder.

We order our first drinks of the night and take a shot for liquid courage. With the music blaring and the colorful strobe lights flashing, I feel like I am twenty again, at a club with my girlfriends.

Janine and Angela remain seated at the bar for our debut song, which makes sharing the one microphone less awkward. Claire knows every word and doesn't need to consult the screen. Lisa seems more interested in dancing and acting out the lyrics. I belt out the words and laugh with my new friends.

Halfway through the song, Claire pulls me closer to the microphone. "Jo, you can sing! You're requesting your solo next."

I glance over at the bar where Janine and Angela sit, immersed in conversation. Janine picks at the label on her beer as she talks, her face solemn. Angela is much more animated and her expression changes from shocked to appalled.

We finish the song in harmony and then I push my way through the crowd at the bar to order my second and final drink for the night. I don't want to have a hangover tomorrow when JP's parents arrive.

As I approach the women, I hear Angela say, "You should probably tell her. She deserves to know."

Janine swivels in her barstool to face me, her eyes wide. "Hey, nice singing."

I make my drink and song requests through the bartender and am about to turn back to the group when Janine pats the stool beside her. "Hey, sit with us."

I comply, adjusting my skirt once I'm seated.

"I ran into your husband on the train the other day. JP, right?" Janine asks.

"Yeah, JP. He hates when I keep the car and he's forced to ride the train to work."

She chuckles. "We only have one car too. Doesn't seem worth it to buy a second." She takes a gulp of her beer. "Yeah ... so, JP was with a girl. Blonde hair?"

I sip on my drink as I contemplate what she is getting at. Is she trying to stir something up? Or is this what girls do for their friends? Spy on their husbands and report back?

"Hmm, probably someone he works with," I suggest.

"Right. She was very pretty."

"Oh yeah? That's nice for her."

It's hard to tell whether she intends to hurt me, but I am left feeling both ugly and concerned. From what it sounds like, she could be describing the graphic designer, Lauren. I'm pretty sure she lives a town over from us, so it would make sense she takes the same train. I turn back to our group who are doing their best not to giggle at the woman onstage attempting Ariana Grande's riffs.

"Sorry, if that came off weird. You're prettier. I just meant she was an attractive-looking woman. And they seemed to be close." Janine pauses to sip her beer. "I'm not trying to gossip. I'm really not like that. I guess I just got a vibe."

A vibe? What does that even mean? JP is just friendly and naturally charming.

"Don't worry about it." I set down my beer. "Time to break the seal," I say and make my way to the washroom. I'm not in the mood to ask follow-up questions, though I'm wondering what she means by *they seemed to be close.*

Janine accosts me in the communal washroom a few minutes later, as I'm reapplying my lip stain.

"I just love that color on you," she says joining me at the mirror.

"Is something up?" I surprise myself with my boldness. My voice comes out strong and assertive. I hold her stare until she breaks eye contact.

Switching her gaze to her reflection in the mirror, she adjusts her shirt. "There's more I should share about the girl he was with. But first, I need to tell you something else. My experience with your husband has been a little uncomfortable, to be honest."

"Uncomfortable?" Is she incapable of using direct language? I feel like this woman is talking in code.

"When I met you both at Lisa's barbecue last year, he was, well, kind of flirty with me."

I don't remember JP even talking to Janine at the barbecue. "He can be overly friendly. Sometimes people misinterpret that."

She shakes her head. "Jo, he made a move on me."

"What? When?"

"It was after you went home, and he stuck around for a while. He kissed me, Jo. I pushed him away once I realized what was happening. Honestly, I was shocked."

My throat tightens and the buzz of the fluorescent light is the only sound I hear. I realize the water I have been washing my hands with has turned scalding hot. I pull my hands from beneath the tap and watch as they turn red.

"Jo? I'm so sorry to have to tell you this. I never expected to tell you but now that we are hanging out, it was just too weird not to."

I can't think clearly. It doesn't feel real. The water from my hands drips onto my suede boots and the tiles. I never thought my entire world could come crashing down in the bathroom of The Landing. I feel like I'm back in high school and I've just found out that my boyfriend Cody cheated on me with a girl from math class, but this is so much worse. I look around for paper towels and end up pushing the nearest stall door open and unraveling some toilet paper until I have enough to wipe my hands dry.

"I really am sorry, Jo." Janine is standing too close to me, blocking the stall door.

"I think I'm going to be sick." I hunch over the toilet, my nausea taking over.

"Do you want me to call you a cab?" she asks.

Tonight was supposed to be my night out. I was supposed to leave my anxious thoughts at home, clear my mind, and have a drink or two.

I push past Janine, bumping her harder than I meant to.

"Ouch," she says, rubbing her arm. "Him and that girl. He had his hands on her leg for most of the ride and when she got off at her stop, he kissed her goodbye."

I shove the wad of wet toilet paper into the garbage bin. "I should go. I think my song's up soon." I leave Janine in the washroom, staring at her perfect reflection.

CHAPTER NINETEEN

There are certain moments in life when you want to show off and tonight is one of them. Whether it's fair or not, I'm mad at Janine for being the one to tell me about JP. I don't want to believe that he tried to kiss her or that he also kissed Lauren on the train. It sucks knowing that the moms—my new friends—will all hear about it by the end of the night. This doesn't stand a chance of being left a secret in our small town.

I stand on the wooden platform with my mic in hand, waiting for the screen on the other side of the bar to display the lyrics. Claire rushes to the stage holding two bright blue shots for us to drink before I serenade the group of strangers. I welcome it, and in one smooth motion, throw back the fruity shooter that is sure to give me a headache tomorrow.

I can admit that I am a good singer. I have a strong voice, and I've always been musical. Amy is the performer of the family, as Mother would say, but give me a microphone and I can run circles around her. My song choice is perfectly suited to my situation—an angsty song about an ex-boyfriend moving on—and I use my anger to channel my inner rock star. I've had enough practice singing Alanis Morissette's *Jagged Little Pill* album. I don't even need to consult the turquoise screen for the lyrics—I know them instinctively, and they've taken on a completely new meaning tonight.

After the first verse, I can tell that I have the audience's attention. My friends root for me at the front of the stage, but the whole bar seems to have inched closer to get a better look. I close my eyes and belt out the first chorus, not holding back. The next thing I know, there's another shot in front of me. I look up to see Lisa with her arm extended, passing me a shot glass—this time a clear liquid, likely vodka. It burns as it slides down my throat. I continue my song, gaining more confidence.

The room spins around me, but I maintain composure. My eyes focus and I notice a group of guys standing with my group, cheering me on. One seems particularly interested and smiles at me throughout my solo. He looks familiar and I'm almost certain I've seen him before. I make eye contact and match his smile. I finish my act, singing the last line solely to him. The bar erupts in shrieks and applauds. Clearly, The Landing doesn't get too many karaoke performers who can hold a note. I break into laughter, forgetting for a moment that my marriage might be a lie.

I join my crew, which has merged with the group of guys. The man eyes me from the spot in the circle. What would JP think if he knew someone else was interested in me? Would he even care? My admirer finally moves beside me.

"Jo, right?" he extends his hand.

"Yeah, and you are?"

"Arjun. I went to Springley. I was a freshman when you were a junior." And now I feel old.

135

"You rocked that song," he continues.

I sway but catch myself before falling. "Thanks. Will you be taking the stage?"

"Definitely not. I just come here for the stale beer."

I chuckle a little too loudly at his joke. "So, you still live in town, then?"

"No, just came back for a buddy's wedding. I live out west now."

I notice the girls have drifted away to give us space, but they huddle nearby, glancing over at us occasionally. I should say goodbye and rejoin their circle. I'm a married woman. I have a baby at home.

I can't shake the growing feeling in the pit of my stomach and talking to Arjun makes it a little less intense.

"It looks like you need another drink," he says, recognizing my empty hand.

"Look at that. I guess I do."

We amble to the bar and take a seat on the only open stools that are side by side. Arjun orders two beers. The room is buzzing around me, and I need to concentrate on sitting up straight on the stool.

"I'm just going to say it. I had a huge crush on you in high school," he says.

The blood runs to my cheeks. "Oh? You liked the older girls?" I feel embarrassed at my attempt at flirting. This is completely unlike me.

"Every guy liked the Baker sisters. My older brother had a huge thing for your sister. Amy, I think?"

"Amy had a lot of admirers."

"You did too, no? You dated that one guy for a while—the one in that band."

I hold the beer in on my tongue for a moment before swallowing. "Cody. The lead singer of the Bristol Strippers."

"The Bristol Strippers," he chuckles. "I forgot about them—they weren't half bad."

Shortly after Mother's death I started dating Cody, a ginger who hid behind black hair dye and liked the attention that being in a high school punk band got him a little too much.

"Yeah, we dated for a while." My stomach churns. I can't tell whether it's from the beer or the thought of my ex.

"It's terrible what happened to him. Tragic."

I slump in my seat. The car accident. "Yeah, it was horrible."

"You were with him, weren't you? I'm so sorry, that must have been horrific."

Why do I feel like I'm back in therapy? I've talked about the accident with countless crisis counsellors and Alice. At this point, I'm just numb to it all.

"I was. Bad storm that night. The car lost control." My voice comes out void of emotion. I don't remember anything after I pulled onto the narrow bridge that crosses over the river near my childhood house. It was raining and the roads were sleek. I was upset. We were fighting, and he had been drinking. He was calling me names again, terrible things. I know I was driving faster than I should have been, but there were no cars on the road, and I just wanted to drop him off and never see him again.

Arjun nods and places his hand on my knee. I stare at his hand and he finds another task for it, grabbing his beer. "Do you ever go visit him?" he asks.

"Cody? No. Not since ..."

He nods again but doesn't say anything else. I wonder if he thinks I'm a bad person for not continuing to visit my catatonic ex-boyfriend. If he only knew the whole story. How can I speak ill of someone who is no longer the person they were?

I continue, feeling like he needs more of an explanation. "I went to visit him for a while after it happened, but no, I don't see him anymore."

I know people from school talk about the accident, and what happened to Cody. Nothing ever happened in our town, so it consumed Springley's hallways my last two years, high school sweethearts in a car crash together. The girl is left with minor injuries, broken bones that heal with time. The guy has severe brain damage and hasn't been himself since. The girl moves on.

What people don't know, except for my family, is that Cody broke up with me the night of the crash. He said goodbye when he told me he didn't love me anymore after we watched the latest blockbuster at the drive-in movie theatre. I should have been the one to do it. He should have begged for me to take him back after everything. He didn't care. He had already made his choice.

I went to see him twice in the hospital, but it was too hard to see him in that state, especially knowing that he didn't want me. When they finally moved him back home for twenty-four-hour care with a live-in nurse, I couldn't bring myself to visit.

I've had enough reminiscing about high school traumas, and I'm realizing how stupid it is to be flirting with some guy.

I slide off the stool. "It was nice catching up. I should really get back to my friends."

"I'm sorry. It was dumb of me to bring that up."

"It's fine. But I should head back. It's moms' night out." I know that my mention of being a mom will end the conversation.

"Gotcha. It was nice to see you. Have a good one."

I can't bring myself to say goodbye to the girls. The talk has probably already turned to my failing marriage. I need to get home, confront JP, and find out exactly what happened on the train.

CHAPTER TWENTY

I exit through a basement door that leads to a patio and I get a whiff of cigarette smoke. The restaurant staff is already anticipating winter; the patio tables are covered in tarps and the chairs have been stacked under the awning. Smokers currently occupy the patio. They stand with their shoulders slumped, heads down, aware that winter is on its way.

There are no cabs waiting outside the restaurant, so I open my rideshare app. Nothing is available. I check the monitor on my phone, and Addison is sound asleep. I climb the stone steps that lead up the hill to Main Street and trip on the last step, falling to my knees.

One of the smokers yells, "Shit, you okay?"

I scramble up and continue to walk at a quick pace with my arms crossed to shield me from the October wind. When I approach the intersection where I will cross to the residential side of town, I get a strange feeling that someone is watching me. I turn around half expecting to see Mother again, lurking in an alley. There is no one in sight. The streets are quiet; nothing but a few leaves rustling in the wind.

I dial Amy's number. I need to talk to someone before I confront JP. I let the phone ring, and it goes to her voicemail. I stumble through a message.

"Ames, it's me. Sorry, I just realized you're probably sleeping. I had a night. I'll call you tomorrow to talk about it. It's JP. I think he's screwing around with a girl at work. I heard it from this mom who lives near me. I don't know what to believe."

I hang up, feeling silly. I should have just waited until tomorrow. I look down at my boots, avoiding the cracks in the sidewalk.

Don't step on a crack or you'll break your mother's back. Don't step on a line or you'll break your mother's spine.

I recite the rhyme in my head that my sisters and I used to sing to each other when we were young. If Mother was being strict, we'd purposely step on a crack and giggle about it. Little did we know her demise would be a fall that would break her neck and crack her skull. Perhaps we willed it.

It is much darker on this side of town. Most of the houses have their porch lights turned off. I have the option of cutting through the park or taking the longer route around it. My feet ache, and I can tell that I have a blister forming. I make my way down the chain link fence lined pebble path that cuts between two houses and spits me out into the neighborhood park.

I walk cautiously on the pathway, trying to avoid making too much noise. When I reach the other side, I realize that at night, the park is home to rebel teens who want to drink anywhere but their parents' basements. There is a group of boys and girls sitting on the jungle gym, passing a joint back and forth, and more near the murky pond.

"Slut," someone yells from the brush near the pond. I assume they are talking about me, but I avoid eye contact and continue to the street on the other side of the park. I wonder if they would say that if they knew I was a mother. Maybe that's the reason why they yelled it. What mother is out walking alone in a short skirt at night?

I walk the longer route since the streetlights haven't been installed yet in the section where new homes are being built. I wish I had never gone to karaoke. I feel like an idiot. Is Janine right? Is JP having an affair with Lauren? Does he love her? My entire body is shaking. I would never be able to look at him the same again. How could I? I'm at home taking care of our daughter and he's kissing another woman in plain sight. It's like he wanted to get caught.

I pass Marjorie's house, which sits in complete darkness. How lonely it must be to lose the love of your life and have no companion. To spend your days painting still life, barely living your own. Is my situation much different? I haven't had JP's companionship in months. Our intimacy lives solely through Addison. Maybe she's the only thing keeping us together. Addison, my beautiful baby girl. I'm not going to let someone take her away from me. I have to pull it together. She's everything to me.

I stumble on the sidewalk. Maybe I'm drunker than I thought. I'm embarrassed that I flirted with Arjun tonight, and that I left Addison to get tipsy at a dive bar. I skipped our evening feeding. She probably didn't take the bottle well and wondered where I was. I didn't get to stare at her tiny features as she nursed. I didn't pet her head as she fell asleep.

And now, I am walking home in the cold with sore feet, feeling like every shadow is someone waiting for the right moment to destroy what little remains of my happiness. I peer into the darkness ahead, trying to decipher the shapes. That's just the mailbox. To the right of the mailbox is just a bush. There's no one lurking near the stone retaining wall that separates our street from the grocery store plaza. It's all in my head.

When I arrive at our house on the corner, I'm relieved that the porch light is on. I make my way up the driveway, but I drop my keys in the process. I crouch, feeling around for them in the dark. Using the flashlight on my phone, I scan the driveway. They are by the front wheel of our car, the yellow tassel of my keychain exposing them. I crawl over to my keys and am ambushed by a wave of lightheadedness. Here come the spins. After a moment of sitting with my head between my knees, I gather enough strength and balance to stand.

With the flashlight still on, I shine the light at the gate to our backyard and confirm that it's shut. I climb up the granite steps to our porch.

It is one in the morning. It took longer than I thought to walk home. I drank more than I should have. If it wasn't for Janine's confession, I don't think I would have accepted the shots and the last beer.

It takes me a moment to unlock the door. I enter the dim foyer, which only gets darker when I turn off the porch light. I remove my heels and feel the immediate ache in the arches of my feet.

Before heading upstairs, I ensure the door is locked.

I catch a glimpse of the bedroom at the top of the stairs and observe the light is on. JP is awake. I hope he's ready for what I have to say.

I enter the bedroom and drop my clutch and leather jacket at the door to the walk-in closet. JP is in bed, propped up against the headboard, typing away on his laptop.

"Hey, I didn't hear you come in. You're a ninja." He chuckles. "How was your night?"

"Janine says hi." I make my way to the bed and take a seat, locking eyes with him.

"Remind me which one Janine is, again?"

Nice try. I let out a laugh. "The one you made out with at the barbecue in the summer."

"What the hell are you talking about?" His cheeks redden.

"Doesn't ring a bell? Janine. Small, pretty, blonde. Opposite of me, I guess?"

"Are you drunk?"

"No, are you?" I retort. He has a glass of wine next to him on the nightstand and I can only imagine it isn't his first of the night.

"Where'd you get this crazy idea from?"

Here we go. Make me feel delusional for suggesting it.

"You're such a prick. Janine. Our neighbor down the street. She told me about the barbecue—that you kissed her. I was pregnant."

"She's obviously lying."

"She said she saw you on the train the other day with a woman. Another blonde. It seems you have a type."

"Come on, Jo. You don't actually believe her. That's ridiculous."

He holds my stare, and I search his face, probing for a sign that he is lying. Then it occurs to me: I don't know what JP does when he lies. Does he look away like Meg? Touch his face like Amy? I don't know these intimate details about my own husband.

"She was with you in Montréal on your trip, wasn't she? Did you stay in the same room? The night you ignored all my calls and texts—you were with her, weren't you?"

"This is insane." He rolls away from me to his side of the bed. He turns off the lamp on his nightstand, leaving us in complete darkness.

I fiddle around with my lamp, and in the process, I knock over a glass of water on the nightstand. "Shit," I whisper, jumping into action to tidy the mess.

"Jesus, how much did you drink tonight? You're hammered."

I run into the washroom to grab a towel and when I return, his light is on and he is already cleaning up.

"I got it," he says. "I think you need to go to bed. Why don't you just go sleep in the guest room? We can make it up for my parents again tomorrow."

"We're not done talking."

"I think we are. You need to sleep off the alcohol. You're practically slurring every word."

That's not true. He just wants time to get his story straight. He thinks if I go sleep it off, he can come up with a reasonable explanation for everything.

"*I'm not done talking.*" I grab the towel out of his hands, forcing him to stop mopping the water up. "Janine said that when the woman got off at her stop, you kissed her goodbye."

"And you're trusting some woman you just started hanging out with? Someone who clearly wants to stir up shit?" He brushes past me, ripping the wet towel from my hands, and heading to the washroom.

I follow. "You're not even answering the question. Were you with a blonde woman on the train and did you kiss her?"

"This is embarrassing."

"Was it Lauren?" I block the doorway, trapping him in the bathroom.

He rolls his eyes and laughs. "No. I can't believe how drunk you got tonight. You're a mother. Do I need to remind you of that? You went out and got wasted. That's just sad."

"I'm not even that drunk and this was the first time I've been out since Addison was born. You were all for it earlier today. Do I need to remind you of how much you've been out in the last few months?"

"That's different."

"How is that different? Enlighten me."

"I can handle my alcohol. I'm not sinking into a depression, blacking out, and thinking I saw my dead mother."

The anger flows throughout my body from my heart to my fingertips. My hands move quickly from my sides and straight to JP's chest, and I push him with everything in me. He stumbles back and falls into the wall.

"What the fuck, Jo?"

My heart is pounding.

I didn't have time to think, I just reacted. I drop my hands defeated, giving him the option to leave. "I want the truth."

"So do I." He pushes past me, turning off the bathroom light. "Go to bed."

I feel my way back to the bed and retrieve my phone from my nightstand. I turn on its flashlight to guide my way to the guest room. Halfway down the hall, the dull hum of the television interrupts the silence. I turn towards the room I just left and a blue glow seeps through the crack beneath the door. I guess it's not bedtime after all.

Poor Jo

Fifteen years old

Amy bounced in the front seat of the car coming off a performance high so strong she was buzzing. She had performed a hip-hop dance, and Jo had sung "Don't Speak" by *No Doubt* at Springley's talent show.

"Amy, you really were the star. They should have put you in the middle." Mother praised her middle daughter as she drove.

Amy beamed. She made Mother proud once again, and all it took was attempting to mimic Beyoncé's latest music video.

"Yeah, I know. It would have made more sense, right? They practically copied me the entire time." Amy was eyeing herself in the visor mirror. She had straightened her platinum hair with an iron and wore thick charcoal eyeliner.

"Stacey's put on a bit of weight since your birthday party." Mother shot Amy a glance, and they both laughed.

Jo traced the roses on her dress with her index finger, mouthing her solo to herself.

Mother caught her eye in the rearview mirror. "Joanna, I'm sorry but I was so distracted by your hair, I couldn't focus on anything else."

Amy erupted in laughter. "Oh, poor Jo. But it's true." She turned around in her seat to face her sister. "Your bangs were sticking straight up the whole time."

Jo waited until Amy was facing the dashboard once again. Then Jo kicked the back of Amy's seat so hard she even scared herself.

CHAPTER TWENTY-ONE

My anxiety has been surging since the fight last night. It swirls around in my stomach, a dull flutter, occasionally building into a tornado when I remember how this all started. When I think about Janine's story, it's like I've missed a step on a stair. I know I'm falling, but it's too late to grab hold of anything. There's nothing left to do but close my eyes tight and brace myself for impact. If it wasn't for the drinks last night, I don't think that I would have been able to fall asleep.

My depression hits me even harder. It lives in my throat as a large lump in my esophagus; it feels as though I've swallowed a piece of bread and it creeps slowly down my chest, getting stuck behind my breastbone.

I can't cry this morning. Maybe because I don't want Addison to think it's because of her. She takes notice of my emotions, seems to know me better than anyone. I hold her upright, her chin resting on my left shoulder. My left arm supports her bum, and my right hand cradles her head. We sway side to side, a mother-daughter dance. My face is next to hers and I press her head gently towards me, so I can feel her chubby cheeks against mine. I burrow my face into her neck, breathing her in, smelling her baby scent: the ivory soap I use during bath time, the delicate laundry detergent I wash her onesies with, the faint smell of my milk. It calms me. I kiss the top of her head, her peach fuzz tickling my upper lip, and I wonder if she'll have thin hair like JP.

We woke up together, Addy and I, at seven. She either slept through the night or I was too sound asleep to hear her stir. Sleeping off last night's bad judgement. I can feel that she missed me, and it makes me feel wanted.

"Let's stay here a while together, okay?"

She doesn't fuss. She lets me hold her. Occasionally, she tries to lift her head up to meet my eyes. She's unsteady; her head is still too heavy for her neck, but I spot her with my right hand and smile with my eyes wide.

JP clears his throat. I spin around to face the nursery door, clutching Addy close.

"Hi," he says delicately, hovering in the doorway. He is very different now that we're sober. I expect that he is trying to gauge my mood or waiting to see what I remember from last night.

I nod my head to acknowledge him, but I can't speak without breaking composure.

"When's naptime?" he asks, stepping one foot into the room.

I retrieve my phone from my pocket and check the time. "Soon. Twenty minutes." I keep it short, so I don't start crying again.

"Do you want me to step in? You can have a shower. We can talk when she goes to sleep."

I desperately need a shower. The waves in my hair have gone limp and they are crusted together with last night's hairspray. A film of stale beer and sweat covers my entire body. I nod and that gives JP permission to enter the room. I squeeze Addison one last time. I wonder if she knows how much I needed this morning with her. I kiss her again and then pass her to her dad. She protests my exit, and JP tries to comfort her with his sing-song voice, as I walk down the hall to our en suite.

I sit on the couch with my wet hair wrapped in a towel, waiting for JP to join me. He brings us each a glass of ice water and sinks into the other side of the couch so that the oversized pillow in the corner separates us. I wonder if he's chosen that seat strategically, so he can grab the pillow for cover if I do anything drastic.

"I'm glad we took last night to cool off. I just thought it would be better for us to be sober for this," he says.

I fight the urge to hit him. I want nothing more than to pummel him until this all goes away. I stare into his eyes, my lips pursed. I'll give him the floor because I need the truth.

"Start talking."

"What do you want to know first?"

"What happened at the barbecue with Janine?"

He looks down at the floor and nods his head. Then he meets my eyes and tells me his side of the story.

"If I'm remembering this right, the barbecue was about a week before your due date. I was feeling the weight of it all."

I let out an audible breath. *He* was feeling the weight of it all.

He puts his hands up in defense. "I know, I know. You were feeling it just as much as me. Probably more. It's just that everything had moved so quickly since we found out you were pregnant and the idea of becoming a dad was too much for me that day. So, I did what I do best. I drank a lot. You went home because you were tired. I should have gone with you, but I stayed and had another drink."

I knew that he would blame it on the alcohol. It's why it's so ridiculous he was disappointed in me last night.

He pauses to sip his water. "When I went to leave, Janine was leaning against the garage. She said something about needing to get away from the noise. I asked if she wanted company and she said sure."

"You're such an ass."

He lowers his eyes, unable to meet mine. "We spoke for a bit. I don't even remember what about. Movies maybe? Honestly, she could have been anyone. I just needed the responsibilities to go away for a night. I wanted to be someone else. So, I leaned in, and so did she. We kissed, briefly."

He looks back up at me, waiting for a reaction. Janine had said he tried to kiss her, not that they both kissed each other, although, it doesn't make a difference. He's admitted that he kissed her. My husband kissed another woman. My husband betrayed me while I was asleep at home, with our baby growing inside me.

The walls feel as though they are closing in.

"We both stopped when we heard someone opening the side gate. That's when I realized what I'd done. I said I was sorry and left. When I came home, I thought about telling you. I wanted to confess everything. But you were asleep, and I didn't want to put any stress on you—"

"Oh, you didn't want to stress me out. What do you think this is? I'm losing my mind, JP." I can't hold it in any longer. I've just discovered that I'm in this alone. He's betrayed me, and even worse, he's betrayed Addison.

"I know. If it makes you feel any better, I've barely seen Janine since. At the grocery store, maybe once. It was honestly a bonehead mistake, and I regretted it instantly."

"You cheated on your pregnant wife," I snap. I breathe in sharply and suddenly it's all too much. The room feels so small. I know this isn't the end of the story. There's more and it could be worse. "What about the other woman?" My fingers begin to tingle.

JP takes a drink of water and expels a deep breath. He drops his head and I get the sense that this is the story he is more afraid to tell. Perhaps this is the woman who means more to him. I watch as he fidgets with his wedding ring—taking it off and putting it on again and I wonder if he's unsure whether he wants to fight for us.

"Who is she?" I press.

"A girl from work," he says. Lauren. It has to be Lauren.

"Are you seeing this *woman*?"

"We've fooled around a few times."

"Have you slept with her?" I close my eyes and clench my teeth, anticipating his response.

"Yes."

The pain in my breastbone sharpens. It's worse than I thought. I need to escape. I push myself up from the couch and pace the room. "God, JP. Why? When did it start?"

He buries his face in his hands, then looks at me through splayed fingers. "Two months ago."

"Are you serious? It's been going on for two months?" That means Addy was only three months old when it started. I was just starting to feel like myself again.

"It's over. I swear. I called her this morning. When you were in Addy's room. I told her that it's over. It's never going to happen again." He secures the ring back on his finger and stands to meet my level.

"Is it Lauren?"

"Does it matter?"

"So, that's a yes."

He shrugs.

I shake my head, trying to erase it all, but it's too late. Everything is ruined. He tries to console me, reaching froward to wrap his arms around me tight. I squirm out of his hold and push him away.

"Don't fucking touch me." If he lied about this, who knows what else he's lied about? "When you said you were working late, were you with her? Did you hook up with her on your business trips? Were you even travelling for work?" Suddenly, it's all too much to process and the room spins around me. The stripes on Addison's zebra ripple and my knees go weak. I fall back onto the couch.

"Jo, are you okay?" JP rushes to my side, moving the oversized pillow so that it can no longer play referee.

I let my head drop between my legs. Breathe. "Was she your escape from us?"

"It wasn't like that. Honestly, it happened a few times, usually after a late night at work and a few drinks. That doesn't make it better, but it's not like I wanted to escape my life with you and Addy."

"Do you love her?" I lift my head. I search his eyes for the answer, but I can't decipher them anymore.

"No," he responds quickly. He's either telling the truth or he anticipated that question. "I don't," he says.

"So, you risked everything, for what? A fling?"

"I don't know what I was thinking, Jo. I guess I was lonely. I can't remember the last time we had sex. The last time we kissed more than a peck on the cheek. Half the time I think you've lost all attraction towards me."

Here I was thinking I was the unattractive one. I sink into the couch and close my eyes. "You realize everything's changed now, right?" I look him in the eyes. "Things will never be the same."

"I'm sorry, Jo." There's desperation in his voice.

"I'll play nice this weekend for your parents but after that, we're done. I want you gone."

"You can't mean that," he says.

The doorbell interrupts us, and I struggle to my feet. "That'll be Amy with the cake."

"I didn't know she was dropping it by today." He follows me through the kitchen.

"Bakery is closed on Sundays, so she had to pick it up today."

"Oh, is she staying?"

"I don't know, JP. They didn't have the fridge space to keep it at their place."

I open the door and Amy stands in front of us holding a pastel pink box. She lifts the lid to reveal a three-tier cake with rose gold embellishments and the words *God Bless Addison*.

"Isn't it gorgeous?" she beams.

"Beautiful," I say, forcing a smile. "Let's get it into the fridge."

The three of us walk back to the kitchen together in an awkward procession. I open the fridge and shuffle some of the contents around. I sacrifice a jar of three pickles so Amy can place the cake inside. All the while, JP stands there, a tagalong to a two-person job.

Addison cries on the monitor and he practically runs up the stairs for something to do. "I've got her," he calls.

Amy raises one eyebrow.

"Up for a walk and a coffee?" I ask.

"Obviously. You need to fill me in after that voicemail last night."

CHAPTER TWENTY-TWO

It's early enough on a Saturday that the café has free tables. A cyclist stops in for his regular order and exchanges niceties with the barista. He finds his seat near the door, presumably where he can watch the bike he left unattended on the street. A woman types furiously at her laptop, deep in thought, letting her tea go cold. Amy and I sit at a four-top against the back window that overlooks the patio, with Addison's stroller parked beside us. Addison sucks on her ice cream teether that is attached to a pacifier clip. I'm glad that I remembered to bring it, otherwise she would be sucking on her toes, which she's been doing ever since she realized she's flexible enough for that.

The patio is set up for anyone brave enough to drink their pumpkin spice lattes in the cold. A girl in her twenties is coaxing her boyfriend to take photos of her in front of a pot of orange chrysanthemums. They've been at it a while and I have a hard time focusing on anything else.

Amy stares intently, waiting for me to give her the details. "So, your message last night …"

"Oh, I'm sorry about that. I don't know why I expected you to be up."

"I'm sorry I missed it. It sounded like you needed someone."

Amy's expressions are animated as I recount the girls' night out. Janine's accusations that turned out to be true. The liquor. Arjun. The girl on the train. The way I left the bar. My walk home. My fight with JP and how he treated me like I was the one in the wrong. How my lapse in judgement—my three extra drinks—were reason enough for him to belittle me. The change in his demeanor this morning. How he seems remorseful now that he is sober.

She shakes her head in disappointment and scoots her chair closer to the table. "Jo, I don't even know what to say. I'm shocked. And it's obviously him who's in the wrong. Anyone can see that." She reaches for my hand.

"I'm not going to lie; I overdid it with the drinks."

"Yeah, but it was your one night out. That doesn't make you a bad mom. And to say that to you? After everything he's done. He needs a good slap in the face." A smirk stretches across her face. "If you want a volunteer, I'm willing."

"I'll keep that in mind." I pick my thumb, and Amy eyes me.

"Are you still doing that?"

"Bad habit." I sit on my hands to stop myself. "I'm starting to think it's me. Like I attract this sort of thing." Ever since my session with Alice, I've been thinking more about patterns. The power dynamics in all my relationships.

"So, you've picked a couple of bad apples. That doesn't make it you."

"Is it just easy to push me around?"

"Are you thinking about Cody again? Is it because Arjun brought him up?"

I pause and think carefully before my next comment. "I'm thinking about Mother."

Amy lets out an audible sigh. I'm sure she'd rather me bring this up with Meg there too. It's easier to convince themselves it wasn't as bad as it was when they are both there.

She smiles slightly and pats my hand. "It's just because the anniversary is coming up. I can't believe she's been gone for fifteen years. I've noticed Meg's been extra maternal lately. I've been burying myself in my play. You've been—well, obviously dealing with a lot. I seriously want to kill JP."

I take a sip of my drink and place the mug down, adjusting it so the handle is at ninety degrees.

I breathe deeply. "Amy, I saw her the other night."

"What do you mean? Like those dreams you used to have?"

"Yeah, but this time it felt different—more real."

She looks at me the same way JP did that night. Skeptical but mostly concerned.

"I'm going to talk to Alice about it. It's probably just because of the anniversary, right?"

She squeezes my arm. "Probably. Talk to Alice though." She pauses to tie Addison's shoe that has come undone.

"Listen, don't tell Meg about this. It will just confirm what she's always thought—that we rushed into things." I sip my drink. "Maybe we did."

"Rushed into the marriage or parenthood?"

I shrug. We did rush into both in a way, but I don't regret anything about parenthood. I look over at my daughter and flash her a big smile. She kicks her feet in excitement.

"I won't let on like I know a thing this weekend. Tomorrow's Addy's day," Amy says.

I sigh. "Now I just need to act normal around his parents."

"Normal? I say tell his mom. It's time she learns her son isn't perfect. What time does their flight land?"

"Two o'clock this afternoon. JP's picking them up from the airport." I check my phone for the time.

Two teenage girls catch Addy's eye. They smile and wave from the line that's formed since we arrived. Amy smiles back.

"Your baby is gorgeous," says one of the girls to Amy.

"Yes, she's so cute," the other chimes in.

Amy touches Addison's thigh. "Thank you. But I'm actually the aunt."

I wave awkwardly, a little annoyed that they didn't think I was the mom. I turn my focus back to Amy who is looking at her phone.

"I have to get going soon for rehearsal," she says.

I nod but don't make an effort to leave. I don't want to go back to JP.

"Ah, what's another five minutes? Let me fill you in on my play."

Mother was always Amy's go-to for discussing theatre. Mother was her biggest fan, after all.

"Jo, it's going to be my big break; I can feel it."

I suspect Amy wants to take my mind off my situation and I welcome the distraction. "You're liking the role?"

Amy lights up. "I love this role. I was born to play it. And you know how I feel about Shakespeare."

"You're a natural with the language. *King Lear*, right? I haven't read that since college."

"It's such a dynamic role for me."

"Remind me who you're playing?" I ask and watch as her elated expression fades. She's told me this before, and I can tell she's hurt that I don't remember. Mother wouldn't have forgotten.

"Goneril," she says and sets her coffee mug down with a thud.

"Right, right. Sorry, I knew that. She's the oldest sister, right? Power hungry? Kind of a bitch?"

Amy's expression softens. "Yeah, I'm using Meg as my inspiration."

We both laugh and it feels good to think of something other than JP.

"And the director is such a visionary," she continues. "He's set it in modern day."

"Oh, nice. I love a good adaptation."

She leans closer in her seat and gets more and more animated. "Yeah, so it's set in New York and Mr. Lear, of Lear Enterprises, needs to decide which of his daughters will take over his media conglomerate."

"Very cool." I am doing my best to feign interest, but I really couldn't care less about Amy's amateur play. She never bothered to share her theatre with me when Mother was around.

"Think HBO's *Succession* but with daughters."

"I love it."

"Will you come? Opening night is a month away."

"Oh, yeah. We'll see how things go."

There's that downward pull of the lips, that crinkle between her brows again. *Wrong answer, Jo.* Amy turns towards Addison and helps her retrieve the teether, which has gotten caught in the straps on her stroller. She sips her coffee and once again, sets it down with a thud.

I do my best to recover. "I wouldn't miss it, Ames. Count me in."

She brightens. "I'm so excited you're going to come. I'll get you reserved seats."

"Doesn't Goneril end up killing the one sister at the end?" I ask.

"Yes. Offstage though. I was hoping he'd let us do something dramatic."

Just like that, I've committed to another night away from Addison. I already feel the anxiety of it. I'll need to pump again. Amy's play will be somewhere in the city. We'll have to decide to either drive or take transit. Maybe I'll be going solo.

Amy helps guide the stroller over the curb, and we cross the street to my driveway. I want to loiter outside until this weekend is over. I can't imagine pretending everything is okay with the in-laws around.

The yard is in a state of seasonal transition; the pink and orange geraniums are now dried and brown, waiting for me to remove them before winter comes. Some leaves have started to fall from the surrounding trees, but it isn't enough to warrant a rake of the yard yet.

I spot a paper cup in the gutter and pick it up to toss it in the garbage bin we keep in the garage. I push the stroller in between Amy's car and our SUV, heading towards the garage door. That's when I notice it.

"Amy, come here."

"What's up?" She walks in between the cars to meet me. "Oh, shit."

Someone has been in our driveway.

CHAPTER TWENTY-THREE

Etched on the driver's door of our SUV is the word *CHEATER* in block letters. I guide Addison's stroller through the pathway to the garage and step on the parking brake. I move closer to our car to get a better look, tracing my finger along the scratched surface.

"It looks like it was done with a key."

Amy kneels and mimics my movements, tracing each letter. She nods, "Yep, someone keyed your car. And I don't think the message was meant for you."

There are only two women who could feel compelled to do this. Janine was with me last night and had her share of drinks. It's possible she didn't like the way our conversation went, but I honestly can't picture her doing this. It would make for some awkward park visits and grocery trips. Plus, from what it sounds like, the kiss, which happened months ago, didn't mean much to either of them.

I don't know Lauren, but I do know their relationship was more involved than one kiss. If JP is telling the truth about ending things this morning, the timing isn't on her side.

"Amy, what do I do?" I ask.

"I'm so sorry to make you deal with this on your own, but I really have to get to rehearsal," Amy says, fishing in her purse for her car keys.

"Right, we'll see you early tomorrow."

She hugs me before getting into her car. JP opens the front door as she is pulling out of the driveway.

"Can I help with the stroller? How'd it go with Amy? Did you tell her about us?"

That's what he worries about. Does my sister know what a lying prick he is? I step to the side to reveal the vandalism. The writing is large, taking up the entire door, and his jaw drops immediately when he sees it.

"What the hell?" He runs over to the car and crouches. He runs his hands along the car he loves so dearly.

"When did you say you ended things with Lauren?"

"This morning." Then, as though he is just realizing what I am implying, says, "She wouldn't do this. No way."

I scoff. "You sure about that? It wasn't here last night."

"No, it's not possible. Lauren is out of town, at her cousin's place." He stands up, shaking his head. "I have to pick up my parents from the airport at two. They can't see this."

I laugh internally as I enter the garage code on the keypad. Did he really think he could keep his affair a secret from his family? I toss the paper cup into the garbage bin, then walk back to the stroller to unbuckle Addison. "I can't see Janine doing this either. It would be silly to do something when she lives so close. What's that expression?"

"Don't shit where you eat." He rubs his brow in frustration.

"That's the one."

He did this to himself. He can explain to his parents why someone defaced the car.

"You said this wasn't here last night when you got home?" he asks.

I pick up Addison and head to the porch. "I didn't notice it. I wasn't looking for it though."

"And you were drunk. And upset."

"Right." I blink hard.

"Jo. Is it possible you did this last night? Out of anger?"

You've got to be kidding me. "Asshole." I shake my head and walk towards the house.

JP runs after me. "Relax. I'm just saying, I wouldn't be upset if you did. You have every right to be angry at me. And you were really drunk."

I can't believe this—he thinks I'm more capable of something like this than his mistress. I turn his way and before I know it, I've slapped him across the face. My hand stings with satisfaction. "No. I didn't key our vehicle that I also have to drive. Call your girlfriend and ask her." I turn away abruptly and head to the stairs.

"Jo, wait a minute, would you?"

I run up the stairs with Addison, not bothering to look back. "I guess that's another good reason for you to get the video camera. Good luck with your parents. Maybe they won't notice!"

CHAPTER TWENTY-FOUR

Margot sits on the end of the couch with Addison on her lap, facing her. She is soaking all of Addy up, compensating for lost time. She kisses each of Addison's fingers, counting them aloud one by one. She rubs her nose against Addison's, humming softly while she does so. Margot has JP's slightly hooked nose, but on her it's more elegant, almost bird-like. She brushes her salt and pepper waves out of her face and then very gently kisses both of Addison's eyelids, whispering, "Grandma's here, darling."

I feel like I've stumbled upon a mother and daughter having a private moment. I doubt they would notice if I left the room. Normally, I'd appreciate the break and a few seconds to myself, but right now I just want to cuddle with my daughter. She's the only thing keeping me from leaving this house and JP.

I rise to clear our plates that carry a few crumbs left over from our apple crumble, but JP stops me. He cups the small of my back and I recoil. He either doesn't notice or pretends not to. "No, sit, please. Leave the clean-up to the guys. You two visit."

This is the most JP and I have interacted since he and his parents arrived from the airport. I've kept myself busy with Addison, with JP entertaining his mom and dad. At dinner, I watched him intently as he laughed at his dad's jokes, bragged about his work, and sipped his wine. I took notice of the way he spoke with his mother, confiding in her as they chopped vegetables. I wonder how a man who is so close to his mother could be disrespectful to his wife.

I reluctantly sit back down on my side of the couch and watch as JP and his dad clean up the dinner that Margot cooked for us. JP moves efficiently, rinsing the dishes from the counter before loading them into the dishwasher. He stops occasionally to look my way and offers an apologetic smile. Margot mistakes his look for a doting husband, enamored with his wife. She smiles to herself when she notices it; *oh, how she has raised a good son.*

Louis moves slowly between the dining room and the kitchen, carrying no more than two dishes at a time. He looks bored out of his mind, and I'm sure he would gladly trade with me, so he could drink his scotch by the gas fireplace.

"Margot, thank you again for dinner," I say, my attempt at visiting.

Margot looks up briefly. "Oh, don't worry about it, Joanna. It's the least I can do." She returns her gaze to Addison. "I don't know how you get anything done with this little angel. I'd just stare at her all day." She shakes her head subtly from side to side and then gets more and more animated when she discovers that Addison finds it amusing. "No, I wouldn't, you're an actual angel."

I relax into the couch, the heat from the fire making me sleepy. My eyes get heavier, and I start to drift off to sleep.

"Oh, I almost forgot. What will Addison be wearing tomorrow for the baptism?" Margot's question jolts me awake.

"Oh, um, a white dress and matching cardigan."

"That sounds nice. Let me show you something I brought in case you want to explore other options." She passes me Addison and heads to the stairs where her suitcase sits. She returns a moment later with a white gift bag, decorated with an embossed silver cross. "Just a little something from Louis and me for her special day."

"JP, do you want to come open this with me?" I ask.

Margot has a habit of assuming anything to do with children or the domestic space is the wife's responsibility. Whenever we see her, she drones on about techniques to make JP's white shirts stay bright or how to brine a chicken so it's tender. I'd like to tell her that I really don't care whether JP's shirts are bright and that chicken is chicken. Instead, I always smile and act interested. Mother taught me to respect adults. There were repercussions if I didn't.

JP joins us on the couch. "What's this, Mom?"

"Just a little something from your father and me."

Louis takes this as an invitation to leave his chores and he retires to the armchair next to the fireplace with his drink in hand. He lets out a big sigh; it's only a matter of time before he'll nod off.

JP takes the lead, removing the white sparkly tissue paper and crumpling it into a ball. Margot looks horrified. "JP, perhaps Joanna wanted to save that?"

JP shoots me a look, worried he's once again messed something up.

"Oh, that's okay," I say as I realize Margot wants me to save the paper. I begin unfolding the crumpled-up balls, doing my best to smooth them out on the couch.

JP reaches into the bag and reveals a delicate lace christening gown with a matching bonnet. "Oh wow, she's going to look so cute in this. You like it, Jo?"

Explore my options.

"It's beautiful. I was just going to have her wear that white dress I bought, but we can put that on her some other time," I say and then I quietly add, "before she turns six months and outgrows it."

"It's completely up to you, Joanna. You're her mom." Margot holds the dress up to Addison, letting it drape over my thighs. "It's eyelet lace. I saw it and thought instantly of Addison."

It's a baby christening gown, who else would she think of?

"She'll look beautiful," JP says.

"Then it's settled. We'll have to get some family photos done in front of the church. Have you hired a photographer?"

"Meg's husband, Derek, is going to take some for us. He has a nice camera."

Margot's silence says it all; how could I not have thought to hire a professional photographer for such an event?

Later that night, Margot asks if she can observe Addison's bedtime routine. She explains how she wants to witness how I do it in case she babysits in the future. I agree and lead her up to Addison's room. She stands at the foot of the change table, occasionally reaching for items she thinks I might need.

"Oh, now that's interesting," she says, as I roll up Addison's used diaper, securing it closed with the two sticky tabs.

"What?" I toss the diaper into our diaper pail, designed to mask the smell.

"In my day, we would dump the poopy into the toilet before rolling up the diaper. Just helped with the smell."

I let out a breath.

"We didn't have those fancy diaper disposals though." She passes me a fresh diaper.

"Thanks." Holding Addison's feet, I lift her bottom up and slide the diaper underneath.

I am opening the diaper tabs, so I can fasten her diaper when Margot interrupts. "Diaper cream? Or do you not usually use that before bed?"

I accept the container with a forced smile. "Yeah, sometimes." I apply a thin layer.

"So how are you adjusting since the last time I saw you?"

The last time I saw Margot, I was wearing oversized pads and gushing blood with every movement. I was sleeping for an hour at a time if I was lucky and wandering around like a zombie. I was crying constantly. Sometimes it was because Addison wasn't latching right, and I was worried my milk wasn't coming in. Other times I cried because I thought she was the most beautiful thing in the world, and I was afraid I wasn't the mom she deserved. No one should judge a new mom in the first month. Yet here I am, feeling the need to defend myself.

"They weren't kidding when they said the first month was tough." I lift Addison up and lay her sleeper on the change table. Margot helps me straighten it out, but she ends up pulling so that it is too high on the table and there is no longer a place for Addy's head to rest. I'm forced to readjust before I can lay her back down on top of it.

"Yes, the first months can be so overwhelming," she says, and she pats my hand. "I hope I'm not overstepping here, but I mentioned to JP that with our retirement, we have ample free time right now." She pauses as if to check whether I'm following.

I nod, giving her permission to continue.

"And, you know, we think the world of little Addison." She squeezes Addy's foot, which I've managed to get into the sleeper.

"Yeah, I know." I smile. It does feel nice to have a grandma for Addison who I know loves her unconditionally.

"So, like I said. I mentioned to JP that if you wanted, I would be happy to stay for a bit to help. Like I did the first couple of weeks after Addy was born. I could cook, clean, give you some relief from baby duty."

"Oh, wow. That's a generous offer, Margot."

"You would be doing me the favor, really. I want to live up to my grandma title. They change so much at this age, and we are missing it all."

I feel completely put on the spot. Would now be a good time to tell her that I just discovered her son is having an affair? "We'll give it some thought," I say and zip Addison's sleeper up.

"Please do. I know JP was warming to the idea when we last spoke. I even packed some extra things if you wanted to try it out for next week."

Warming to the idea. I had hoped to make JP the bad guy and break the news to her that we don't need a live-in grandma right now. I don't want someone taking over my routine. I pick up Addison and bring her to the rocking chair.

Margot follows me. "Joanna, I heard about the recent incidents." I open my mouth to speak, curious if JP has also mentioned his adultery, but she continues. "Now, before you say anything, I want you to know I don't judge at all. It's tough being a new mom, and I realize JP travels a lot. But, Joanna, you need to accept help when it is offered. Let go of your pride. It will be better for Addison."

There's no ill intention with Margot's offer. I realize that, but I'm left feeling like a failure. It seems to come naturally for so many moms. All of the moms on my social feeds post blissful photos of their babies wrapped in delicate neutrals, draped in their arms in front of airy backdrops. They appear to be wearing no make-up but look effortlessly beautiful. Motherhood looks good on them, just like their baby bumps did. They don't need live-in in-laws to help because they are losing their minds.

"We'll think about it, Margot. I usually nurse her before bed, so if you don't mind ..." I position Addison so her head is in the crux of my arm and begin unbuttoning my blouse.

"You and JP talk and let us know. In the meantime, I'll plan to stay in the guest room for a few extra days." Margot bends down to kiss Addison. "Tomorrow is a big day. Get some rest." She pats me on the shoulder before leaving the room.

She's right, tomorrow carries more weight than I'd like to admit. Tomorrow, I will return to the place where I said goodbye to Mother.

CHAPTER
TWENTY-FIVE

We mount the stone steps of the church I went to every Sunday as a child. I steady myself, leaning against the brass railing and peek over the cake I carry to ensure I don't bump into anyone. I follow the procession of white-haired women wearing pastel pantsuits and bald men supported by canes. The average age of the congregation is eighty years old. Everyone moves slowly. God will wait for them.

I remember how heavy the golden-painted wooden doors were as a child. I used to lean on them from the inside with all my might, barely nudging them an inch. Today, I am thankful they are propped open by the bodies of the ushers who greet us.

Once inside the doors, we step onto mint-green linoleum. They haven't updated the flooring in decades. JP climbs the stairs with Addison in his arms, followed by Louis. Margot and I head downstairs to the entertainment hall, which is nothing more than a windowless room with an adjacent kitchenette.

On baptism days, the families are welcome to use the space to host guests following the service, but every member of the congregation is also invited to join. That is part of the tradeoff of getting to use the space for free. Margot carries a tray of veggies and fruit, and I shuffle slowly behind her with Amy's opulent cake.

The basement holds a permanent smell of cheap coffee and hard-boiled eggs. The room is set with rectangle tables and burgundy banquet chairs. I picture Meg arriving an hour early to set it up with Derek as the boys run laps around the church.

Meg pokes her head through the doorway of the kitchen. "Jo, good, you're here. Wow, look at that cake. I'll need to make room in the fridge."

Margot and I squeeze our way into the small kitchen. Meg opens the fridge to reveal five trays of crustless sandwich quarters—cucumber, egg, tuna, and ham—on thin bread that's been dyed soft pink. I never could quite understand why Protestant women think dying the bread makes the sandwich more appealing.

"Those look beautiful," Margot says.

I nod in agreement, but my mind is elsewhere. Being back here gives me the strange sensation that Mother is close by. Meg still brings the boys to Sunday service every so often, but the last time I entered the building was for the twins' baptism six years ago. Meg served the same sandwiches.

Meg squeezes the fruit and veggie trays onto the top shelf of the fridge and stands up, shaking her head. "I don't think the shelf is tall enough for the cake. What if we put it out on display? On the table in the foyer?"

I nod and she leads us back out to the stairs. We spot Amy outside of the Sunday school classroom. She kisses her fingers and touches them to a gold plaque on the door. After Mother's death, they dedicated the room to her; the plaque reads: *In loving memory of Carolyn Baker.*

Meg joins Amy, embracing her from behind. "I miss her, too," she whispers. Margot rubs my back. The look she gives me tells me that JP has divulged at least some of the details of my complicated past.

That's when my fingers start to tingle. Cold drops pitter-patter down my hands, and I am back here on that rainy day we buried Mother. I can see the coffin. Closed casket. Mother's crumpled body. Her eyes wide open. Blue ice. The blood pooling beneath her head.

I shake my head to make the visions go away. There is a rush of heat and I pull away from Margot to give myself space. The air is stuffy, each breath coming harder. She asks me if I'm okay, but her voice is muffled like we're underwater. *Calm down, Jo, calm down.* My heart thumps heavy in my chest as if it's trying to escape so it doesn't have to feel the weight of this moment.

My arms go limp, and I let the cake fall to the floor.

I hear a shriek.

I reach for the railing of the stairs but miss it.

Margot says, "She's fainting."

I think I call for Addy. That's when it all goes black.

I lean against the wall with my knees up. My head hangs between my legs. Where am I? JP crouches in front of me, fanning me with a folded piece of paper.

"Jo, are you okay?" I no longer feel the breeze on my face. JP has stopped. He lets the paper that was previously used as a fan fall to the floor. *St. Andrew's Presbyterian*. The church program now lies a few inches from my feet.

"You fainted, sweetheart." Margot sits beside me, rubbing my leg. "You took quite the spill."

The right side of my body throbs. A scrape marks my forearm from elbow to wrist.

I fell at Mother's church. Addison's baptism is today. The pieces of today slowly come into form, like a puzzle.

"Is Addison okay? I dropped her. How could I have dropped her?" My words come out in hysteric wails.

Amy steps into view. She sways from side to side, holding Addison. I try to stand to get near her, but my knees go weak. I sit back down and drop my arms to my sides.

Meg moves closer, holding a plastic cup. "Drink this, Jo, it will help."

I take a gulp. It's not water. It's sweet. I let the liquid dribble down my chin. "I dropped her."

"What's she talking about?" I hear someone whisper. It could have been Margot.

"She's delirious." Meg sits down on the other side of me still grasping the juice. "Addison is fine. You weren't holding her. Drink some more juice."

JP leaves my side. "What happened before she fainted?"

Addison fusses, and Amy kisses her on the head. "It's okay, baby girl. I think she had a panic attack. She came out of the kitchen with your mom. She dropped the cake, and then she fell. She's dealing with a lot right now."

I look around me. There it is. The cake lies in a pile by the stairs. Layers of buttercream, vanilla cake, and strawberry compote are smeared across the mint tiles. It reminds me of the smash cake photo shoots so many moms do with their kids on their first birthdays. The rose gold, fondant flowers, and the words *God Bless Addison* are still intact.

Margot rises to join the conversation. "She was clearly overwhelmed being here. I don't know why everyone thought this was a good idea in the first place - having Addison's baptism at *this* church."

Meg is up now, and I'm left alone. I whimper to myself and sip on my juice.

I hear more voices and they build into arguing. Meg says something about the church being special to Mother. JP says I owe Mother nothing. Meg's face gets stern, and she goes quiet.

Amy chimes in with, "Perhaps there are other things on Jo's mind, JP. Something you want to share with the group?"

"I want my baby!" I yell.

Everyone stops arguing and stares in my direction. Amy looks around at the others, as if she is waiting for permission to pass my daughter to me.

JP grabs Addy and joins me on the floor. "Here she is, Jo." He passes her to me but spots her as one would do with a newborn being held by their sibling for the first time.

"I'm sorry, Addy, I'm so sorry," I say, looking down at her in my arms. Her ice-blue eyes are just like Mother's.

Margot pets my head and tucks me into bed. "You just get some rest. You fed Addison not long ago and JP says you have some milk in the freezer we can use."

"I'm so sorry, Margot. I know today was important to you."

"Don't you worry a thing about it." She pats my head one more time and then leaves me in the room to rest.

I roll over onto my side. I'm exhausted. I honestly couldn't care less about missing the baptism. I only agreed to it because JP's family insisted, and Meg said it was the right thing to do. She kept saying that everyone at the church was asking when Carolyn's granddaughter was going to come so that they could meet her. I don't know if this is true. I never did get to talk to anyone.

After my spell at the church, I remained in the basement with Margot. JP and my sisters brought Addison upstairs where they went ahead with the baptism. Derek flashed his camera at our incomplete family. Margot cleaned up the cake and offered me a plate with some of the top layers that never touched the ground. I even ate one of the fondant flowers. I saved Addison's name.

We left immediately after the ceremony. Meg and Amy stayed to serve coffee and sandwiches and reminisce with Mother's friends. They wouldn't miss me. Meg and Amy were always the favorites. Mother made sure that stuck, even outside of our home.

I was quiet on the car ride back to our house. JP drove with his father in the passenger seat. Margot was sandwiched between me and Addison's car seat. It's a good thing she's tiny, otherwise the drive would have felt even more claustrophobic. I looked out the window and thought about how our car still says *CHEATER* on the driver's door. I watched the town I grew up in go by in a flash. We always used to say you could hold your breath from one end of the town to the other. After that, I pretended to sleep. Margot and Louis agreed she would extend her stay indefinitely.

An alert comes through on my phone from Amy.

> I hope you are okay. I'm sorry if I overstepped with JP. Let's plan a walk or a park date this week.

I stare at the screen for a while and all I can come up with is:

> I'm sorry I ruined the cake.

As if that's the most important thing.

A message from Meg follows. I suppose they were talking and agreed they should both reach out to me.

> Sending you love. The photos turned out great. Addy looks beautiful. Derek is editing and will share soon.

I imagine what the photos might look like from today. I picture myself carefully curating a gallery for my social feeds. Then I think of the captions I will write alongside the photos. *Today, Addison got baptized at Mother's old church. Here she is held by my sister Meg, wearing a christening gown picked out by my mother-in-law. And here I am sitting on the floor of a musty church basement, eating floor cake and drinking apple juice.*

THE LORD DETESTS LYING LIPS

Eight years old

Mother sat at the front of the class, waiting for a volunteer to raise their hand. It was almost time for arts and crafts and the stack of Noah's Arc illustrations sat on her desk waiting to be shaded in. If no one volunteered, it would mean Jo, the daughter of the teacher, would be forced take a turn.

"Joanna? Would you like to share about a time you were dishonest?" The arch in Mother's eyebrows reminded Jo of the rainbow on the worksheet.

There were a few uncomfortable giggles. What child is going to volunteer that information in the house of the Lord?

Jo twisted her face and shrugged. "I can't think of anything right now, Mother."

Mother raised her eyebrows, and the rainbows took shape again. "It's Ms. Baker in this room, Joanna."

More giggles filled the room.

She and Jo both knew there was something Jo could share. That is why Mother chose honesty and integrity for this Sunday's lesson. She knew Jo had lied about wetting the bed. She knew that Meg had helped Jo switch the sheets with fresh ones from the linen closet. Jo had thought that Mother was going to let it go when she hadn't brought it up.

This was Jo's punishment.

Jo pressed her hands between her thighs in prayer position. "One time I lied about taking Amy's doll. I wanted to play with it but she wouldn't let me."

Mother nodded and paced the front of the room. "Anything more recent? Something you'd want to ask the Lord for forgiveness for today?" Then she looked at the class and smiled. "That lie would have been quite some time ago. Amy hasn't played with dolls in a few years."

Mackenzie, the minister's daughter, shot up her hand. Jo offered her a look of thanks but when Mackenzie dismissed her, Jo realized the other girl simply wanted brownie points for volunteering.

Mother nodded and Mackenzie sat up tall in her seat and flung her braid behind her shoulder. "I told my grandmother that her butter tarts were the best I've ever tasted last week, but it's not true. I tried butter tarts at the fall fair and they were ten times better than hers."

The redheaded boy in the front raised his hand then. "Ms. Baker? Is it okay to tell a white lie if it means protecting someone?"

Mother had lost control of her lesson. It would be hard for her to bring it back to Jo.

She politely responded to each child's question and handed out the coloring pages and crayons. When class was over, she told the children to bring their drawings to the front. Mother wanted to display them on the bulletin for a week and they could collect them next Sunday.

Jo didn't like to be the last one with Mother. It was better to disappear into the group. When she slid her drawing on Mother's desk with six students still behind her, Jo thought she would have an uneventful walk to the sermon.

Mother put her hand on Jo's before she could escape. "Joanna, next time you wet the bed, please don't be afraid to tell me. It's nothing to be embarrassed about."

Jo's body grew hot. She wanted to scream. Mackenzie gasped and a few snickers followed. The boy with the red hair had a red face to match. Mother freed Jo's hand and recited her lesson to the class. "The Lord detests lying lips."

CHAPTER TWENTY-SIX

I sit in the waiting room at Alice's practice, once again wearing casual clothes and loafers while her assistants are dressed to the nines. Today, the young man wears a loose knit, black sweater that falls to his knees with slim leather pants and the woman wears a jean romper with chunky straps and wide legs. I don't know when I got too old to be fashionable. Maybe I never was.

It's only been one week since my first mandated therapy appointment, and I'm apprehensive about filling Alice in on everything that has occurred in the short time. Since we last spoke, Mother has consumed my thoughts. I'm awash in memories from childhood and visions of Mother's lifeless body. I can already anticipate what Alice will say. *The fifteenth anniversary is coming up; it's completely normal for you to be thinking about her more.* How do I tell her that I saw Mother in the flesh? I'm not sure there's a reasonable explanation for that.

While I'm on that topic, what is the explanation for the strange occurrences around the house? Since the backyard fiasco, there's been another incident where Addison's moved—this time from the crib to the bassinet. Then there was the gate being left open and Addison's belongings thrown across the yard. I really don't think the hour-long session can handle all of this. Not to mention my panic attack at the church two days ago and my husband's affair.

JP senses my breathing is escalating and pats my leg. He is probably worried I will faint right here in the waiting room. Although that could give him a chance to chat up *Jean Romper*. She is blonde, after all.

JP insisted on joining me today for "support," but his presence just adds to the tension. This wouldn't be possible without Margot, our temporary live-in babysitter, which is a thing now. He sits a little too close to me, asking me questions of concern like, *Are you warm? Do you need something to drink?* I consider answering yes to see how he will solve each one. There's no vending machine in view, and I don't think he can convince the fashion twins to adjust the heat.

Alice appears in the doorway of her office and gives me a warm smile. "Hi, Joanna. Come on in." I rise to follow her and JP offers a small wave.

She meets me halfway, entering the horseshoe of reception chairs. "Is this JP? Are you joining us today?"

He stands. "No, I'll wait out here. Unless Jo needs me."

She nods. "It's nice to meet you. Perhaps you can join us during one of our future sessions."

I follow Alice and when I arrive at her office, I glance back at JP. He has already moved on and is now invested in his phone.

Once we are seated on the leather chairs with the natural sunlight streaming in and making the dust dance in the air, Alice asks, "How has your week been?"

If she only knew what a weighted question she just posed.

Then it comes out—the word vomit. *Here's a question, Doc, am I losing my mind if I keep seeing visions of my dead mother, I don't remember events that have taken place, and instead of appreciating having my mother-in-law to cook and clean for me, I want her to fly home and take my cheating husband with her?* It is something to that effect but probably even less cohesive by the time it makes it out of my dry mouth. I lick my lips to signal that I've finished.

If she's freaked out by my confessions, she doesn't show it. First, she grabs me a paper cup with water from the cooler. I guess my dry mouth was obvious. She speaks calmly and gently. She asks if I've been taking any medication. I tell her only prenatal vitamins and magnesium at night. Nothing of concern there. She mentions sleep analysis might be beneficial and that she can refer me to a specialist for that. I figured that was coming. I'm not really looking forward to sleeping in some medical building, hooked up to sensors, but I'll cross that bridge when we get there.

"With the anniversary looming, I'm not surprised you are thinking more of your mother. And being back at her church could have been triggering for you," she says.

"Do you think this will all go away soon?"

"We'll keep an eye on it. Are JP and your mother-in-law helping around the house with Addison?"

"Truthfully? It's a bit much. It's nice to have the extra hand, but I don't feel like I can be myself."

Alice asks how I would feel about JP joining us during the session next week—if I would be comfortable with that. I fixate on the word *comfortable*—it doesn't seem fitting. Tolerating is perhaps more accurate.

"I can also refer you to a marriage counsellor. Her office is just a few blocks away." I'm not sure I even want to try to fix things with JP. He stopped trying months ago.

As I'm leaving her office, I realize that I didn't tell Alice about mommy dearest paying me a visit at the house, how I almost touched her face before she escaped out the back door. I tell myself I just forgot—that I'll bring it up next week.

On the way home, JP suggests we stop for ice cream and I'm mad that I want it because I'd really love to tell him to fuck off.

CHAPTER TWENTY-SEVEN

JP and his mother are changing Addison's diaper when I wake up from my afternoon nap. If I wasn't annoyed with them both it would actually be cute. They've started mandating more rest periods for me. Margot wipes a generous layer of diaper cream on Addison's bum and JP distracts Addy with facial expressions I've never seen him do before. All three of them laugh together until they notice me and then JP and Margot go quiet.

"My turn to tag in?" I ask.

"Sure, if you'd like," JP says, and he steps aside.

Since the baptism, it feels like everyone is walking on eggshells around me. Even my own sisters haven't been by. That could also be because they had words with Margot at the church. My solace now is my daily walk with Addison, the only time when I'm allowed to be alone with her, and even that comes with challenges. I'm forced to dodge the neighborhood moms regularly. I've been ignoring Claire's texts since karaoke night. I imagine Janine has filled them all in by now.

I intercept Margot, taking hold of the pants she is about to dress Addison in. "Thanks, I've got it from here."

Margot moves to the other side of the room to sit on the rocking chair to fold laundry.

"I'm going to take Addy for a walk to the park," I say, pulling the leggings up over Addy's adorable chubby thighs.

JP hovers near the change table. "Want me to come with you guys? I'm taking the car in to get the door painted, but we could go when I get back."

Margot chimes in. "Oh, good, you were able to get an appointment? I still can't believe someone vandalized your car."

"Stupid teenagers. Probably drunk. A dare on their walk home from the bar." JP looks at the ground. He never told his mother.

I slam the drawer shut. "*Teenagers*? What the fuck, JP?"

"Joanna!" Margot shrieks as if she's never heard that word before.

"You need to tell your mom the truth."

Margot's eyes move from JP to me, back to JP again. She holds one of Addy's sleepers to her chest and it hangs lifeless.

JP cowers and turns towards his mother. "Mom, we should probably go talk."

"Do it here. I want to hear you tell her." I pick Addison up from the change table even though I still need to put her shirt on.

"Okay, the reason the car says *CHEATER* on it is because ..." JP crouches so that he is eye-level with Margot. "I cheated on Jo."

Margot gasps and drops the sleeper.

"It's over now. It was someone from work—"

"Well, the one was from work. There was also a mom who lives a street over."

JP's head drops and he talks to the floor. "She's right. There was an incident with one of the neighbors in the summer. That's over, too."

I maintain focus on Margot, watching her look of shock slowly fade.

JP puts his hand on his mother's knee. "Seriously, Mom, it will never happen again. I promise." JP looks more desperate for his mother's forgiveness than mine.

Margot rises and pushes past JP. She walks over to me and wraps her arms around me and Addison.

"I'm sorry," she whispers. "You don't deserve that."

I let her hold us both, relaxing into her embrace. For once, I think she is on my side.

CHAPTER TWENTY-EIGHT

It's been a couple of days since Margot learned of JP's affair. Her coldness towards him has gradually turned tepid. It must be hard to stay mad at her only child, who also happens to be her best friend.

JP accosts me in the foyer as I'm zipping Addison up in a sherpa onesie, headed for a walk around the neighborhood.

"How about a trip to Pine Farms to pick up some pumpkins for the porch?"

"Fine," I say. This is unlike JP, who believes these types of seasonal outings to be overpriced and kitschy. I guess this is *in the doghouse JP* trying to make things right. It's going to take a lot more than a visit to a pumpkin patch to get him out of that.

The leaves have turned the warmest of colors and it wakes my heart up. Why decay makes me happy, I'm not sure, but I'm certainly not the only one who gets swept up in the autumn season. The farm is packed. With only two weeks until Halloween, I'm not surprised that our entire town has made the fifteen-minute drive north to the quaint, family-owned farm.

I wear Addison in my wrap, and we make our way through the harvest activities. We stroll through the corn maze, and JP runs a few meters ahead with the intention of jumping out to scare us. He ends up popping out from the golden husks just as an elderly woman and her daughter walk by. They scold him for his prank, and I cover my laughter with a cough as I saunter past them, pretending I'm there alone with my baby. The moments where Addison and I are on our own feel right—like this is how it's supposed to be. The warmth from the sun is on my face, and I'm resting my chin on the top of Addison's head.

When JP joins us, I tense my shoulders. My heartbeat quickens and my stomach wrenches.

We trek through the farm field to the pick-your-own pumpkin patch and choose three pumpkins, one for each step leading up to our porch. We attempt a photo of Addison, leaning her against one of the pumpkins, but she falls over and face plants. We don't bother trying again.

JP suggests we have a cider at the restaurant, a café housed in a small wooden cabin. Out back is a porch that overlooks the forest the farm is nestled in. We sit outside on a picnic table, sipping on cider, Addison resting in my lap.

JP's leg is restless, bumping up and down like he's doing some sort of stomp dance routine. He has something on his mind. I catch his eye and offer a slight smile -- the most I've given him in a week. "How's your cider?"

"It's good. Hot. I burned my tongue." He blows on the murky amber drink and then attempts another sip.

"Yeah, that's the thing about cider. You don't add anything to cool it down. Not like coffee, with milk." Is this really the type of conversation we've resorted to? "Or cream," I add, but it doesn't make it any less forced.

I breathe in the cool air, letting the scent of baked goods and burning leaves fill my nose. The moment feels too perfect for us, like we aren't deserving of it.

"How have you felt about my mom helping out?"

I have to admit, it's been more than helpful having Margot around; having another adult to talk to during the day has felt nice. I can't talk to JP anymore. She helps with dinner, laundry, and general tidying, plus she's on hand if I need to use the washroom or take a break. Coincidentally, Addy has started sleeping through the night, something I didn't expect to see for a while. Getting eight hours of uninterrupted sleep has made me feel more like myself, but I don't want to live with my mother-in-law forever.

"It's been nice having the help. I feel bad that she's spending her retirement doing Addy's laundry, though."

"She's loving it. Told me this morning how the time she's had with Addy is exactly how she pictured retirement."

"Right. But this isn't a permanent solution, JP."

"What if we could have it both ways? Mom's help whenever we need it and our own space as well." I hate when people refer to their own parents as your communal parents. Your mom is not my mom and calling her *our mom* doesn't make it any truer.

"What do you mean? Like, your parents moving here?" I have visions of them buying one of the houses being built down the street. That would be way too close.

"I was thinking of us moving to Montréal." He lowers his head, fiddling with his mug, and then returns his gaze to me.

I spit my drink out, taken aback by his proposal. With my napkin, I mop up the cider saliva that has splattered over the picnic table. "I wasn't expecting that. This is Addy's home."

"Just hear me out. You're not in love with your job, and PR is something you can easily do anywhere." I raise my eyebrows in response. It's laughable that he thinks moving will solve our problems. "The Montréal office needs some extra care right now, so this would mean I wouldn't have to travel as much." He takes a gulp of cider, forgetting it's still scalding. "Damnit, that's hot. I think it would be a fresh start for us."

"Is this just so you don't have to face Lauren at the office?" I haven't asked about Lauren and how the office life is treating JP. I've been partly afraid of the answer. He comes home right after work, though, and drives more, so I can only imagine it's less than ideal.

"No, it's not that. Although, would it be such a bad thing for me not to see her every day?"

I shrug, and adjust Addison's hat, which is no longer covering her ears.

"My mom even offered to look after Addison full-time when you go back to work."

"You mean after I'd find a new job in Montréal." He's forgetting that tiny piece of the puzzle that I would now have to spend nap-time job searching.

"I don't think it's a terrible idea to have a family member close by if anything were to happen to us."

"What's that supposed to mean?" My arm sticks to the apple cider residue on the table.

"It's life, Jo. Shit happens. You have to plan for that. My mom and dad would be there if we needed them, is all I'm saying."

"What about my sisters? I always thought one of them would be Addison's guardian. Also, what's going to happen to us?"

"Meg has her hands full with the boys, and Amy? I just don't picture her having a lifestyle that fits."

"Well, she doesn't need to have a lifestyle that fits right this second. And what does that even mean? Just because she doesn't live in the 'burbs and have a typical nine to five job?"

A couple sitting at the table over eyes us and JP lowers his voice. "Okay. Clearly, we have some things to talk about. It was just an idea to help you out. You have to admit it wasn't working before."

"Please, elaborate." I want to hear him say it. I want him to look me in the eye and tell me that I haven't turned into the mother he expected. That I'm a disappointment. Then, I can enlighten him on how he has failed as a partner.

"You want to get into this here? Fine. I'll say it. I'm worried about you. More importantly, I'm worried about Addy. You're freaking me out, to tell you the truth. And I'm going to tell Dr. Lui when we meet. Because if I don't, who knows what will happen the next time you're left alone with Addison."

"Are you fucking kidding me?" My voice comes out louder than I intended.

The old woman and her daughter walk by our picnic table, the daughter shaking her head to advise us once again that we've ruined their visit.

As we pay our bill, I contemplate our conversation. JP wants to move across the country. JP wants me to leave my job and my family. JP wants to make his parents Addison's guardian. I squeeze Addison closer. This doesn't sit right.

CHAPTER TWENTY-NINE

Margot enters the dining room carrying the pot roast she's been braising all afternoon, and places it in the center of the table. Steam rises from the meat, and the smell of thyme and rosemary permeate the air. She returns a few minutes later with roasted potatoes and carrots in serving dishes that match the china plates she set; all items she picked out and purchased for us as a wedding gift last winter. It's an elaborate meal, but she insists that she will only do this on Sundays. How many more Sundays does she expect to be here for?

JP and I are quiet during dinner. Margot makes small talk, asking how our day went at the farm. We skip over Addy's face plant and our fight, instead focusing on the weather and the freshly pressed cider. JP drinks a few glasses of wine, and I watch the liquid get lower, the line moving dangerously close to the bottom of the bottle. Addison spits out her carrot purée, still getting used to the solid foods I introduced last week.

I consider having a glass of wine just so JP is forced to open a new bottle if he wants another glass. I want him to disappoint his mother again. I want her to be in my corner. I excuse myself from the table and go to the kitchen to defrost one of my freezer milk bags. I dig around for a minute but discover there are only two left. I could have sworn I had at least eight, each with about four ounces of breastmilk.

I enter the dining room with a puzzled look on my face that Margot picks up on immediately.

"Joanna? Is everything okay?"

I lower into my seat, contemplating whether drinking a glass will be worth the second last bag. "Yeah, it's fine. I just need to pump more milk; I'm running low on my stash."

"Oh yes, thank you for the reminder. I was going to tell you that. I noticed you were running low when I made a bottle for Addy last night."

I'm caught off guard with a mouth full of potatoes. "I'm sorry, what did you say?"

Margot shifts in her seat. "I fed Addy a bottle last night. She had fussed and I didn't want to wake you."

"What time was this at?" I open the app on my phone to watch the night summary video that I started dismissing once Addy began sleeping through the night.

"I think it was around three o'clock. It was honestly no trouble at all. It's better that you get your full night's rest."

JP smiles at his mother and dishes himself another helping of carrots. "That's nice of you, Mom."

"Was this a one-time thing or have you fed her before during the night?" I look down at my phone trying to find the previous night's video summary, but it is no longer available.

Margot smiles at me sweetly. "There's been a few nights, but don't worry about me."

I push my chair out and it screeches across the hardwood. "That is not okay, Margot."

JP drops his cutlery to the table. "She was only trying to help you, Jo? You're being rude."

I return to my seat.

Margot puts her hand on JP's, "It's okay, honey." Her smile dissolves. "Joanna, I'm so sorry if that makes you uncomfortable. My room is close to Addy's so I can hear her cry right away, and the first night it happened, I did wait a few minutes before I went in. In fact, I tried to wake you. I opened the door to your room and called your name, but you were sound asleep. After that, I guess I got into the habit of taking over the night feed for you." She blinks hard and then looks at JP to see if he's still on her side.

Addison lets out a cry, and I shove another spoonful of purée into her mouth. She allows it to roll around on her tongue for a minute before spitting it out.

I place the spoon down. "Addison hasn't been sleeping through the night? You've been doing the night feed? What, like every night, since you moved in?"

"Not every night. I'm sorry, I really didn't think it was an issue and I was actually trying to help you wean her. That's what I did with JP. He was breastfed too and would wake up in the night for a top-up for the longest time."

JP grabs the wine and pours the last of the bottle into his glass. He looks uncomfortable with the fact that his mom is now talking about how she used to breastfeed him.

Margot eyes JP's glass and then directs her attention to me. "It's so much harder to wean a baby when you're breastfeeding. How can you really tell whether they are drinking less each night? With the bottle, you can gradually cut back. Last night Addison only had two ounces, so soon enough she will be sleeping through."

"Let's hope so, because now I probably can't even produce milk at night; it's been more than a week since I've had to." For someone who is such an expert on breastfeeding and weaning and diaper changing and every other thing to do with raising a child, you'd think Margot would have thought of that. She's gone and thrown off my milk supply.

Margot stands up and as though she is speaking to a room full of guests, announces in a cheery voice, "Who is ready for dessert?" Then she pats my hand. "The pie you picked up from the farm looks delicious."

"JP picked out the pie," I say. I attempt to feed Addy one last bite of the carrot. When she spits it out another time, I slam the spoon down.

"Relax, Jo," JP says.

I retire to bed before both JP and Margot. Shortly after I nurse Addy to sleep, I move into our room to read. If Addison is still waking up during the night, I'll need to start going to bed earlier again. I'm going to miss my eight hours of sleep, but I'm not okay with letting my mother-in-law take over the night feeds. It feels unnatural that I should be sound asleep while Margot feeds Addison a bottle in our rocking chair, cuddling her as she drifts off.

A light knock on the door barely catches my attention. "Joanna, are you awake?" Margot asks in a small voice.

"Come in," I say.

Margot walks into the room grasping a mug she bought for my baby shower emblazoned with the words, *Mom, Wife, Boss.* Three titles I'm finding hard to live up to lately.

"I made you some chamomile tea." She searches my nightstand for a coaster and then opens the drawer to reveal books, hand cream, and my magnesium vitamins.

"You can just set it down on the nightstand."

She places the mug on the bare wood and then eyes the pills. "Do those help you fall asleep?"

"They seem to. It might just be a placebo, but I haven't had as much trouble falling asleep."

She closes the drawer and then sits down at the foot of the bed. "Joanna, I'm sorry about everything you are going through right now." She uncrosses her arms to brush her silver bangs to the side and then crosses them once again.

There are a few things she could be referring to, but I don't know how much JP has confided in her and I don't want to reveal anything that she isn't aware of. I clutch the mug, feeling the warmth against my hands. I sip the golden liquid. She's steeped it for too long and it's bitter.

"It's nice, isn't it? Chamomile is my favorite."

"Hmm." I nod.

"Good for sleep, too," she says.

She waits for me to take another sip before continuing the conversation. "I hope you know that even though I love my son very much, I'm appalled by JP's recent behavior. I raised him to be better than that."

This is a heavy conversation for bedtime and I'm not sure where she is going with it. It might simply be her way of absolving herself from his actions. I take another sip even though I'd rather drink my water.

She scooches a few inches closer to me. "I hope in time you can learn to trust him. I do believe it will never happen again."

I'm not sure I want to stick around to find out. "It will take some time."

"Of course, in time. For Addison's sake."

For Addison's sake. Why do people always say that, for the child's sake? As if being miserable together is better than being happier separate? The truth is that if it wasn't for Child Services' interest in us, I probably would have kicked JP out already. I don't think that would look good. I understand that I'm under a microscope. I have to make it look like we are a functioning family.

"Joanna, do you know why I decided to move in?" she asks.

This sounds like a trick question. "To help out with Addison."

"Yes, of course. It really is true that it takes a village to raise a child. Selfishly, though, I moved in so that I could spend more time with my son and my granddaughter. I think a part of me always hoped that JP would find his way back home once he started his own family. Perhaps that was naïve of me."

"It makes sense that you'd want him close."

"Especially now that I'm retired. I'm noticing how lonely the city can be."

"Margot, I think I know where you're going with this. I don't know what to say. *This* is our home."

"Of course, I understand. It's your first house."

"It's more than the house. My family is here." The house itself is just starting to feel like ours. It hasn't even been a year since we moved in, and we still have unpacked boxes in the basement, but I could never move out east and say goodbye to Meg and Amy.

"All I ask is that you think about it. Not tonight, of course." She stands up to leave. "Are you still working on your tea?"

I take another gulp of tea and swallow a leaf that escaped the confines of the bag. I clear my throat. "I'm still working on it. Thank you, Margot."

"Sleep tight, Joanna." She wanders to the door and then turns back to face me. "Oh, so tonight, do you plan to wake up for Addison's night feed?"

"I do." I glance down at the word *Mom* on my mug; it is made up of little peach roses. "I'll feed Addison tonight, and each night going forward."

She nods and then closes the door behind her. I adjust the volume on my phone to the maximum level, hoping to ensure that I'm first to the scene when Addy stirs.

CHAPTER THIRTY

"Joanna, wake up!"

The lights are bright in our room, and I'm being shaken awake.

"I have no idea what's wrong with her. This isn't normal." JP stands over me, his hands on my shoulders.

"What's going on?" I mumble. "Am I dreaming?"

Addison's angry wails echo from the monitor beside me. Margot stands wide-eyed at the end of our bed in a long-sleeved, flannel night-gown. She sways from side to side like she can't decide what to do next. "I'll go feed Addison." She shuffles out of the room and down the hallway, her slippers scuffing the hardwood until she reaches Addison's carpeted floor.

JP drags me up by my arms so that I am in a seated position, but my head still hangs backward towards the pillow and when he lets go, I fall back down on the bed. He tries again but my body is dead weight. He pulls me faster and harder until I end up crumpling forward, my head and shoulders slumped towards my knees.

"Are you on something? Why are you so out of it?" he asks.

"I was sleeping. What time is it?" I rub my eyes; they are heavy and opening them takes effort.

"It's 2:30 in the morning. What's wrong with you?"

I finally make eye contact with JP. His face is tense and his lower jaw juts out. I've never seen him look so angry. What did I do to make him this mad? Then I feel a sharp sting across my left cheek.

He looks at his hand, realizing what he's done. "I'm sorry."

I'm completely awake now, and I sit there shocked, holding my face. "What did I do?"

"I needed you to wake up. I was going to call an ambulance. You were dead to the world, Jo."

Addison's cries have lessened, but they still come through the monitor as out-of-breath whimpers, and Margot is shushing her, trying to calm her down.

"Did you take something before bed?"

"She needs her mother," I say to the monitor as if it can hear me, but JP's hands return to my shoulders, preventing me from getting up.

"Not like this, she doesn't. What did you take?"

"What do you mean? Nothing."

"Are you on drugs, or something? Sleeping pills?"

"No." I focus my view on the nightstand. The drawer is still open, revealing my magnesium pills and the mug sits half empty with Margot's chamomile tea.

"I took one vitamin, and your mom made me tea."

He leaves the room and I lean back against the headboard. What happened tonight? Why couldn't I hear them? How did I not notice Addison crying?

JP is now with Margot in the nursery and their words come through the monitor.

"Is she okay?" The right side of Margot's body sways in and out of frame as she rocks Addison.

"I don't know."

"Does she normally sleep that soundly?"

"No, something's off."

"Did she take something?" She asks.

"Tea?"

"That's harmless," she scoffs.

"I've never seen her like this before."

"I hope I'm not overstepping, but I think she needs help."

"Maybe I should take some time off work?" he asks, as if she is an expert on the matter.

"I think she needs *professional* help."

They continue for a few minutes, whispering about my state of mind, whether I'm capable of taking care of my own daughter, and how Margot will stay another two weeks. JP mentions our appointment with Alice the next day and how he plans to bring everything up.

The volume was loud on my phone. I should have heard Addison. I turn out the lights and let my heavy eyes shut once again. I don't remember JP coming back to bed.

The pain from JP's slap lingers like a bad taste in my mouth. JP snores softly in the next room, drawing in more breath than he expels. The sound of dishes being put away in the kitchen is underscored by Fleetwood Mac. I wonder where Margot gets her energy.

I stare out the window of our washroom, trying to make out the road that runs alongside our house. A thick fog crept in overnight, like the one that clouds my mind. The tops of the cedar trees that line our fence peek above the white haze.

Sitting on the ledge of the bathtub, I search my phone's browser for the side effects of overdosing on magnesium glycinate. The results aren't surprising—nausea, diarrhea, stomach cramps—possible side effects for most over-the-counter medications. Then I look up whether magnesium glycinate causes drowsiness and don't find much. I research the effects of mixing magnesium with chamomile tea—again, no substantial results.

Last night wasn't normal. Someone is messing with me. Did Margot slip something into my tea? Was it my pills? They're just magnesium—I think. I look up images on my phone of magnesium glycinate pills, and more specifically the brand that Meg bought me. Most of the photos I find are just the product shot of the branded bottle, but there's one image that features the pill. They are small, white, and circular. They look like the pills I've been taking fairly consistently for the past three weeks.

JP and I are supposed to go for a joint therapy session with Alice today. If we go, he will tell her about last night's incident. If Alice thinks I'm unstable, she'll be forced to update Child Services. I need more time to sort things out.

I turn on the hot water and run a washcloth underneath it. After I ring it out, I place the warm cloth on my head. Next, I find the thermometer in our medicine cabinet and run it under the hot water stream, until it reads 101 degrees. Finally, I wrap myself in my housecoat and reenter the room, pretending to be sick. It's all very Ferris Bueller of me, but I'm desperate.

"JP, are you awake? I really don't feel well."

He looks at me with one eye squinted.

I approach him slowly and hand him the thermometer. "I have a fever—one hundred and one, and the chills."

He looks skeptical at first, then touches my forehead with the back of his hand. "You're a bit warm. Do you remember last night?"

"Vaguely. I remember being half-asleep, kind of delirious. I was fighting my body to wake up."

"Maybe you're coming down with something. Here, lie down." He pats the bed beside him.

I crawl into my spot. Hugging my pillow, I let out a small groan.

"You were really out of it last night. You slept through Addy's cries. It took us so much to wake you. Mom ended up feeding Addy the bottle because you were kind of useless."

Useless? I think the guy who can't figure out how to feed his daughter a bottle is the useless one. It's convenient how he leaves the slap out of the story.

I lift my head up slightly. "I think I might have the flu. I feel nauseous."

"I'll get you some water." He retrieves my glass from the nightstand and runs to the washroom to fill it.

So far, this is working, but I have to play this next part wise. "Shoot, what time is it? We have an appointment with Alice this morning. I should hop in the shower. Maybe that will bring the fever down."

JP returns with the water. "I don't think we should go if you're sick. Can't we reschedule?"

"Maybe we should. I'll give her a call and see if we can move it to next week."

He feels my head again with the back of his hand, and I worry that the temperature has lowered. "Why don't you rest? Mom and I can watch Addy. I blocked my calendar for the appointment, so I have some time before I have to go to the office."

I let out another groan. "Okay, call me if you need anything. You can use the last of the milk for Addy." I pull the covers up to my chin. "It's freezing in here." I may have laid it on a little strong, but JP doesn't question me.

I text Amy and beg her to stop by with dinner tonight. Until I can figure out what happened, I will not be eating or drinking anything that Margot puts in front of me. Last night's conversation encroaches upon my mind. Margot wants us close—she wants JP and Addison close.

What if this is her way of getting exactly what she wants?

CHAPTER THIRTY-ONE

After a quiet dinner slurping soup, Amy and I excuse ourselves to take Addison for a walk. We leave Margot and JP on the couch where they are watching a rerun of *Jeopardy*.

The rain stopped an hour ago and the fog has let up, but the sidewalk is covered in puddles and soggy leaves.

"So, June Cleaver is getting on your nerves?" Amy pushes the stroller over a worm and its carcass gets stuck to the wheel. It hangs on for a few rotations and then half of it falls off on the sidewalk, the other half squished into the treads.

"Margot's been sneaking Addison bottles at night. She said she didn't want to wake me. That's a little messed up, isn't it?"

"Wait, what?" Amy stops abruptly, unable to focus on two tasks at once.

"She would hear Addy cry and would just go ahead and feed her without me knowing."

"That's insane. She can't do that."

"Well, she did and has been, for over a week now."

"I hope you said something to her. Who does she think she is—Addison's mother?"

"JP thought I was being irrational."

"JP is a jerk." Amy resumes pushing the stroller. "Sorry, I'm not over the cheating."

"You and me both."

"Did you tell her it bothered you?" She pauses at the intersection. "Which way do you want to go now?"

"Let's go to the park. We can sit for a minute if the bench isn't soaked."

We push the stroller toward one of the benches that overlooks the murky pond. I wipe the seat down with a burp rag from the stroller's undercarriage and we sit down next to each other. Addison sleeps, nestled in the stroller positioned in between us.

"Something really weird happened last night," I say.

"Weirder than your mother-in-law sneaking Addy a bottle?"

"Surprisingly, yes. Addy woke up Margot again, and this time she came in to wake me, but I was incoherent."

"That's strange. You were just really tired?"

"This is going to sound crazy, but Margot had made me a chamomile tea earlier in the night, and I don't know... I felt like I was on something."

Amy covers her mouth. "You think she drugged you?"

"How insane does that sound?"

"I don't know her very well but there's something kind of off about her. She seems too—"

"Perfect?"

"Exactly."

"I hope I'm not right. But then what was it? Is something wrong with me?"

Addison stirs and Amy moves the stroller back and forth in response. "I'd talk to your doctor."

"I'm on thin ice though. All I need is Alice telling Child Services I'm unstable."

"She's your doctor though, Jo. Her priority is to help you."

I stare off into the pond, imagining what it would be like if the builders had gone through with the proposed design. Would I come here more often to reflect if there was a flowing fountain? The water I'm looking at —cloudy, dingy, morose—it feels more fitting to my situation.

"The timing was really weird too," I continue.

"Timing?" she asks.

"When Margot brought me the tea, she was talking about how she wants us to move to Montréal. She wants to be closer to JP and Addison."

"This woman has a lot of nerve. She moves into your house indefinitely, tries to convince you to move closer to her, and then takes over caregiving for your daughter? She's overstayed her welcome if you ask me."

If only it was that simple. Just tell Margot to leave? Maybe it's time I stand my ground.

"It's getting dark; we should head back." I'm now well aware of the scene this park becomes at night. Soon enough the teenagers will turn this bench into their speakeasy.

As we start to walk away, we realize each of us assumed the other was pushing the stroller. "Oh, Addy." I run back to get the stroller. "You're so quiet, Mama almost forgot you."

By the time we get back to the house, it is Addy's bedtime. Amy stays to help me with Addison's bath and her nighttime routine. She holds Addison while I fill her baby bathtub. The water runs loudly, and I close the door to muffle our conversation.

"One more thing that's been on my mind. JP has been saying some things. Suggesting we make concrete plans for Addison if something were to happen to us. It's definitely something you have to do when you have kids, but it just feels ... icky."

"What does he suggest you do?"

"He thinks his mother would be an appropriate guardian for her."

"But she's old."

"That's what I said. I told him I'd want you and Rich. If you were up for it."

Amy's eyes widen. "Really? I would be so honored. You know I'd love her like my own."

"I know. That's why I'd want you. If I die a horrible death," I say, laughing off the serious moment.

"If Margot tries to drug you again and it goes wrong," Amy adds.

"Too far. I have to sleep in the same house as her, remember."

"Did you do any snooping? See if you could find anything in her bag?"

I raise an eyebrow. "I haven't had a chance yet. She's always around. Wait—"

I run to the counter where she keeps her make-up bag. I open the pockets and sift through her toiletries—toothbrush, dental floss, night cream. Inside one of the pockets, I discover a canister of pharmaceuticals.

"Amy! She has pills."

"Of course, she has pills, Jo. She's old."

Inside are the usual suspects: ibuprofen and antacid—but there are a few white circular pills I don't recognize. "I wonder what these are for."

Amy swaps Addison for the pills. I turn off the tap and undress Addy for her bath. Amy inspects the pills and consults her phone.

"Anything?"

"Risedronate—it's used for osteoporosis."

"How can you tell?"

"I checked the imprint code on the pill. If I were going to drug you, though, I wouldn't leave the pills lying around. She'd be smarter to hide them in her purse or suitcase."

"That's comforting." I lower Addy into her bath, and she lets out an unearthly scream. I immediately retrieve her. "Baby girl, what's wrong? Is it too hot?" I dip my hand in the water. Shoot. How did I not notice it was boiling?

Amy feels for herself. "Jesus Jo, that's scalding." She wraps a towel around Addison. "Is she okay?"

"I don't know. She wasn't in it for too long," I say.

Addy continues to let out horrified screams. She looks at me like I've betrayed her. I pass her to Amy. I feel hot and overwhelmed. I want to escape. "I need a minute."

I rush to the en suite bathroom in our bedroom and splash water on my face. I slump down onto the toilet seat lid. I can't do this anymore. Amy knocks on the door, forcing me to return to reality.

Addison wears a sleeper now and is no longer red in the face with anger. Amy holds her close. "Are you okay?"

"I honestly don't know." Everything is taking up space in my mind. I can't focus on the simplest tasks because I'm too busy trying to figure out what's happening to me.

"She's okay now. She was playing with the little fish toy. I got a few laughs."

"Thank you."

"I think you just need to slow down. Take a minute."

I nod but it's easier said than done.

Amy helps me put Addison to bed. She sits on the floor beside the crib while I nurse. Perhaps it's moral support, or perhaps she fears for her niece.

After Addy is safely in her crib, we watch a film adaptation of *King Lear*. Amy's play opens in less than two weeks, and she is excited to take the stage. I fall asleep halfway through the movie, and Amy wakes me when it's over.

I tell Amy to leave me on the couch. I'd rather not sleep in the same bed as JP. I turn up the monitor on my phone and skip the magnesium vitamin.

CHAPTER THIRTY-TWO

I wake to the sound of Margot opening the blinds. With each pull of a cord, the room gets brighter, until she stumbles into the living room and gasps. "Oh, my goodness, Joanna. You scared me. Did you sleep on the couch?"

I scramble to a seated position. "Yeah, I fell asleep watching a movie."

"Sorry I woke you." She retreats to the kitchen, leaving the blinds drawn by the couch.

"Did Addison wake you last night?" I ask and grab my phone to consult the baby monitor app.

"No, she didn't. I assumed you took care of her night feed." She rummages through the fridge.

"I think she slept through the night." Maybe Margot's bottle feeding has helped Addison wean. I won't admit that to Margot, though.

"Good for her. That's great. Do you want some eggs?"

"No, thanks. I'll make myself some toast later."

JP joins us downstairs, dressed for the office. "Morning." He drops his briefcase on the counter. "Jo, you never came up to bed."

"I fell asleep on the couch." I finish Margot's task and open the rest of the blinds in the living room. The day looks promising, with only a few clouds in the sky.

"Eggs, honey?" Margot asks JP.

"I'm good, thanks. I'll grab something at the office."

I fold last night's blanket and retrieve the nursing bra I had ditched on the floor. Addison cries out over the monitor.

"There's Addy. She'll be hungry." I move past Margot and JP en route to the stairs.

"She slept through the night," Margot says, catching JP up.

"Nice. Good job, Addy. Well, I'm off then. See you both tonight," he says, following me out of the kitchen.

I run up the stairs, coming to Addison's aid. She lets out an excited scream when I enter her view.

"You did so good last night, babe. You're such a big girl now."

I change her diaper and zip up her onesie. When I am opening her blinds, I notice JP at the foot of the driveway next to Addison's stroller. He hunts through the undercarriage and reveals what appears to be my purse. He opens it up, looks inside, and then heads back to the house.

JP calls me from downstairs. I wanted to nurse Addison in her room, away from the action of Margot making breakfast.

I step into the hallway and yell, "What's up? I'm about to feed Addy."

"Did you forget to put the stroller away after your walk last night?"

I follow his voice to the foyer. "No, I brought it back inside. Why?"

"You sure? It was left on the driveway. Addison's bear was in the seat and your purse was in the undercarriage." He passes me my purse. "Doesn't look like anything was taken."

I set it down on the entryway table and poke around in it. Wallet, keys, everything seems to be in order.

"I don't even think I brought my purse on our walk last night, and we definitely didn't bring her bear." I'm sure I brought the stroller in. Amy was with me, so she would have held Addison for me as I lifted it inside. I can't imagine the two of us forgot; I would have at least pushed it up to the porch.

"You have to be more careful, Jo," he says.

"I brought it in. Amy would have backed over it if it was left there. She was parked behind us in the driveway."

Margot joins us in the foyer. "What's going on?"

"Jo left the stroller out all night with her purse in it."

"Oh no, was anything stolen?" Margot asks.

"I did not, JP!" Addison starts to cry at my outburst. "I brought it in the house. I know I did."

"So, what then? Did you do it in your sleep? I really don't have time for this, I'm late for work." He tosses the bear on the table and exits, leaving the front door open.

I run to the door and slam it shut.

Margot wrings her hands. "Everything okay, Joanna?"

"Everything's fine." I retreat upstairs to feed Addison.

As Addison nurses, I text Amy.

> We brought the stroller in last night after our walk, right?

Amy responds a few minutes later.

> Yep. We had to wipe off the dead worm, remember?

She includes a worm emoji and a skeleton with crossbones.

She's right. I used a damp paper towel to clean the wheel.

> It should be by the door.

> JP found it at the end of the driveway this morning with my purse in it. Tell me I'm not going crazy.

I put my phone down and move Addison to the other breast. The chime of Amy's text prompts me to pick up my phone.

> Do you think Margot took it out for a stroll last night? Keep an eye on her, Jo.

I'm relieved that I have someone on my side. Someone who believes me. I open my phone browser and search for outdoor home surveillance. It's time I take this into my own hands. If Margot is up to something, I'm going to find out.

FUCHSIA FUSION

Thirteen years old

Mother's room looked like the aftermath of a New Year's Eve party. Feathers from her down pillowcase chased each other around the room like confetti. The blush curtains had been torn and pulled to the floor. The ripped wallpaper fluttered like a butterfly's wing, the air from the register giving it life. There was profanity written on the mirrors in Mother's lipstick in what looked like Jo's handwriting.

"She'll kill you," Amy said, shaking her head at the state of the room. "She will actually kill you, Jo."

"It wasn't—I don't remember."

Meg rushed in with a large trash bag and cleaning supplies. "Amy, you're on garbage. Throw the pillows out, anything torn. When the bag's full, throw it into one of the neighbor's trash bins." She tossed the bag to Amy, then rummaged through the cleaning caddy. "I'll do the mirrors. Then, I'll vacuum."

Jo stood in the doorway of the room, still pondering what had happened. Meg looked up at her from where she knelt by Mother's full-length mirror. "Jo, get out of here. Just disappear for a while."

Mother would be back from church soon, but Meg and Amy would move fast. They'd think of something. Some excuse for the curtains and pillows. Jo trusted them more than she trusted herself.

Jo remembered their fight. Mother had discovered photos of Jo and her best friend dressed in lingerie, posing, much like the covers of Mother's romance novels. Their prepubescent bodies barely filled the A-cups.

They had played around with a roll of film, wanting to see how they looked. Jo had dropped off the film and picked it up herself but forgot to hide the stack of glossies where Mother wouldn't look.

When Mother called her daughter a slut, Jo couldn't contain her anger. After Mother left for church, Jo punched her pillow. She punched it enough times she had burns on her knuckles.

It was Jo who trashed the room. Of course it was Jo. But she had no recollection of it. She certainly didn't remember writing *die, bitch* on Mother's mirror in Fuchsia Fusion.

CHAPTER THIRTY-THREE

Margot is on her way out the door to replace the milk when she pauses and turns on her heel like she's forgotten something. "Why don't I take Addy with me?" she asks.

"You're just running across the street," I say.

"I might stop off at the drug store and pick out a few Halloween decorations."

The house only has the three pumpkins we grabbed at the farm last week. They're still uncarved.

Margot walks towards me, reaching for Addison. "I bet Addy would find it exciting. The bright colors, lights, and sounds," she says.

I haven't had time to search for more evidence that Margot drugged me. This is the perfect opportunity to go through her suitcase. I dress Addison in her fleece snowsuit and help Margot set up the stroller in the driveway. Neither of us mentions the incident from two nights ago, although I'm sure she is thinking of it when I buckle Addison in where the bear had previously sat. I wave goodbye from the driveway and head back inside to begin my investigation.

Amy's probably right—Margot wouldn't leave the pills where I could stumble upon them. I open the door to the guest room closet and drag the tan leather suitcase into the room. I unzip it entirely, letting the front of the bag fall to the floor. There are a few compartments—Margot's suitcase is high-end with a built-in garment bag and shoe organizer. One by one I undo each zipper, shoving my hands deep inside the sections. In the fifth pocket, I feel something. I pull my hand out to reveal a foil packet that I assume was once full of pills. There is only one left.

The white pill is small and round with an imprint code etched on the back. When I look up the code on my phone, it spits out results on zolpidem tartrate—a sedative-hypnotic drug, a prescription pill for helping people fall and stay asleep. I read the drug description over and over until the words no longer make sense. Part of me wants to jump up and down shouting *I knew it, I knew it. I'm not losing my mind!* Then I realize what this means. My mother-in-law is drugging me.

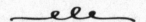

With JP at a client dinner, Margot and I are forced to make small talk over spaghetti Bolognese. I found a jar of JP's meat sauce in the freezer and defrosted it, so Margot wouldn't be tempted to get *creative* with a home-cooked meal.

Margot and I sit across from each other at the counter. She delicately twirls her spaghetti with a fork. I shovel heaps of the noodles into my mouth, so I can maximize the time feeding Addison mushy peas and get away from Margot as soon as possible.

Margot presents the decorations she procured earlier in the day in between bites and sips of her Chardonnay. I play along, pretending I'm not freaking out that we are alone in the house.

She dabs her mouth with a Halloween napkin she also purchased at the store. "You'll love this one." She reaches into the plastic bag and pulls out a rustic-looking wreath made from grapevines. Silk sunflowers and orange and yellow leaves intertwine through the vines, and at its center is a burlap ribbon tied into a bow. "Isn't it beautiful? I could have gone with something spookier, but I thought this would work well into November."

"It's nice." Please just keep your hands where I can see them.

"I saved the best for last."

We'll have the most decorated house on the block with the amount she's bought—spider webs, pumpkin string lights, foam gravestones, and a ghost projection light that may induce seizures.

"Baby's first Halloween." She fastens a black and orange bib around Addison's neck without bothering to remove the bib she already has on.

"Cute." I shove the last bite of spaghetti into my mouth.

"Since you made dinner, I'll handle the clean-up," she says.

"No argument here." I remove Addison's bibs and release her from the highchair. "I'm going to give Addy a bath."

"Oh." She sets down the plates by the sink. "Do you want a hand?"

I'm already halfway to the stairs. "I've got it," I call back.

Addison holds the rubber duck to her mouth while I wash behind her ears. I move to her neck and wipe away dried peas from her crevices.

Margot pops her head in the doorway. "Sorry to interrupt this sweet moment." She enters the room and towers over us, looking down at the bath scene. "I just need to take my medication."

I shuffle on my knees to face her and watch intently as she digs through her makeup bag. She pours the pill from the canister onto her open palm and tosses it back with a gulp of water.

"What's that you're taking?" I ask.

"That was for my bones. Osteoporosis runs on my mother's side."

"Margot, do you take zolpidem?" I watch her closely to see if she offers a reaction.

She stares blankly. "Zolpidem? What is that?"

"Sleeping pill."

"No. I've never had much trouble sleeping. Can't sympathize with you there, dear."

She turns back to the sink and grabs her toothbrush and toothpaste. "You don't mind, do you?" her reflection asks.

"No, we're almost done." I retrieve the second washcloth and move to Addison's diaper area.

Margot watches herself in the mirror while she brushes her teeth. When she is done, she rinses her mouth with water. She begins her nighttime regime, applying a series of thick creams with a white paddle that resembles a miniature spatula.

I lift Addison out of the bath and place her onto the change table where her towel is outstretched, waiting to engulf her.

"Margot, you've heard of zolpidem," I say.

"You just told me it was a sleeping pill. Is this something you've been thinking of taking?"

"It's a prescription drug." I guide Addison's limbs into the sleeper.

"Your doctor might consider prescribing it to you, but I don't know if that would be a good idea right now. You should really be alert in case Addison needs you during the night."

I glare at her through the mirror. Maybe I'd be more alert if my mother-in-law wasn't drugging me.

She doesn't seem to notice my expression and continues combing her hair. "Is that safe to nurse on? Those are questions you'll want to ask your doctor."

Did you do this research before you slipped it to me?

Margot lets out an audible yawn.

"I'm not looking to go on zolpidem or any sleeping aid," I say as I fasten the last snap on Addison's sleeper.

Margot sets down the comb and rubs her eyes. "Did I miss something? Why are we talking about zolpidem?" She yawns again.

I hold Addison in my arms, swaying from side to side. It's time I confront my mother-in-law. "Margot, I found the packet in your bag. All but one pill used?"

"Which packet?" Then she slumps down on the ground, her back against the vanity.

"Margot?"

"I feel strange. I just need to lie down for a moment—" She falls to the floor with a thud.

Shit. That happened faster than I thought it would. How am I going to get her into bed?

When I swapped Margot's osteoporosis pill with the sleeping pill from her suitcase, I wanted to ensure she was knocked out for the evening, so she couldn't do anything to me. I didn't think I'd have to put her to bed myself. Her wine must have made its effects stronger.

I place Addison in her crib in the nursery and she protests with a wail. I run back to the bathroom where Margot lies unconscious. Okay, I can do this. I drag Margot by her arms, which are stretched above her head. She looks lifeless. The way Mother looked when she ... I close my eyes tight as Mother invades my thoughts. I can see her like it was yesterday, lying dead on the library floor. *Stop it, Jo.* Don't let her take over your mind. I brace myself on the bathroom vanity and focus on my breathing. I have to move quickly before JP gets home.

Margot slides easily on the hardwood but when we get to the carpeted floor of the guest room, there is more resistance. Addison's frustration increases in the next room, her cries interrupted by shallow breaths.

A car door closes outside, and I fall to my knees. JP is home earlier than I expected. I run to the window and spot a silver sedan in the driveway. It's Monica from Child Services. A surprise visit while my mother-in-law lies drugged on the guest room floor. *Oh God, not now.*

Monica will arrive at the door imminently. I pull down the covers of the bed. Margot is still in her slacks and sweater. There is another car door followed by a peppy beep, our car locked up for the night. It's JP, home early from his dinner. Please, whatever you do, JP—don't let her in yet.

The front door swings opens, and JP and Monica step inside.

"Jo? Mom?" JP calls from downstairs.

Monica's voice is faint, but it sounds like she says she wants to meet JP's mom. Addison is still crying in the next room. JP and Monica will hear her and come up. I kneel behind Margot, positioning my arms underneath her armpits and try to lift her up with all my might. She's not a big woman, but it's dead weight, and I have no choice but to release her back to the floor.

"You upstairs, Jo?" JP shouts. "It's probably Addy's bedtime," he says to Monica and I hear him climbing the stairs.

I don't have enough time. I'll have to roll her under the bed.

"I'll come up with you," Monica says. "We can start our inspection up there."

Fuck.

I push the last of Margot under the bed and pull the bed skirt down again. I shut off the light and close the door. I run into the nursery, just as JP reaches the top of the stairs.

"In here. Putting Addison to bed."

I rescue Addison from the crib and bring her to the change table, pretending I'm just starting her bedtime routine. JP and Monica enter the nursery.

"Hey, Monica is here for a visit," JP says, greeting Addy with a kiss. She hits his face in frustration.

"Hi, Monica. Sorry, I'm just about to get Addy in bed." Addison's eyes are red and wet with tears. "She's not a fan of bedtime." I laugh.

"Who is?" Monica chuckles. "Hi sweetheart." She rubs Addison's arm. "I won't be long today, just wanted to check in since it's been a couple of weeks since we last met. Things are going well?"

I zip up Addison's sleep sack and hold her to my chest. JP heads back into the hallway.

"I think she's asleep, JP." I try to keep my voice calm but it comes out rushed.

JP opens the guest room door a crack. Then he pushes it open and turns on the light. "Mom's not here. Where'd she go?"

"Oh, she mentioned something about going to the pharmacy. I guess she's not back yet." I'm surprised at how natural my lie comes out. "She ran out of her osteoporosis pill." That seems logical.

I switch my attention to Monica. "Shall we take a look at the house and then head downstairs for a cup of tea?" I need us to move away from the guest room before JP finds Margot shoved under the bed.

"Sounds great." Monica follows me out of the nursery.

Other than my mother-in-law being unconscious, Monica chose a good time to check in. The house is spotless from Margot's incessant cleaning. After our tour, I pour Monica and myself a cup of tea, and JP offers to put Addison to bed.

"Dr. Lui said you've been making great progress." Monica sips her tea.

"That's great to hear. I think so, too."

Upstairs I hear a faint ringing. Margot's phone. JP must be checking in on her. Where is it? In her pocket?

"Should JP be here too? Let me go see if he's done with Addy." I excuse myself and run upstairs.

JP stands in the hallway, holding two cell phones. "Mom left this in the bathroom. It's weird she didn't take it with her."

"She must have forgotten it. The pharmacy's just a quick trip. She should be back any minute. Come downstairs, Monica has some questions."

JP doesn't follow me. "Did she walk there?"

"I guess so." I continue towards the stairs.

"How long ago did she leave?"

"I don't know. She was still here when I started Addy's bath, so she hasn't been gone long."

He reluctantly follows me downstairs.

"Maybe I should drive there. Take a look for her. I hope everything's okay."

Monica stands up when we enter the kitchen. "Is everything alright with your mom? We can wrap this up now. I think I have everything I need."

This is good. Monica will say goodbye and then JP can go look for his mom at the drugstore. Meanwhile, I can get her into bed and pretend she returned while he was out. Foolproof plan. I just need to make sure she stays asleep.

CHAPTER THIRTY-FOUR

JP anxiously waits for Margot to wake up. I, on the other hand, pray that she'll stay asleep until he leaves for work. I don't know what she remembers from last night and I'd rather he not be around when she finds herself in the guestroom bed fully clothed.

JP puts his cereal bowl in the sink. "She's still not up. I hope she's okay."

"Maybe she caught what I had," I offer.

"I have to go. Text me when she's up?"

I feel a pang of jealousy that he cares more about his mother than me. I barely nod and watch as he heads to the front door.

Today is the day that I tell my mother-in-law to pack her things and get out of my house. It's lucky that I intervened last night. Who knows what would have happened if she had used the last sleeping pill on me?

I managed to get her into bed eventually. I hope she doesn't remember falling asleep on the bathroom floor.

The door to the guest room swings open and I make my way to the foyer. Margot walks sheepishly across the hallway above.

"Margot—good, you're up."

She clutches the railing and takes cautious steps down the stairs. "I don't remember going to bed last night."

"You felt sick in the washroom, so I helped you."

"That explains my clothes." She rubs her head. "I have a splitting headache this morning."

She must have hit her head on the tile when she fell.

"I hope you didn't catch what I had."

"I might take it easy today. I know I promised I'd take Addy to the mall." Margot reaches for Addison but I hold her close.

"Child Services came last night. They said that I'm doing really well and don't need help anymore. You've done so much, but I think it's time JP and I get back to our normal routines."

Margot's lips part. "Oh? JP thinks so, too?"

"Yes. You can stay until Halloween, then we think that you should go home."

Margot nods to herself. "I'll need to book a flight. That's only two days' notice."

"I can help you with that today."

"Are you sure you can handle the responsibility again?" She reaches for Addison. "We wouldn't want anything to happen to Addy—"

"Margot, back off!" I turn away, shielding Addison from her. "I am Addison's mother. Not you. It's time you leave."

"As you wish, Joanna." Margot's voice is cold.

"I'm off to my appointment." Before she can say anything about watching Addy, I say, "I'll be bringing Addison with me."

Addison is at that adorable age, all wide-eyed and curious. She sits on my lap, trying to reach for a glittery orange pumpkin on Alice's coffee table. She blows bubbles, sending slobber down the front of her romper, and giggles when Alice greets her in a high-pitched voice. Addison provides just enough of a distraction that I can pretend I'm doing better than I was last week, and Alice won't think twice about it. I'm so close to having Child Services off my back. I just need to fake that everything is fine for another month and I'm sure they'll close my case.

"I hope you don't mind that Addy came along this time. I had trouble finding a sitter today," I say.

"Not at all. It's so nice to see you with her. You really light up."

"Thank you. She's at such a fun age right now. I'm loving it."

Her eyes narrow slightly and then her smile returns. "How are things this week? You're feeling better after your bug?"

"Yes, thanks for rescheduling. I'm feeling much better. Addy has been sleeping through the night, and honestly, getting that uninterrupted sleep has made such a difference."

"Oh, I can imagine. So, you've been sleeping well. And you're still not taking anything for that, right?"

"Right. I've been falling asleep better and sleeping through the night now that she is too."

This is a lie. The past couple nights have been more than rough for sleep. And it has nothing to do with Addison. I've stopped taking anything before bed including the magnesium pills. I only drink a glass of water if I've poured it myself. I stay up until both JP and Margot are asleep and then I wait. I wait to make sure neither of them tries anything. I don't take my eyes off the monitor. I usually fall asleep after hours of this. I get maybe three hours a night, then I wake up and pretend I've slept. I pretend I'm fine.

I look up and realize Alice must have asked me another question. She sits on the edge of her seat, her eyebrows raised. "Joanna?"

"Sorry, I guess I'm a bit distracted with this one." I kiss Addison on the cheek and smile. "What did you ask?"

"Any memory lapses since we last spoke?"

"No, actually. I think the sleep is helping with that, too."

She nods. "That's great. I bet you're feeling more like yourself."

"Absolutely."

"How have you and JP been? You were hurting the last time we met. Have you had a chance to communicate those feelings to him?"

I almost laugh out loud. I think about the conversations JP and I have had since I saw Alice last. Most of the time we are civil, but we keep to ourselves. We co-exist, going about our days. This will work for now, until my case is closed. After that, I can serve JP with divorce papers and ensure Margot never comes near Addison and me again. "Joanna?" Alice asks.

"It's going to take some time. I'm not ready to forgive him yet."

She nods in agreement. "Just let me know if you'd like me to refer you to someone for marriage counselling."

We are too far gone for that.

Alice stops me at the reception desk when I am booking next week's appointment. "Normally we'd meet next week."

I nod, consulting the calendar on my phone even though it's been wide open since I went on leave.

"I just wanted to check with you if you'd rather meet again later this week. Maybe even on Friday?"

Friday is November second, the day Mother died. I don't like to plan anything for that day. Usually, Meg, Amy, and I get together. I imagine it will be the same this year.

"Next week is fine. I'll be with my sisters on Friday."

November second. A day where I felt both horror and relief. Best to put it out of mind.

CHAPTER THIRTY-FIVE

Margot waves to us from the doorway, the cat ears she's wearing slightly off-center. "Bye, my little pumpkin," she says to Addy, who we've dressed in a burnt orange ball, her head and limbs poking out of the holes Margot left when she knitted the costume.

Margot abandons the large plastic bowl that holds just about every type of mini chocolate bar there is and trades it for her phone. "Wait, one more photo before you go, and why don't you stand with her on the stoop next to the pumpkins?"

I reluctantly pose on the stoop, looking down at Addison, so I don't have to face the camera straight on. I imagine this is what my photos will look like for the next ten years. Me in the background, always looking at Addy, always wearing an awkward smile.

JP hauls the stroller down the steps and unfolds it once he gets onto the driveway. "Thanks again, Mom. We'll just do a loop of the block."

I'm still surprised he thinks I could manage that action while sleeping.

"Take your time. This will be fun!" Margot claps her hands and resumes her position at the door. She has been masking her disappointment about going back to Montréal. I caught her wiping away tears while she changed Addy this afternoon. I have no remorse and can't wait until she departs tomorrow.

I join JP in the driveway and buckle our pumpkin into the stroller. Poor Addy; I'm sure she'd much rather be on the boob right now, drifting off to sleep. Instead, Margot has insisted that we parade her around the neighborhood, showing off Margot's knitting skills. At least I can collect candy to eat later tonight while I watch Jamie-Lee Curtis run away from her estranged brother.

As we travel down our driveway, we pass a witch, a ballerina, and a girl who I'm assuming couldn't decide between a mummy, a princess, and a soccer player, unless there is a new television character I'm unfamiliar with that wears a jersey, tiara, and bandages of gauze.

"Are we *actually* going door to door?" I ask as I push the stroller across the street to the sidewalk. The fallen leaves make a crumpling sound beneath the wheels.

"I don't know. She was just trying to be nice." He takes a hold of the stroller and maneuvers it over the curb. "Let's just walk around the block for a bit."

It doesn't take very long for someone to stop us and tell us how cute our baby is. "Oh, my God. How old is she?" a woman asks as she holds hands with a five-year-old Queen Elsa.

JP and I both hesitate in a game of chicken, hoping the other will jump in to answer. Neither of us seems to be in the mood to talk lately.

"Thank you. She just turned five months," I finally say.

"Well, she's an absolute doll. I miss those days." Then, she gets pulled away by the *Frozen* preschooler who, to be fair, just wants to fill her pillowcase with sweets.

"I feel like your mom would love this more than us."

JP smiles slightly. "I think you're right."

"Let's go to Marjorie's. She'd like to see Addy."

We park the stroller at the foot of Marjorie's driveway, and I carry Addison to the door, showing her the orange twinkling lights that are draped over the cedar shrubs. Marjorie opens the door before we can ring the bell. I imagine her standing at the window with her candy bowl in hand, anticipating every visitor—much like Margot will be doing at our house.

"My little Addy dressed as the cutest pumpkin that I ever did see."

"Happy Halloween," I say as I bounce Addy in my arms, hoping to get a smile out of her so that I can make Marjorie's evening.

"Here, take a candy, Joanna. You too, JP."

Marjorie thrusts a bowl toward us that is filled with square caramels and molasses kisses. I wonder where she even found these dated holiday treats. I accept a caramel to be polite.

"Can I hold her quick, before you move on?" She passes the candy bowl to JP.

"Of course." I hand over Addison who looks back at me in fear.

"Look at this lattice stitch," Marjorie says, admiring my mother-in-law's craftsmanship.

A couple of superheroes run up the steps and JP is forced to take over candy duty. He holds the bowl down at their level and lets them each grab a handful.

Marjorie passes Addison back, distracted by what she has just witnessed. "One candy each! They need to last the night." She snatches the bowl back from JP, and we take our cue to move on.

After fifteen minutes of weaving through the streets of our neighborhood, we head back east to our street. We pass the park. Instead of hosting young kids in costume, it acts as a meet-up spot for the older kids in town. They are mostly wearing their street clothes; the odd kid holds a character's prop, and a few wear masks.

"Guess we're going to have these kids coming to our house soon. Better go relieve Mom," JP says with a sigh.

"I'm turning the lights out once I put Addy to bed. I don't want them waking her up."

Addy rubs her eyes as if she's understood what I've just said.

"That's right, little one. It's almost bedtime."

When we turn onto our street, I notice a couple of moms and their kids. It's exactly who I've been avoiding the past couple of weeks. Claire leads the group, dressed in a silver unitard and heels, her hair falling in waves beneath a funnel hat. She holds Charlie in a lion costume and is followed closely by her daughter, Madeline, who is dressed as Dorothy from *The Wizard of Oz*. I scan the group for the Scarecrow, but instead I find Lisa holding hands with the fifth Elsa we've seen. I wonder if any of the *Frozen* queens will get mixed up tonight and go home with the wrong mom.

"Jo! I'm so sorry; we should have invited you to go door-to-door with us. I didn't think you'd be going out with Addy this year. How freaking cute is that costume though?" Claire is just as confident as ever, even in her skintight, metallic one-piece.

Lisa joins us and tickles Addison's pumpkin belly. "Addy is so cute."

"Thanks, and no worries. This was a last-minute decision. JP's mom is staying with us and insisted we take Addy out."

JP hangs back a few feet, pretending to be engaged in an email. He must realize the awkwardness of this situation and, to be honest, I'm relieved that he leaves us to talk. I survey the scene to see if Janine is nearby.

"It's just us tonight," Claire says, pulling down her onesie that has been slowly riding up since she stopped to talk to us. "Serene didn't bother bringing Oscar out."

Lisa moves in closer, pulling Elsa with her. "Angela decided to stick to her neighborhood even though we have way more houses here. She's going to get half the candy we do."

The word *candy* makes the preschooler Dorothy jump up and down. "More candy, more candy!"

Claire, unfazed by her daughter's outburst, says in a voice slightly above a whisper, "Oh, you haven't heard. Janine and Paul are splitting up. You didn't hear this from me, but there's another guy. It's a real mess."

"That's horrible." I look in JP's direction, and he just stands there acting aloof. Is this another guy, or did Janine's husband find out about the summer barbecue kiss? I don't even want to think about the alternative—that both Janine and JP played down their little rendezvous. Maybe it was her who wrote *CHEATER* on my SUV, or maybe it was the husband? The questions keep popping into my head until Addison starts to cry.

"I'll catch you up on it another time. I better get this one to the next house before she turns into the Wicked Witch." She motions to her daughter who is stomping around in her ruby slippers.

We say goodbye and then cross the street to our house. Next door at Claire's, a grown man is shelling out candy, dressed as the Scarecrow.

I throw the KitKat wrapper, aiming for the plastic bowl that sits on the other side of the couch, but it falls short and floats to the floor. Each time I snatch a mini chocolate bar from the Halloween stash, I move the bowl farther away. It's my attempt to discourage myself from eating another one, but unfortunately, it isn't working.

My phone rings and I'm forced to eat the entire chocolate bar in one bite. I answer with my mouth full, but it's only Amy.

"What's your favorite scary movie?" she says, disguising her voice.

"Very funny. I obviously have your name in my contacts, loser."

She bursts into laughter, and I can tell she's been drinking. I hear voices and psychedelic funk playing in the background.

"Are you calling me from a party?" I ask.

"Maybe. I wanted to see how Addy's first Halloween was. You never sent me a photo of her as a pumpkin."

I consult my phone and select a couple of pictures of Addy. "Okay, I'm sending them now."

"…Got them! She's so freaking cute," she says into the phone and then her voice sounds muffled and farther away. "This is my niece. Isn't she adorable?" She is showing the room the pictures I just sent.

"Amy? I should let you get back to your party," I say, feeling a little jealous that my Halloween is eating a ton of candy and watching a scary movie solo.

"No, I want to talk. I'm going outside so I can hear you better." I crawl over to the bowl and choose an Aero bar, then I push the bowl another few inches away and settle back into my seat.

"Can you hear me?" she asks. "You sound sad, what's going on?" My sisters can always sense my mood, even over the phone.

"Oh, Ames. I honestly don't know what to believe anymore."

"With Margot? She's leaving tomorrow, right? She'll be gone soon, Jo. Everything will go back to normal then."

If only that was true. "I found out that the woman JP kissed is leaving her husband. Now I'm worried it might have something to do with JP."

"Which one? The graphic designer?" Amy hiccups and then coughs to cover it up. "I didn't think she was married."

"No, not Lauren. Janine, the mom who lives down the street. The one he kissed at the barbecue. Apparently, her husband found out about a guy. What if it's JP?"

"Did you ask him?"

"I asked if there was more to the story, and he dismissed it. He said he's told me everything."

"How do you know this woman is leaving her husband?"

"Gossip. Claire, my neighbor mentioned it."

Party guests yell in the background and then Amy shouts, "Happy Halloween!" She resumes her normal volume. "I think you should try to get more info from Claire. Maybe she knows more than she's letting on."

"Yeah, maybe. It doesn't make sense though. If JP and Janine were having an affair, why would she tell me about their kiss? Why risk her reputation, and her husband finding out?"

"Maybe she wanted to get caught."

"Maybe, but it still seems like self-sabotage."

Amy's voice gets louder and more animated. "Ooh, maybe she found out about Lauren and was jealous and wanted to ruin their relationship. So, she told you about it, so you'd confront him, and he'd end it."

Amy might be onto something. "That would explain the keying of our car."

"Yeah, it was her way of sending him a message. Maybe she's a stalker!"

On the television screen, Jamie-Lee Curtis is trapped in a closet and Michael reaches through the door, trying to attack her. I grab the remote and turn the volume down a few notches.

"I think I have to talk to Claire. Maybe she has more details."

"I'm sorry, sis. What's this girl's last name? I want to look her up."

"Oh, please don't do anything. We don't know for sure."

"I'm not going to do anything," she laughs. "I just wanted to see what she looks like. Oh, shoot. I got to run—it's my turn for beer pong." Amy disconnects.

I open my text messages and write Claire.

> So nice bumping into you tonight! We need to finish our chat. I'm dying to hear about you know what...

I hate myself for stooping to this level. Encouraging secrets and perpetuating the gossip but all the trust has vanished with JP. That's the real problem.

It doesn't take Claire long to respond.

> Yes, it's a real mess. Let's set up a coffee. Free this week?

I was hoping she'd just text me the guy's name, so I could be done with it.

Maybe she doesn't know who it is, only that there's another guy. Either way, I need to find out what she knows.

> How about tomorrow? 10:00 a.m. at Steeped?

Claire sends a series of emojis—smiley face, coffee cup, piece of cake, dancing lady—that I assume to be her way of saying yes. I respond with a thumbs up because as far as I know there is no emoji for: *I'm already dreading our coffee date because what I find out may just push me over the edge.*

CHAPTER
THIRTY-SIX

I sit at a four-person table at Steeped, waiting for Claire to arrive. It is the first of November. A date suspended between two morbid observances—All Hallow's Eve and the anniversary of Mother's death. The dreary weather is fitting.

Claire is ten minutes late. I went ahead and ordered my drink when I first arrived and answered *here* when the friendly barista asked me whether I wanted my drink to go. I figured if I ordered without Claire, we could avoid the awkward dance of who would be buying the drinks. And I'm glad I did. The wait would have been much less enjoyable without sipping an Earl Grey latte from an oversized yellow mug.

Claire bursts through the door at the front of the café, causing everyone in the bustling room to look in her direction. She wears a red pea coat and is wrapped in a cream wool scarf and matching mittens, and a hat complete with a faux fur pompom. She looks as though she has stepped out of a holiday movie, especially in the quaint setting.

She waves at me from the door and calls out so that everyone can hear, "I'm so sorry I'm late. We had a poo-catastrophe. It was everywhere."

Oh, Claire. Not something you should yell at an establishment that serves refreshments. The poor guy at the table beside me is eating a double fudge brownie.

She begins removing layers to reveal a dark green blouse. "Oh yay, they have the holiday menu. To brulée, or not to brulée? That is the question." She chuckles at her attempt at wordplay. "Let me go order, and I'll be right back. P.S. such a good idea to leave the kiddies at home."

It was my suggestion that we come on our own. I thought it would be best to have a distraction-free conversation, in case this gossip affects my family. Claire returns with a snowman sugar cookie and the brulée drink, which she insists that I try. "It'll change your life, Jo."

It tastes like burnt sugar and I am happy to return to my more dignified drink, which is creamy and soothing with a subtle flavour of bergamot and citrus.

"How is Madeline liking her Halloween candy?" I ask.

"Would you believe me if I said it's almost all gone? Sweets don't last long in our house."

Sadly, I relate to this notion all too well. "I ate most of our stash last night. I have no willpower." I wonder how much small talk I'll need to engage in before I can ask about Janine and the affair. My nerves can't handle the unknown.

Claire leaves my query irrelevant when she dives right in. "So, Janine. I didn't want to say anything in the middle of the street because you know, people talk."

I find it more than amusing that she doesn't recognize herself as one of these people, but I nod, encouraging her to continue.

"Okay, so the night of karaoke after you left, we ran into Scott Marino."

"Scott Marino?" I recognize the name.

"New Corvette guy? Mid-life crisis guy, whose wife Linda left him? He lives on our street."

"Ah, yes." My interactions with Mr. Marino have always been limited to the odd wave when we are both putting the garbage out or small talk about the weather when we happen to check the mail at the same time.

"Well, my suspicions were correct. Linda left him because he was having an affair." She bites off the snowman's head.

"With Janine?" I almost shout with glee. Janine and Mr. Marino are having an affair, not Janine and JP.

She nods and continues to chew. "Yes, ma'am. It was so obvious that night. The way they were looking at each other. And Janine left the bar seconds after he did. Naturally, I had to follow and see for myself."

"And?" I almost feel bad about my excitement.

"I saw them making out on the corner of Main Street and King."

"Oh, wow—"

"There's more," she says with an all-knowing smile. She takes a sip of her liquid sugar before she continues. "I saw them get into a cab together after the kiss, and then drive away into the night. By the time I got home, the lights were off at Scott's, so it was hard to say whether they went home together. The next morning when I was out for a jog, and I saw Janine leaving his house in the same clothes as the night before."

"Yikes." Another marriage is falling apart.

"I waved to her of course. She waved back and then I think she probably realized it was time to come clean to Paul."

I think back to the night I saw Janine walking by our house. She was probably on her way to see Scott.

"Did you talk to her about it after? How do you know she's leaving Paul?" I ask.

"Word travels fast. Paul works with Tammy, who is a neighbor of Cindy, who is a stylist at the Prism salon."

I know none of these people, but don't bother asking for clarification. It really doesn't matter who they are.

She continues, "I went there to get my highlights done, and normally I'd go to Sheila, but she's on vacation so, I went to Cindy ..." She pauses and I feel pressure to comment on her hair.

"Oh, yeah, I meant to say something. Your hair looks nice. I like the color."

"I just ended up getting a cut, because it's risky to go to someone new for color." I don't bother correcting myself. *Just tell me what you've got, Claire.* "Anyway, Cindy heard about it from Tammy."

"The neighbor."

"Yes, and she said that Paul broke down at work. Told her that Janine had moved out."

"And in with Mr. Marino?"

"No, she's moved in with Angela for the time being. I imagine they'll want to move somewhere else—her and Scott. How awkward would it be to live a street over from your ex?"

I look at my phone, and it's nearing the time I agreed to be back at the house. "Shoot, JP has to go to work now."

"Aw, boo. Let's do this again soon, okay? We've missed having you around."

"I'd like that," I say as I gather my purse and head to the door.

I know I should feel relieved. Janine is leaving her husband for Mr. Marino and my husband isn't involved. Why do I still feel sick to my stomach? Why am I disappointed?

CHAPTER THIRTY-SEVEN

I'm convinced there's nothing scarier than an empty house in the suburbs.

The only noise is the howling wind and the autumn wreath banging against the front door. The sun has gone missing, but it's not hiding behind ominous grey clouds. Instead, the sky is pure white, like the universe sucked up all the air, and the trees and buildings are next to go.

The street is empty except for what's left of autumn's fallen leaves, chasing each other down the sidewalk. The vibrant reds, oranges, and yellows have further decayed to brown shadows that crumble to dust under your shoes. A few of the houses across the street still wear their Halloween decorations—soggy cobwebs in clumps on the Millers' shrubs, a cardboard skeleton barely hanging onto the Marinos' garage light. Rotting pumpkins are left at the end of driveways, rejected by the garbage pick-up this morning.

There wasn't a soul out on our daily walk around the block. The empty house is further proof that I'm alone. My only form of company is fast asleep. I finally have a second to myself but that's just it. I am alone, and I realize I haven't talked to anyone today. I've forgotten what it's like to be alone with my thoughts.

I sit in silence at the front window, urging my eyes to stay open, fighting the sleep I wish I could succumb to following a few short hours of rest last night. I order myself not to think of Mother, but the anniversary of her death weighs heavy on my heart. I have to believe I will get through the day with no issues. I have no other choice, as no one is here to help me. Margot left yesterday morning and JP is at work, followed by a client dinner. I haven't even heard from my sisters today. I battle with my internal duologues—the sane, practical me, versus the sleep-deprived, losing-my-mind, me. The latter dominates the conversation.

Wow, Addy has been down for a while. *I hope she's not sick. Maybe she's teething, or having a growth spurt. Maybe she'll finally hit the twenty-fifth percentile for weight.* If she isn't gaining weight, I could always supplement with formula. *Then I would fail. I wouldn't get those monthly breastfeeding badges from the parenting app.* Who cares about the badges? It's not like anyone sees them. *If I stop breastfeeding, it will be harder to lose the extra weight.* That can't be a reason, I'm not that selfish. *Why is the door to the basement open? I don't think it was open this morning. It definitely wasn't—it never is.* Should I go down and check it out? *It's moments like these that I wish we had a big dog. Was the door open before we went for our afternoon walk?* Relax, you're freaking yourself out again. *Why didn't I lock the front door when we went out? What if someone came into the house?* It was a quick walk around the block; no one snuck into the house. *How am I supposed to know when Addy wakes up with this stupid monitor running updates all day? Show me my daughter!* Surely, I'll hear her stir. *I'm trapped in this house; JP was supposed to leave me the car.* He's out late tonight, so I guess it makes sense for him to take the car instead of the train. *If he drinks too much, he'll end up leaving the car at the office and taking a cab home, anyway. What time is it? 4:00 p.m. That can't be right. I put her down at 2:30 p.m. What have I been doing for the last hour and a half? I have nothing to show for it. I must have fallen asleep. I blame the couch. Maybe I should go check on her. She will definitely wake up. As soon as she smells me, it's over.* I would hear her if she woke up. I don't really need the monitor. Her cries are loud; they would travel through the silent house. *What if she's sleeping on her tummy and she can't flip over, and her neck gets tired, so she puts her face down, and then suffocates? It's decided; I'll check on her.*

The wreath scratches against the door, building with intensity until the lock turns and the door swings open. Amy steps into the foyer, taking shelter from the wind. Her hair is a mess of auburn waves. She is holding a grocery bag and wine bottle.

"Just a tad windy out there," she says when she notices me on the couch.

"Oh, thank God it's you. You scared me," I say, clutching my chest.

"I didn't want to wake Addy if she was sleeping."

"She is. Thank you for being quiet." I guess I've freaked out enough on my sisters when they've rang the doorbell during nap time.

"I brought you dinner. *Us* dinner. Meg's coming too. We thought you might want company."

"I really do."

Taking the wine bottle from her, I lead her into the kitchen. "Is this for now or later?" I ask, tempted to numb my anxiety with a glass or two.

"Can you sneak a glass now?"

"Yeah, let me pump first." I set the wine down on the island counter and make my way to the cupboard where I keep my breast pump. "I may have to switch over to bottles completely. She's drinking less and less from me. Whenever I give her a bottle she downs it, but if I offer the boob, she's not interested."

"Maybe she wants her mama to have her life back. She knows you miss the wine."

"It's because of Margot. She really messed things up when she started feeding her bottles at night."

"How has it been since she went back home?"

"Good. I mean, this is only day two. It's a little weird being on my own though. I guess I got used to having her around."

"It's what you wanted though, right?"

"Definitely. I couldn't trust her after I found the sleeping pill." I remove my shirt and secure the funnels to my breasts, now resembling an udder of a cow being milked.

Amy reaches into her grocery bag, revealing ingredients one at a time, waiting for me to utter a guess as to what she'll be cooking. Fresh linguine, parmesan cheese, walnuts, butternut squash. "And Meg's bringing a charcuterie board."

"What time is she coming?"

Amy consults her phone. "She said she'll be here in half an hour." She gathers a cutting board and knife and takes her position at the island. She carefully teeters the knife back and forth until she cuts the squash in half. "Alright, let's hear it. There's more you're not telling me."

"Huh? I don't know."

"You do and you'll tell me," she says, matter-of-factly. "Otherwise, you'll have to share in front of Meg."

She has a point. I'd rather keep the conversation light when Meg joins; chat about girls we went to high school with and the television shows we are binging.

"Where to begin? I haven't showered in three days."

Using a spoon, she scoops out the seeds of the squash. "I know, I can tell. After this chat you are hopping in the shower." She dumps the seeds into the organic bin. "Go on." She methodically peels the squash, and I find it oddly therapeutic watching her.

Maybe it's time I tell her everything and stop kidding myself. Let her know I think I'm losing my mind. That I've forgotten who Jo was before there was Addy. That my relationship has crumbled, although I'm sure she can guess that much is true. I wonder what she would say if I told her I'm afraid to be on my own in the middle of the day and that I feel lost when Addy goes to sleep, like I don't exist when she's not around. Every day feels the exact same. It's sort of like *Groundhog Day*—I'm forever in a loop, but I'm not trying to sleep with Annie McDowell, I'm just trying to sleep.

She interrupts my thoughts. "I think you're putting too much pressure on yourself."

"What do you mean?" The pump tugs at my nipples with urgency, so I turn it down a level.

She sets the peeler down. "You're one of the hardest-working people I know. You always have been. I'm worried you are treating motherhood the same way you treated school. You're not being graded. Remember how you burnt out your senior year of high school? You're moving in that direction. You just need to love that little baby. That's all she needs."

"I do love her. More than anything in this world." It's the only thing I'm sure of. It's the only thing I know to be true.

Amy collects the peel in her hand.

"And I'm not trying to be perfect. I don't know ... I just want to make sure I don't end up like ... *her*." I stare directly at Amy, studying her reaction, but she doesn't acknowledge my words. She picks up the knife and starts chopping the squash into cubes.

I don't know why I bother bringing it up. So often, I try to make her and Meg face it straight on. I would just love for them to admit it for once. *Yes, our mother was a manipulative control freak and, unfortunately, because you were the youngest, or most strong-willed, or looked like Dad, you got the brunt of it.* Nothing. She just keeps on chopping the squash, her fingers stained yellow.

"Remember Jody Vance?" She spreads the squash cubes onto a pan. "She got pregnant in high school. What was she, like fifteen?"

"Yeah, grade ten."

"Those fucking fertile teeny boppers."

It's true. Most teenagers go through adolescence trying to *avoid* getting pregnant. Then they grow into mature adults, figure out their shit, and spend their thirties trying desperately to start a family. It's sort of a sick joke.

"My point is, if Jody Vance can raise a child, you can, and you'll do a hell of a better job."

I really don't find this the least bit comforting.

I glance at the two bottles that hang from my breasts. I've pumped about four ounces. "Okay, that's good for a bottle. Hand me the wine."

"Go shower first. I wasn't kidding when I said you smell."

I close my eyes and let the hot water stream down my face. I'm happy to have a moment to relax and to have my sisters help me take my mind off everything. I didn't realize how lonely I was until Amy showed up.

I grab my shampoo from the shelf and squirt a generous amount on my hand. The smell of coconut and banana fills the steamy shower. I reach for my loofah sponge and allow it scrub away my thoughts. I clean my mind of Mother. I wash her down the drain. Tonight is about being with my sisters and Addy. The day isn't so heavy if I have them by my side.

Addy should be up and wanting to see me, and I have a glass of wine waiting for me downstairs. I turn off the tap and hear the front door close. That'll be Meg.

I towel off in the washroom and put on my robe and slippers. Then I poke my head out of the bedroom. Meg is removing her shoes in the front hallway.

"Hey," I call. "I'll be right down, but you guys go ahead and have a glass of wine."

Meg looks up. "Amy's not here yet?"

I tiptoe out of the room into the hallway. "She's in the kitchen."

"Her car's not here; did she take the train?" Meg walks towards the kitchen, her arms full of groceries. "Amy?" She steps back into view. "She's not here."

"That's weird. She was prepping dinner."

Meg checks her phone. "Oh, she texted me ten minutes ago. She forgot to get sage, so she ran to the store. I'll get the appetizers together."

Why would Amy leave while I was in the shower? Could she not have waited until I got out? Addy must be awake. I shuffle down the hallway towards her room, but I don't hear a sound. I glance at the time on my phone. She's been asleep for more than two hours. Maybe she's coming down with something. I slowly open the door, trying to avoid the usual creak of the hinges. Her room is dark, and the air is warm and stuffy. I tiptoe into the room. She's not awake, but I want to make sure she isn't on her tummy. When I get close to the crib, my stomach drops and panic sets in.

Addy is gone.

CHAPTER THIRTY-EIGHT

"We need to go find her, Meg. Now." I try to stand and she guides me back onto the kitchen stool. She forced me to sit down after I had started pacing frantically around the house, impulsively wringing my hands. "I knew it. I knew someone's been messing with me. I should have trusted my gut. And now they've taken Addy." Water drips from my hair onto the countertop.

"Calm down, Jo. Let me try Amy again. She probably took her with her to the store. Maybe Addy woke up after you hopped in the shower." She dials Amy's number on her cell again; it's the third time she's tried her in the past five minutes. "Amy! Good, I got through. Do you have Addy with you?"

I lean in close, so that I can hear Amy on the other end. "Does she? Put it on speaker."

"Okay, you need to come back right now. Addison isn't in her crib—"

"She doesn't have Addy? Put her on speaker." My voice comes out shaky and I feel my hands going numb. I rub my thumbs against the other fingers to try to get the feeling back. *Don't you dare do this now.*

Words fall out of Meg's mouth in a rambling sentence and I have a hard time following. "Okay, why don't you do a quick drive around the neighborhood? I don't even know what we're looking for—should I call the cops, do you think? Or maybe JP first?" She switches her attention to me. "Jo, do you think JP might have come home early. Maybe he has her?"

"We have to go look for her. Someone took her," I say.

"They can't have gotten far. Amy's only been gone five minutes," Meg assures me, but her eyes are wild.

Then a horrible realization washes over me and it's as if someone has punched me in the abdomen. I hunch over the counter. What if someone *did* come in while we were at the park? What if I did fall asleep on the couch, and they took Addy before Amy arrived? Addy and her kidnapper could be anywhere by now.

"Meg, I think someone snuck in here when I took Addy for a walk because the basement door was open when we got back and it's never open." I run to the basement door and peer into the darkness. "They must have taken her at some point this afternoon. I might have fallen asleep on the couch. I'm not sure. Meg, we have to go now."

"Okay, we will, I promise," she says and then directs her attention back to the phone. "Amy, did you see Addy at all when you were here?" She pauses for Amy's response. "Okay, what about on the baby monitor?" Another pause. "I don't know if we should call the police yet ... Because what if—" She moves towards the front of the house and quiets her voice. "What if it was Jo?" she whispers. She exits the front door.

Does she think I did this, or that someone's moved her again on me, trying to make me think I've sleepwalked? Meg loops around the side yard to the back porch and then enters through the sliding glass door.

She returns to the kitchen out of breath. "Jo, hunny, where do you keep your stroller? Usually at the front door, right?"

My mind is racing. "My stroller ..." Where did I put the stroller after the walk?

Meg grabs my shoulders. "Jo, I need you to think. Walk me through your day. Where did you go for a walk?"

I can't think. I keep worrying if Addy would be warm enough outside in just a sleeper. Meg offers me a glass of water and then nods for me to drink. After I do, she puts the glass down on the counter and says, "Tell me about the walk."

"We went to the café, and I got a latte."

"Okay, good, good." She stops to text something. "Where else did you go?"

"The park. I sat down on the bench and finished my drink."

Again, she sends a text. "After the bench? Did you walk anymore, or did you come home?"

"Home. I came home because it was cold, and Addy was falling asleep, and I wanted her to have her nap in her crib because I wanted her to be able to stretch out."

"Okay, great. And when you got home? What did you do with Addy and the stroller?"

"I took her out of the stroller, and I brought her upstairs because she was still sleeping. I might have left the stroller in the driveway. Is it there?"

"No, it isn't there. Then what did you do?"

"I put Addy in the crib to see if she would keep napping. I don't remember dressing her in her sleep sack. I didn't want to wake her, so I think I put her in the crib without one."

"Do you remember what time this was at? When you took your walk and when you got home?"

"We need to go, Meg. We're wasting time."

Meg nods frantically, like she's finally registered the gravity of the situation. "Okay, go get some clothes on. We'll walk around the neighborhood, and Amy will keep searching with the car."

She calls Amy again, and I head upstairs. I hover for a moment on the landing, listening to her one-sided conversation.

She's ditched her calm demeanor and speaks to the phone with an intensity that makes my heart flutter. "Any luck at the café? Okay, we are going to retrace her steps and walk towards the park ... I don't know, Amy. This wouldn't be the first time she blacked out like this ... Why don't you try JP now? I don't want to scare him, but we need to let him know. If we don't find her soon, we have to call the police. I'll take another look in the house."

Do they think I did this? That I did something to Addison and blacked out?

I relaunch the baby monitor app on my phone. Maybe it captured footage of Addy that will confirm when she was last in the crib. Nothing. The app hasn't worked all day because of the updates. The last time it displays her image is in the video summary when I got her up for the day at six in the morning.

I throw on a t-shirt and leggings and rush back downstairs. Meg is standing in the front hall with her purse on her shoulder, ready to go.

She grabs my jacket and guides my left arm into it, followed by my right, like I am one of her kids and we are late for hockey practice.

"Great, let's go. You lead the way. Take me on the route of your walk," she says.

"Meg, I didn't do anything to Addy." I stumble out of the door, looking back at her.

"I know, sweetie, I know. Let's go find her, okay?"

Outside, the wind brushes past us with an urgency that matches the pit in my stomach. Meg's hair swirls around in front of her face but the wind has a harder time moving mine, which is still sopping wet. I dart across the street, not bothering to wait for Meg. I don't think twice about which direction to take; I just trust my instinct. One foot in front of the other. I continue my hurried jog but at some point, my left toe catches a ridge in the sidewalk, and I stumble to the ground.

Meg helps me to my feet. "Slow down, Jo. You need to stay calm."

"I think I know who has Addy." I hunch forward, with my hands on my knees, trying to catch my breath. "It has to be her," I say to myself.

"Who?"

"Margot."

Isn't it often family? Anytime I've received an amber alert on my phone, the victim's last name matches the suspect's. An ex-husband, estranged uncle, senile grandfather, and in this case, my jealous mother-in-law.

Meg looks down at her phone and types something. "Didn't Margot fly home?"

"Maybe that's what she wants us to think."

It's true that Margot took a cab somewhere with her suitcase yesterday morning, but I haven't had a video chat with her since she got home, so we don't know for sure.

"Okay. She doesn't drive, right? She doesn't have her license?"

I nod and resume my mission, this time at a fast-walking pace.

Meg matches my stride, linking arms with me. "If she doesn't drive, she'd have to be walking with her, right? So, that's what we'll keep doing. We'll walk." She pats my arm. "Take me on the route you took today."

Why is she so fixated on my route? "I told you; I went to the café. It's past the lights up here." The crosswalk flashes a red hand, urging us to wait for the next green light but I run across without hesitation, forcing Meg to sprint to keep up.

"Wait up," she yells. "Amy already checked the café. She wasn't there."

I spin around to face her and discover she's texting someone on her phone again. "Okay, so what? You want to walk to the park? Where's Amy, has she seen anything? Maybe we should have taken your car."

"I think it's time we call the police." Meg's phone rings, and she lets out a sigh. "It's JP. Let's go to the park, okay? Take me the way you went." She answers the phone, and her voice jumps an octave higher. "Hey, JP." There's a pause as she lets him talk. His voice sounds assertive, but I can't make out the words. "We haven't called the cops, no. We wanted to get a hold of you first. Amy is driving around the neighborhood, and I have Jo with me. We're retracing her steps from the walk." She bites her lip. "I already checked the yard."

"Ask him if he's talked to his mom lately." I nudge her arm, but she ignores me.

"What's your ETA? Okay, we'll keep you posted on everything. See you soon." She shoves the phone back into her purse.

"Why didn't you say anything about Margot? Why don't you believe me?"

"Which way to the park?" Meg asks, keeping her eyes fixed straight ahead.

"Listen to me!" I shout, forcing her to stop. "I know it's her. We have to call the police."

Meg turns to face me. "If we call the cops, they'll inform Child Services. You understand that, right? If you ... if you left her somewhere ... Jo, they will take her away."

"I didn't do this, Meg! I didn't do anything to Addy!"

She gives me a small, sad smile. "Okay, I believe you. Let's go find her."

As we near the park, the wind picks up, and we are forced to dodge a cardboard box that has escaped a neighbors' recycling bin. The sky is darker now. It's nearly half past five and we don't have much daylight left. It will only get colder into the night. A fleece sleeper won't provide much protection for a five-month-old. I just have to hope that wherever Addy is, whoever she's with, she's safe and warm. To the east of the park sits the strip of row houses in a half-finished state. The polyethylene sheets that protect them from the weather whip violently, and we have to shield our eyes from the dust that fills the air.

Meg's phone rings and she stops to answer, shouting over the howling wind. "Did you find her? Where are you? Is she okay?" Meg asks.

At the same time, I look up and spot the stroller parked by a bench, facing the murky pond. I can't tell whether Addison is in the stroller, but I know it's mine because of the turquoise caddy that is secured to the handlebar. I sprint through the playground, ducking under the monkey bars, and hopping over a slide to get to the other side where my stroller taunts me. When I make my way to the front of the stroller, I'm horrified to find that it's empty.

CHAPTER
THIRTY-NINE

"Jo, I'm over here!" Amy waves from the bench a few feet away from the stroller. "She's okay. I found her buckled into the stroller. All by herself out here. I'm just warming her up." Addison snuggles inside Amy's wool coat. She doesn't have a hat on. Who would do this to a baby? How long has she been out here for?

I trip over my feet trying to reach them and crawl over the bench, landing beside Amy. I open her coat and reach for my daughter. Amy pulls the fabric from my hands and closes her coat. "She's freezing, Jo. Just let her warm up."

Addison cries for me and I unzip my coat to provide a warm nook for Addison to nuzzle inside. Once again, I open Amy's coat. "Give her to me. I'll keep her warm," I say, and Amy obliges. Addison is wearing the fleece onesie as I remembered. Her body feels warm but that might be because I'm cold from being outside.

Meg slides next to Amy and whispers something to her. They move away from the bench, and I don't bother to try to listen. I hold Addison close and kiss her everywhere that isn't covered by the onesie. Her forehead, her eyelids, her cheeks. I have my baby back, and I don't want to let her go.

Meg approaches cautiously. "We need to get her home now, Jo. Make sure she's okay. Amy has her car; you can hold her on the drive, alright?"

I nod and follow them to the sedan, which is parked across the street from the construction site. Amy places the folded-up stroller into her trunk. Meg opens the passenger door and helps me climb in with Addison. She finds her seat behind Amy who starts the car and pulls out, down the dusty road.

Back at home, we crowd the change table in Addison's room to inspect her. She looks perfectly fine. We remove her sleeper to check for marks, but her skin is flawless. Her diaper is full of pee, which makes sense since I changed her more than three hours ago before our walk. We measure her temperature, and it's an average reading for an infant. She giggles when I blow on her belly. She seems completely unfazed by the event.

I gather her up in my arms and carry her to the chair to nurse her. Amy and Meg leave the room, but remain close by, on the other side of the door. Again, I hear hushed voices, but I don't care. I have Addison back and that is all that matters in this moment. She pats my chest as she nurses and looks at me intently. It's as if she wants to keep her eyes on me for fear we'll be separated again.

"Never again, my love. I will always protect you. I promise you that. You are my forever."

She bats her eyes and makes a humming sound that tells me she feels safe. Her eyelids get heavier until she cannot hold them open anymore. She finally surrenders, closing them. Her long eyelashes are now two fringed curtains, hiding her blue eyes. I kiss her cheek softly, and I finally feel safe, too.

A car door slams in the driveway and not a moment later, I hear JP climbing the stairs. His feet stomp down the hallway until he reaches the nursery door.

As he opens the door Meg says, "She's okay, everything's okay."

Addison pulls away from my breast and lets out a cry.

JP falls to his knees at the rocking chair. "Thank God, you're okay." He steals Addison from my arms and cradles her against his chest. He rises to his feet and paces around the room, ignoring the fact that she'd prefer to be in her mother's arms. Addison's cries become more exasperated.

"Someone start talking," he says, his eyes searching the room. Meg and Amy hover awkwardly in the doorway. Meg looks at Amy, and she nods.

"I came here around a quarter past four. Jo was sitting in the front room. I think maybe I woke her when I came in." Amy eyes me to see if we're aligned.

"No, I was awake when you came."

"Addy was napping, but the monitor wasn't working, and Jo said Addy had been sleeping for a while. We talked for a bit, and I started to prep dinner and Jo hopped in the shower."

I rock back and forth in the chair even though Addison is no longer in my arms. JP continues to bounce her around the room and her cries lessen.

Amy takes a step into the room and leans against the change table. "That's when I realized I forgot to bring sage. I needed it for the next step in the recipe."

"I don't know why you didn't wait until I was out of the shower, though. You knew I'd only be a few minutes."

"I know, I screwed up. I thought I could pop over to the store across the road before she woke up. I shot Meg the text when I left the house at …" she consults her phone, "A quarter to five." She turns to face Meg as if she is passing her the baton to continue.

"I got here ten minutes later. There was only a small window when neither of us was here, and Jo was in the shower. Jo called to me when I walked in and then she went to check on Addy and that's when she realized she wasn't in her crib. We don't know when Addy was taken from it because the monitor hasn't been working today."

JP shakes his head. "Why am I paying for a premium subscription if the thing never works?"

I guess it is my turn. My side of the story. My chance to convince the jury that I didn't leave Addy at the park, that I could never do that to my daughter. Someone must have come in the house and taken her at some point this afternoon before I discovered her empty crib at five.

"The monitor isn't broken, but it had scheduled updates today. Anyone with the app got a notification about it this morning. JP, Amy, you both would have gotten that."

JP sighs. "Okay, fine. So, what are you saying? Someone snuck into the house during a fifteen-minute window between a quarter to five and five when Amy had left, Meg hadn't arrived, and you was showering? You realize how ridiculous that sounds."

I stop rocking in the chair. "I know what you are all thinking. Since Amy never saw or heard Addison when she came over and because the stupid app has no proof she was ever in her crib, you all think I left her in her stroller at the park."

Only JP meets my eyes. "Did you?" he asks.

"Absolutely not."

Meg comes to my aid. "Tell us exactly what happened, Jo. We want to hear your story. We want to believe you."

"Then believe me. I didn't leave Addy in the park." I stand up from the rocking chair to meet their level. "We went for our walk just after lunch. First to the café. I had my usual drink. I used my credit card, so there's that if you need to verify times, or whatever. Then I drank my latte on the way to the park. I sat on the bench for a bit.

"We went back, the long way, past Marjorie's. She wasn't outside. No one was today, because it was gloomy and cold. I checked the mail. Then we came back, and I realized Addy had fallen asleep. I unbuckled her and brought her up to her room. I didn't bother putting her in her sleep sack because I didn't want to wake her. I placed her in the crib. This was at two thirty.

"I went back downstairs and cleaned up the mess from lunch. I meant to go back outside to deal with the stroller, but I forgot. I sat on the couch for a while, and then Amy came."

JP looks at Amy. "I'm guessing there was no stroller in the driveway when you got here?"

Amy shakes her head and looks down at the ground. "No, it wasn't there."

"The mail!" I yell.

Three pairs of dumbfounded eyes shoot my way.

"The mail. I put it in the undercarriage. I had the stroller with me when I checked the mail on the way home. It will be there."

It is in the undercarriage. Nestled safely in the inside pocket is our water bill and a stack of realtor flyers. Finally, I have proof. *Enough to make them believe me.*

After I nurse Addison, I hear the three of them talking in the kitchen. JP thinks of it first.

"What if she checked the mail on the way to the park, not after?" he asks. Even Amy doesn't come to my defense.

THE MIRROR TELLS
THE TRUTH

Sixteen years old

The shower head had turned off and the flood of water subsided, save a few drips that continued to plop against the porcelain bathtub. Jo leaned her forehead against the door and knocked gently. She needed to brush her teeth, but Mother had been in the bathroom all morning.

"Come in." Mother gave her permission.

Jo pushed open the door a crack, and the steam rushed to escape the room. Mother sat half-naked on the toilet seat lid, her nude underwear a few shades darker than her pale skin. Her hair was wrapped on top of her head in a towel. Jo averted her eyes when she saw Mother's breasts. Somehow, they were still perky at forty-five and after three kids had sucked them dry.

Mother glanced up from where she was sitting. "Joanna, they are just breasts. You'll get them someday, I hope. You'll need them to compliment your frame."

Jo looked down at her developing breasts and then dropped her gaze to the floor. She crossed her arms.

The smell of talcum powder overpowered the small room. Mother set the nail file on the bathroom counter and then walked towards the mirror on the bathtub's sliding door. She unwound her hair from the towel and using it, she wiped the steam away from the mirror.

"Come here," she said and held out her hand.

Jo grabbed it without thinking. Even after all these years, Jo was drawn to her. Her hands felt smooth and warm and, for a moment, comforting. Jo had considered forgiving her for everything.

Mother led Jo to the mirror. "We've always been so different, haven't we?" She eyed their reflections.

Jo locked her knees, unsure of Mother's intentions.

"There must be something you inherited from me." She tilted her head to the side as she pondered the thought.

Jo looked away, unable to face the mirror.

"Certainly not my frame." She abandoned Jo's hand. "Nor our features. We have different complexions. We carry ourselves differently, too—"

"I think we're more similar than you'd like to admit," Jo said, surprised by her conviction.

Didn't they have the same temper? Hadn't they both said cruel words to each other at the peak of an argument? They shared a wall between their bedrooms. Jo heard Mother's cries at night. They were both lonely. They were lost. They each had a hatred for themselves that ran deeper than any bond. It was what tore them apart and simultaneously knotted them together.

Mother's eyes met Jo's in the mirror and for the first time, it appeared as though she was truly seeing her daughter. They stayed that way a while until Mother turned away and resumed her position on the toilet seat.

"I'm not sure what you mean." Mother shrugged. "We are nothing alike."

"Is that it, then?" Jo asked.

"I'm not sure I understand your question." Mother looked tired. Worn out. Her hair had started to grey at the roots, and her skin had lost its elasticity at her neck.

"Is that why you love Meg and Amy more than me?"

Mother tucked her lips inside her mouth, and Jo noticed the deepening wrinkles on either side, like a parenthesis.

"Because I'm different from you? Or because I'm the same?"

Mother chewed on the inside of her lip just like Meg. She held her head angled slightly to the left as Amy would. But Jo knew that inside, Mother was hurting just like Jo. Inside they were the same.

Mother glanced towards the light as she contemplated her next words. "You don't always choose who you love and how deeply you love them." She held Jo's stare until Jo caved.

When Mother left the room, Jo borrowed the metal nail file.

CHAPTER FORTY

J P and I sit in silence on the drive to Amy's production of *King Lear*.
Amy had made dinner reservations for us at an Indonesian tapas
restaurant near the theatre, where she plans to join us for drinks before
her call-time. The event marks the first time JP and I have done anything
social in weeks. It's also the first time I've left Addison's side in three days,
since the incident at the park.

"I wonder if I should have set up the tablet with Addison's monitor,"
I say aloud, but not necessarily to JP.

He keeps his eyes on the road. "Meg will be fine. Addy's in good
hands."

I try not to take that personally. Shouldn't a child's own mother be the
best option? Unfortunately, I know all too well that's not true. I don't
think I was ever in good hands with Mother.

JP doubting me isn't new. It's been like this since the original complaint to Child Services just over a month ago now, but seeing my sisters'
reactions the other day winded me.

I pull up the menu for the restaurant on my phone. The cocktails sound tasty. There is a gin-based drink with lime, served with a chili pepper. The dinner menu looks promising, and tapas allow you to try a few different plates. It does mean that I will have to share with JP, and therefore we must agree, which has been a challenge for us lately.

"Amy says we are best to park at the theatre and then walk to dinner. It's down the street."

JP nods and pulls off the highway. "We're ten minutes away if you want to let her know."

I send Amy a text.

> Be there in ten. Can't wait for opening night!

I would never tell Amy this, but going to dinner and her play is the last thing I want to be doing tonight. Leaving Addison is giving me serious anxiety and I have to fight the urge to check in with Meg. We left them forty-five minutes ago, and I've already texted her three times, disguising my concern as information I forgot to tell her. Once she puts her to sleep in an hour, I'll have to resist consulting the monitor all night.

> I've got you guys the best seats in the house. Five rows up and in the center. I might be a few minutes late. Reservation is under your name.

JP holds the door for me, and I'm taken aback by this small gesture. I mumble a thank you and then step into the brightly colored restaurant that is a welcome change from the muted greys of the street. The walls are covered with funky geometric shapes in lime green and blue. The floor-to-ceiling industrial bar is lit with magenta and orange and there are tropical plants hanging from the pipes of the exposed ceiling. A single cushioned bench wraps around the perimeter of the room, which is quite narrow but still deep, and small wooden tables separate the bench into distinct seating areas.

A woman with more facial piercings than I can count approaches us with a clipboard. "Did you call ahead, loves?"

"We did. Reservation for Baker," I say.

She consults the list and scrunches up her face when she can't find it.

"Girard, maybe?" I ask.

JP laughs to himself. He's been trying to get me to change my name since we got married almost a year ago. Half the time I forget which name I've used for what appointment.

"Yes, here you are. Follow me." She brings us deep into the restaurant, which is bustling for a Tuesday night, and finally stops at one of the tables. She takes a moment to light the tea lights and then places down two pieces of cardboard with tonight's menu scribbled out in blue ink. "When you're ready, you can place your order at the bar."

"You and Amy take the bench," JP says and sits on the wooden chair opposite. He picks up the menu. "What's good here?" he asks, as if I come here often.

"Maybe we should wait for Amy. She'll know what to order."

I consult the menu even though I've already had a thorough look online. Dragging my forefinger down the cardboard, I scan the cocktail list until I find the gin drink that piqued my interest.

"Wine menu?" JP asks me as he looks around the table for another piece of cardboard.

I shrug. "I think their specialty is cocktails."

Amy runs through the door, letting the cold air from outside creep in. She removes her layers as she scours the restaurant for JP and me. Her auburn hair is wrapped in a tight bun, and she is wearing her usual black leggings and tunic.

"You made it," she beams and greets me with a hug before joining me on the bench.

"Your hair is different, is that for the play?" JP asks, perking up slightly.

"It is. I get to wear a wig. It stays on better if I wear my hair like this. You guys need drinks. I usually get the *Bandrek Stormy*; it's so good."

"I want the *Gadang Gimlet*," I say and then chuckle at the alliteration.

JP sticks his nose in the menu again. "I'll take the Stormy one, too."

Amy heads to the bar to order our drinks, and I check my phone for updates from Meg.

"This place has a neat vibe." JP scans the restaurant. "I should bring clients here sometime."

"Leave it to Amy to find the trendy places."

Amy returns with JP's and my drinks and then goes back to the bar to retrieve her own.

"It's a bit hands-off though, isn't it? You order at the bar, and you have to bring your own drinks to the table?" he asks.

Amy sets down a bowl and sits beside me. "Prawn chips and peanut sauce."

"So, opening night. How are you feeling?" I ask.

"Really good. Dress rehearsal went off without a hitch yesterday."

"And Meg's coming Saturday night?" We had discussed this briefly before we left her at the house. Meg had mentioned she was getting a sitter who lives across the street, so they could go for dinner and then the show afterward. I asked what one charges to look after four boys and Meg said she usually had to pay for the sitter and their friend to tag along.

"Yes, she and Derek and Rich are going to come to the final one."

"That's a short run, no?" asks JP who takes a big sip from the straw in his drink. "This is delicious by the way."

With a few more sips, he nearly empties the highball glass, the lime left floating in a shallow pool of ice.

"It's pretty typical. The rent on these theatres isn't cheap," Amy says. "Want another? Or feel like trying something different?" She nods at his empty glass.

"Sure, I'll be adventurous. When in Indonesia, right?" He laughs.

A few minutes later, Amy returns with a cocktail in a copper mug and back-up—a server follows closely behind and sets down two shots.

"Jo, I didn't think you'd be drinking much tonight." She passes one shot glass to JP and carries the other to her seat. "I, however, need the liquid courage before I take the stage. But I'll stop after this. Can't be slurring Shakespeare."

I sip my drink and watch as JP throws back the shot and then downs his second cocktail. Amy recommends a few sharing plates for us and places the order through the bartender. She returns with another shot and cocktail for JP.

"Oh Ames, I don't know if JP wants another," I say, starting to lose track of how much he's had.

"Uh oh, boss says no." She laughs and nudges JP.

"You can drive home tonight, right?" He swallows the shot before I have a chance to answer.

Amy reclaims her seat beside me, oblivious to my annoyance. What is this chummy behavior with JP? She seems to have forgiven his indiscretions. I sip my drink and set it down with a thump.

"So, what's the plot of the play? I don't think I know this one," JP asks.

"Just wait an hour and, you'll see for yourself," I say. That's like going to a movie and asking the person who rips your ticket how it ends.

"Oh, it's fine, Jo. It's set in modern-day New York. Lear owns a media conglomerate and needs to choose one of his three daughters to be CEO. Then, it's a power struggle between us sisters. I end up killing the one—"

"Don't tell him the ending. It'll ruin it for him," I jump in.

"Oh, I'm intrigued. How do you do it?" he asks, paying no attention to my plea.

"Sleeping pills and vodka," she says without missing a beat, then looks at her phone. "Shoot, I have to run. See you guys after the show."

Ten minutes later, our food appears on the bar and the bartender calls us over to get it.

The theatre is nestled underground below a barber shop and seamstress. The entrance is almost hidden, and the exterior stairs look like they lead to a subway station, not a playhouse. Once inside, I display our tickets on my phone to a teenager, who I imagine is volunteering so he can network with the actors and directors.

The modest lobby is painted black and features framed headshots of actors who have graced the stage. I don't recognize anyone. There is a small bar with a random assortment of refreshments for sale: house wine, bagged peanuts, chocolate mints, and cheese and crackers. JP purchases a plastic cup of red wine that he says tastes like three blends mixed into one. I have the chocolate mints, and they are chewy and stale.

I get a notification on my phone that there is movement on Addison's crib, and I click to launch the app so I can watch Meg perform the bedtime routine. I feel a little guilty watching her without her knowing, but sitters have to expect that technology is always a witness. She holds Addison, who is dressed in her sleep sack, and chooses a story from the easel bookshelf. Then they disappear from the frame to presumably read the nursery rhyme. A few minutes later she returns, rocking Addison. She sings her a lullaby in a soft, sweet voice and then when Addy is asleep, she kisses her on the head and places her in the crib. The lamp goes off, and the night vision kicks in.

Meg sends me a text.

> Bedtime went great! Your little angel is asleep.

My shoulders soften for the first time tonight, and I finally feel like I can relax and enjoy Amy's show.

The teenager who was accepting tickets calls out in a wavering voice, "The show is about to start."

We follow the other guests into the theatre and find our seats, marked with standard white paper and the words *RESERVED FOR GIRARD* in black marker. We didn't really need the signs as the theatre is less than a quarter full. I consult the monitor one last time—Addy is sleeping soundly on her back. I then silence the phone before placing it in my purse, which I slide under my seat.

JP follows my lead. "Oh right, don't want to be the guy whose phone goes off during Amy's soliloquy." He turns off his phone and shoves it in his back pocket.

The house lights go dark, and a warm glow illuminates the stage, bringing the props into view. The stage is set as an office. A long table stretches across one side of the stage. Swivel chairs are placed around only three sides of the table, and the side closest to the audience is left empty so that each actor is in view. On the other side of the stage sits a single desk and chair, once again facing the audience. A partition separates the two set pieces, so we can assume that they are distinct rooms. JP lets out an audible yawn, and I shoot him a look. I imagine he will be asleep before act two.

The play begins. Two men stand in front of the boardroom table and discuss Mr. Lear's plan to hand over responsibility of Lear Enterprises to his daughters. The lines are a mismatch of Shakespearean and everyday language. I didn't expect the director to be so lenient with the original material, and the English nerd in me is having a hard time enjoying it.

Mr. Lear enters the room in a suit, followed by his three daughters, dressed in a similar fashion. I scan the stage for Amy, looking for her auburn hair, and then I see her, a vision in white. Dressed in a snowy blazer and matching pencil dress, Amy leans against the table, her face lit up by the glow of the stage lights, perfectly framed by a platinum blonde bob. It's like Mother is standing before me, and my heart begins to race.

I think back to the night that she visited me at the house. It was her, but she was younger. I feel the familiar tingle in my hands. If I don't get out of this room, I will faint. Amy steps forward, speaking to her father, but angled towards the audience. She breaks into a soliloquy, and I feel

Mother in every word she says. Then, I feel her eyes on me. It's like I am the only one in the audience. She stares right at me, and she smiles.

JP turns towards me. "She's one of the main characters? Nice."

"I need to leave," I say, making my way to my feet. I grab my purse beneath the chair. "Excuse me, sorry. Excuse me," I say as I maneuver my way down the row, bumping into knees and tripping over purses along the way. JP mutters under his breath as he follows me.

When I make it to the lobby, I collapse into an armchair. JP joins me. "What's going on?"

"Water," is all I can muster, and he runs to the bar. He returns a moment later with a plastic cup of tap water. I drink it in three gulps and then try to steady my breath. "We need to leave. Now," I say.

"Did something happen? Did you get a text from Meg?"

I shake my head no. "We just need to get home."

"Okay, but you've got to catch me up. What's going on?" He is rubbing my back and it is making me feel worse.

"Let's walk to the car. I need fresh air."

He helps me to my feet and lets me lean on his arm. We make our way to the exit, and the teenager tells us we won't be allowed to return until intermission. JP dismisses him with a wave of his hand, and we escape into the cold night.

I consult the monitor on my phone; Addison is fast asleep. I dial Meg's number, but she doesn't answer.

"We need to get back to Addison."

"I think we need to calm down before we drive home. Let's grab a coffee somewhere first, okay?"

I continue in the direction towards the lot where we parked our car. I don't know what is going on, but I'm certain I need to get back to Addison. When I see the car, I fish around in my purse for the keys.

"Jo, you can't drive like this. You're not well."

"Well, you're drunk." I wonder if, for the first time, JP regrets drinking. "Excuse me," I say, pushing past him and making my way to the driver's door.

"Seriously Jo, you can't leave like this."

"You don't have to come, but I'm driving home to Addison."

I start the car and JP trots to the passenger side. He opens the door and climbs in. "Okay, let's go, but please, just take a breath."

It Was His Fault

Sixteen years old

Cody was wasted when he pulled up to the house in his tan pick-up truck. He stuck his head out the window and raised his eyebrows, asking if Jo was coming or staying. When Jo hopped in the seat beside him, she could immediately smell the beer on his breath. She was his second choice. He had already been out with his bandmates and was forced to leave early when Jo called him in tears.

They rode in silence to the drive-in movie theatre where the new *Spiderman* film was playing. He didn't bother asking Jo why she had been crying. They watched the first ten minutes before he opened the cooler of beer that was hidden under a flannel blanket in the truck bed.

"Why didn't you answer my calls last night? Or call me back today?" Jo asked, fiddling with a bottle cap he had discarded on the floor.

"Can't we just watch the movie? Why does everything have to be so dramatic with you?" He took a swig of his beer and let out a sigh.

Finally, he gave in to her continued questions. He told her he wasn't into the relationship anymore and would rather spend his Saturday night with the rest of his buddies getting high in one of their garages. He told her he cheated on her, had hooked up with Erica from math class.

"I can't do this anymore with you. It's tiring," he said, defeated.

Jo couldn't help thinking about the timing of it all—less than a month after they had sex for the first time.

By this point he'd crushed four bottles, so Jo offered to drive home. As they drove, it started to rain, and Jo wondered if the drive-in would get washed out.

"Are you going to come into my house for a bit?" Jo asked. She wanted to talk things out. She needed closure. Was he planning on dating Erica? What did she have that Jo didn't?

"I don't think that's a good idea." He drummed a beat on the dashboard, oblivious to the fact that he'd just flattened her heart.

He asked if Amy was home for the weekend from college. Why did it matter if her sister was home? She narrowed her eyes. Had he always had a crush on Amy? Was his goal that if he hung around with her, he could get close to Amy?

Jo stepped on the gas pedal harder, letting the speedometer climb. Cody ceased his drumming and braced himself on the armrest.

"Slow down, Jo. Please."

She ignored him, flying around the corner. She didn't bother to brake as she turned onto the narrow bridge that travelled above the river.

She asked him if he still loved her. He said he wasn't sure that he knew what love was yet.

It was his fault that she veered too close to the guardrail that night. It was his fault she crashed into the river.

CHAPTER
FORTY-ONE

When I wake, the sun is too bright for my eyes. I open them slowly, one at a time, trying to get accustomed to the light. My head throbs, and nausea overwhelms me. I try to prop myself up when I hear a familiar voice. It's Meg. She rushes to my side and guides me back down.

"Take your time, Jo. You're okay, but you've been in a car accident," she says, petting my hand softly.

"What day is it?" I ask, my mouth parched. I look around and it's clear I'm in a hospital room. I'm wearing a blue gown and there is an intravenous drip inserted in my hand. Yellow gerbera daisies sit on a table next to me, their cheerful appearance mocking me.

The last time I was in a hospital was when Addy was born. *Addy*. "Where's Addy?" I ask, finally pushing myself to a seated position.

Meg fiddles with a button on a cord and the head of the bed rises to meet me. "She's okay. She's at your house. Amy's watching her."

"Amy?" I ask. "She's performing her play."

I left her play, but I don't remember why. I remember going to dinner. I think I only had one drink. JP had more than enough for both of us. We walked to the theatre and waited in the lobby. I think we went into the auditorium to sit down. Perhaps I felt sick? I recall leaving in a rush, but I don't remember the drive home.

"Sweetie, that was last night. You and JP were in a car accident driving home from the play."

Yes, that's right. I drove home and JP came with me. "Is he okay?"

"He's here, too."

I look around the room. There is no sign of him. Maybe he went to get coffee. "He's in the ICU. They are doing everything they can. He hasn't woken up yet,

but they are very hopeful," she says.

My stomach tightens. "I think I'm going to be sick," I say, and I scan the room for something I can use other than the vase holding the daisies.

Meg passes me a cardboard bed pan and gets into position to hold my hair back. After I'm done, I wipe my mouth. "Was it my fault? The accident? Do you know what happened?"

"It was not your fault." She sits back down on the chair next to my bed. "A complete fluke, really. Your tire came loose, and you lost control of the car."

This doesn't seem real. I might be dreaming. I close my eyes long and hard, expecting to be in my bedroom when I open them again. I'm not. I am still very much in the hospital, Meg staring back at me with puppy dog eyes.

"Do you want to try and drink some water?" she asks, passing me a Styrofoam cup with a straw.

I take a sip and welcome the cool liquid. "Was there anyone else?"

Meg shuffles her seat closer to my bed as if she didn't hear the question. "Anyone else?"

"Involved in the accident. Did we hit another car?"

"Oh, no. You didn't," she assures me. "You hit a telephone pole, actually."

I nod. It wasn't my fault. It was a fluke. JP will be okay. They are hopeful.

"Can I see JP?"

"Let me go see if someone can grab your doctor."

A few minutes later, a young woman wearing scrubs and a white overcoat enters the room, followed by Meg. The doctor smiles at me and makes her way to my bed.

"Hi, Joanna. I'm Dr. Volchuk." She presents a small flashlight, which she shines into each of my eyes. It's even brighter than the sunlight. "How are you feeling?"

"Sore. My head hurts. Everything kind of hurts."

"Yes." She nods again. "That's certainly to be expected. You have some bruising and lacerations from the airbag deploying, and you've sustained a severe concussion."

"That doesn't sound good," I say, looking at Meg for a second opinion.

"You lost consciousness following the accident, which is typical with more severe concussions. Are you still having trouble remembering the accident?"

"Yes," I say reluctantly, aware that these answers might affect my discharge.

"Memory loss is common with a grade three concussion—generally surrounding the event and potentially with your short-term memory. We'll keep you overnight to continue to monitor, but you can likely go home tomorrow. I understand that you have a little one at home."

I nod. I hope Amy will bring Addison to see me today. I don't think I can wait until tomorrow. I need to express my milk desperately, my breasts engorged after missing a couple of feedings. I wonder if she's feeding her formula. I don't have any milk in the freezer.

"I'll come back and check on you later. A nurse will bring you some medication for the pain."

Meg follows her out of the room.

My eyes are heavy, and I let them close.

When I open them again, a nurse is in my room, fiddling with something on the table beside me. She slides a paper tray over that resembles a muffin liner, containing two pills.

"Acetaminophen," she says. Then she passes me my water cup. "For the pain." She swivels the table that was beside me, so that it now lies across the bed above my lap. "Your lunch is here, too." She leaves the room once I've swallowed the pills.

The daisies have been moved to the window ledge and the blinds are lowered. If it wasn't for the lunch in front of me, I'd have no idea what time it is. I poke around at the tuna casserole. I eat a few bites and then the apple sauce and dinner roll. The nausea returns, and I regret eating all that food. I push the table away but my ribs ache in the process.

With some time alone, I inspect the body parts that are visible to me. My forearms are bruised and almost look burned, likely from the airbag. I probably threw my arms up to block my face. My upper body feels achy all over, but my head is the worst—a constant throbbing consumes me and makes it hard to focus on anything. My milk has begun to leak and two wet circles have formed where my nipples are. I pull my sheet up for cover.

Meg enters the room holding a cup of coffee. "Oh good, you're up. I was debating waking you because I couldn't stand the thought of you having to eat cold tuna casserole."

"Sorry, I fell asleep again, I guess."

"Don't apologize. You're supposed to be resting. Do you want me to open the blinds?"

"Sure."

The room is once again bright, but it doesn't hurt my eyes as much as it did before. Meg returns to the seat beside the bed, holding a card and a small pink gift bag. She hands them to me. "Amy brought this in when she came to see you last night."

"Amy's been in? I don't remember that."

"Yeah, I stayed with Addy overnight and Amy came here after her play. She said you were asleep. When it got late, she went home to get some rest."

I open the card first. It was clearly purchased at the gift shop because it looks very similar to the one that stands next to the daisies. The picture is a watercolor painting of some northern cardinal birds. It reminds me of something Marjorie would paint. I open the card and it's blank, leaving room for Amy's note:

I saw this at the bookstore and thought of you. I don't know if you've read it since, but I remember you clutching it closely that day. I remember everything about that day. I hope it brings you some comfort (or at least helps the time go by while you're at the hospital). Please get better soon, sis. Xoxo Amy.

Inside the bag is *The Bell Jar* by Sylvia Plath. I haven't held a copy of this book since the day Mother died. I take a deep breath and my ribs protest. I wince and Meg retrieves the items from me, placing them on the side table.

"Sorry, maybe now is not the time for gifts," she says. "Why don't you lie back down."

"It's okay; I appreciate it. Are the flowers from you?"

"Yeah, I just wanted something to brighten up your room. I know how depressing these hospital stays can be."

"They're pretty. Is Amy going to bring Addy by?"

"I don't think so. It's just—we don't have a car seat in either of our cars. Your doctor said you'll be discharged tomorrow morning. I'll come pick you up and drive you home then."

"Can we go see JP?"

"Yes, we can go if you're up to it."

After a trip to the bathroom to express my breasts and wash my face, Meg pushes me in a wheelchair to the Intensive Care Unit on the third floor. When we arrive, we check in with a receptionist and are directed to clean our hands before entering JP's room.

The lights are dim and it is quiet, save for the beeping of a few machines that surround JP's bed. He would look peaceful if it weren't for the scrapes and bruises covering his face. I understand that his side of the car took most of the impact.

A nurse advises that we can move closer and that I can talk to him if I'd like. He isn't responsive, but that doesn't mean he can't hear and understand. Meg wheels me as close to the head of the bed as possible, and I'm brought back to the accident all those years ago and the few times I visited my ex.

I had such guilt when I first saw Cody lying in the hospital bed, comatose, but by the last time I visited him, I didn't feel bad anymore. It wasn't vindication—though I'll admit, sometimes I do think about the things he said to me and the way he treated me, and I wonder whether karma played a role in it all. It was more so a feeling of numbness. If I truly allowed myself to feel everything—if I thought about how one jerk of the steering wheel propelled us head-on into the guardrail and had rendered Cody completely helpless for the rest of his life—I don't think I'd be able to get up in the morning.

Looking at JP is different. I feel pity, I feel remorse, but mostly, I ache for Addison. I don't even want to consider the possibility of her not growing up with her father like I had to. The crash wasn't my fault, but something doesn't feel right about the tire. I don't know if I can accept this as a freak accident. Something in my gut tells me there's more to it. I need to remember what happened last night.

"Can I touch his hand?" I ask the nurse.

"Yes, you can hold his hand if you'd like. Some people remember feeling comforted by that after they gain consciousness."

I gently lift his hand and place mine beneath it, our palms now pressed together. "JP, it's Jo. We were in an accident last night. I'm so sorry. But you're going

to be fine. We're going to get through this."

It feels weird not hearing a response in return; JP always has something to say.

"I'm staying here, too. Just two floors up. Addy is at home with Amy. Meg is also here."

Meg approaches the side of my wheelchair. "Hi, JP. It's Meg. The team here is taking excellent care of you. You are in great hands. Your parents are flying in today, and they'll be visiting shortly."

I hadn't even thought about Margot and Louis. Their only son in a coma in the ICU. I'm thankful that Meg has called them. I would not have wanted to deliver that news, especially since I was the one behind the wheel. I grab Meg's hand and squeeze it.

We stay for another half hour, and then I run out of things to say and grow exhausted. Meg wheels me back to my room. It is close to two in the afternoon. She says she will stop by my house to check on Amy and Addison and will return tomorrow morning to drive me home. I thank her and settle back into my bed. I drift off to sleep thinking about Addison, who must be wondering where I am. I'm hopeful I'll remember everything about last night when I wake.

READING SYLVIA PLATH

Sixteen years old

Jo's jeans rubbed the fresh wound. It had become an itchy sting, like scratching a mosquito bite too hard. She really should have sterilized Mother's nail file before she decided to drag it across her inner thigh.

Amy and Mother walked ahead, Amy filling Mother in on the play she was rehearsing. *At college they had a costume department and a costume designer who measured the actors and would sew something from scratch.* Mother listened intently because she was truly interested. Jealously grew inside Jo like an illness, and she didn't know who of—Mother, because Amy wanted nothing more than to make her proud, or Amy, because Mother was always proud of her.

They headed upstairs in the library to the fiction section. Everyone split up. Meg wanted to scour the magazine section, and Amy had her eye on a Russian author that her new guy was into. Jo found Sylvia

Plath's *The Bell Jar* and decided to read the first chapter on the secluded second-floor landing. She settled into the stained floral bench, leaning back against the marked-up wall. She rested her arm on the windowsill that overlooked the park.

Three pages into the book, Mother spotted her and approached with a stack of her own selection.

"Sylvia Plath?" she asked, moving closer.

"Yeah," Jo said, displaying the cover.

Mother scoffed.

"What's wrong with Sylvia Plath?"

"Don't tell me you're depressed now."

"I like her poetry. I've never read her novel."

"So cliché, Joanna. You've been moping around all day," she chuckled. "And now you are sitting in a corner of the library reading Sylvia Plath."

She shook her head and moved towards the steep staircase that led to the first floor.

Jo followed. "Mother," she called. "Mother." Her voice echoed throughout the enclosed staircase. Mother turned around on the third one.

"Please don't do anything dramatic this weekend, Joanna. We've got too much going on with Amy home."

CHAPTER FORTY-TWO

A my greets us at the door, holding Addison. A lump creeps up my throat, and I try to swallow the guilt of spending two days away from my daughter. She lets out an adorable shriek, the sound immediately warming my core. I steal her from Amy and hold her close, unable to control the sobs that follow.

I am overjoyed at the thought of being reunited with her, but worried JP is not here with me. I know we aren't in a good place, but he's still Addy's father.

Amy squeezes my shoulder and then extends her arms out. "I was just about to change her diaper. Why don't we go upstairs, and we'll get you settled in your room?"

Reluctantly, I pass Addy back to Amy. I understand I'm still weak and lightheaded, but I'm her mother. I should be changing Addy's diaper. I miss kissing the soles of her feet as she lies on the changing table. Meg nods in agreement and helps me up the stairs. Amy and Addison follow closely behind.

They reveal the plan moving forward through cautious words barely above a whisper—Meg and Amy will take shifts staying at the house with me and Addison until I recover—doctor's orders. They will also drive me to the hospital for regular visits with JP. Amy will take the first shift today and Meg will return this evening, so that Amy can perform in her play. Meg will stay the night in the guest room, and I will sleep in my bed.

Amy joins me in my room after she puts Addison down for her nap. I fiddle with my hospital bracelet, trying to rip it off. It makes me feel like I'm still a patient. I want to get back to our routine as quickly as possible. I want to feel like I'm in control again.

Amy places two pills on the nightstand along with a glass of water.

"Nurse Amy here." She laughs in a higher pitch than usual, and I suspect she is uncomfortable. "You can take these every four to six hours. Don't go operating machinery though, okay?" She sits down on the bed. "Sorry, bad joke. How are you feeling? Meg said you don't remember much from that night."

I nod. "I remember our dinner and going to your play. I'm sorry I missed it. I know I left in a rush. Maybe I felt sick." I try to lighten the mood. "I did have those questionable chocolate mints they were selling."

She laughs, and then her smile fades. "Jo, I lied to Meg. I told her that when I came to see you that night at the hospital, you were asleep the whole time. Truth is, we spoke. You were out of it, on pain medications, but you kept talking about JP."

I don't remember any of that. I scour my brain for the puzzle pieces that make up that night but cannot locate any conversation with Amy.

"JP?" I ask. "What about him?"

She wets her lips and then shakes out her shoulders like she is warming up at rehearsal. She takes both of my hands in hers, and I make note of how cold they are.

"You said that it was him. That he had been messing with you all this time. The sleeping pills, Addison's kidnapping. I don't know how you discovered it, but I think that's why you left the play in a hurry."

I shake my head. That can't be right. My stomach twists into a knot. No, that doesn't sit well. What could I have discovered that night to make me think that? "Do you think the accident was—?"

"Not really an accident? I don't know. It is strange that your tire came off. It seems a bit coincidental. I talked to Rich, and he said that the likely cause would have been loose lug nuts. It's possible for them to loosen over time, but it's also possible to loosen them yourself." She lets the thought linger in the stale air of my bedroom.

"Why would he do that and then get into the car with me?"

She shrugs. "I have no clue. I'm just telling you what you told me. You were convinced JP had something to do with it all. Maybe he thought it would look suspicious ... similar to the accident you and Cody had?"

I can't imagine JP putting his life at risk in the off chance it would look like I was responsible. He thinks far too highly of himself to do that. I need time to remember everything. It will come back to me; I know it will. I just need time.

"I should get some rest," I say and lie down.

She nods once, barely noticeable. "Don't forget to take your medication. It will be wearing off soon." Then she leaves me to contemplate everything I've just learned.

———ello———

I roll onto my stomach, hoping the new position will ease my pounding head. I dozed off for a while, and it's been too long between medications. I feel for the pills and the water glass that Amy left on the table beside me.

The sound of faint singing travels from Addison's room. Soft and gentle, a lullaby. I slowly stand, my head spinning, and steady myself by holding onto the wall. With careful steps, my aching body makes its way down the hall toward the nursery. I push open the door a crack and Amy and Addison come into view, rocking in the chair by the window.

Amy kisses her forehead. "Hush little baby, don't say a word, Mama's gonna buy you a mockingbird."

She looks up and notices the door ajar. "Jo, is that you?"

I push the door open wider.

"What are you doing in the hallway? Come in. Addison just woke up," she says.

I take a step into the room, feeling strangely unwelcome. "I just woke up too. Heard you singing."

"Sorry, I hope we weren't being too loud." She bounces Addison on her knee and Addy lets out a giggle. "And if that mockingbird don't sing, Mama's gonna buy you a diamond ring." Amy returns my stare. "Do you remember that lullaby? Mom used to sing it before bed."

"No, I don't remember that at all," I say, but she is no longer focused on me.

She holds Addison on her lap, her arms wrapped around Addy's back. "And if that diamond ring is brass, Mama's gonna buy you a looking glass." Amy kisses my daughter softly on the forehead and then rubs their

299

noses together. "And if that looking glass gets broke, Mama's gonna buy you a Billy goat."

A strange feeling grabs me by the throat, suffocating me, and I am compelled to protect Addison. I move farther into the room. "You take a break, Amy. You've done so much. I'll take over now."

Amy keeps her eyes fixed on Addison and then smacks her lips together repeatedly, pausing occasionally to make a surprised face. Addy giggles each time, unaware of the tension building in the nursery. "No worries. I'm enjoying this. Why don't you have a bath?"

I step closer, now in arms reach of them. "I'd like to spend some time with Addy." I hold out my hands, but Amy ignores me.

"Seriously Jo, have a bath." Her voice comes out sharp and assertive. She softens slightly. "You smell like hospital. When you're done, you can take over, okay?" She directs her attention back to Addison. "Hush little baby, don't you cry, Mama's gonna sing you a lullaby."

I stand a couple feet away from them, watching Amy hold my daughter like she is her own. Watching her play house. An ache grows in the pit of my stomach, and my limbs feel like paperweights. Once again, my body betrays me. I stumble backward, reaching for the crib to steady myself. I grab hold of the ledge just in time. *Don't faint, Jo.*

Then, as if I'm looking through a slide viewer, with a click, everything I've forgotten returns to my mind's eye. The night of the play. I remember how Amy looked in the spotlight. The white dress, the blonde wig—Mother's twin.

"Jo, you're so pale. Are you okay?"

Amy was in the house that night while I slept on the couch. She escaped through the back door with the diaper bag. She threw it in the yard and left the gate open. I didn't hallucinate. I didn't sleepwalk. It wasn't Mother.

"You ... it was you." The words get caught in my throat.

Amy looks at me with wide eyes and pulls Addison closer to her chest.

"You were here. I thought you were Mother, but it was you."

"What are you talking about? You're not making sense."

How could I have missed this? It was Amy. That hot summer day—the day that got me into this whole mess with Child Services, Amy woke me up with her call. It was only then that I realized Addison was on the porch. Amy arrived soon after because she was close by—maybe just around the corner.

"Did you call Child Services?"

"Jo, you're scaring me." She rubs Addison's back in a frantic circle.

She had known we were napping. She had a key to get in. I clasp my hand to my mouth. "Did you move Addison outside that day, in that heat?"

"Jo, you're talking about something that happened months ago. I think you need to go rest. You're delirious."

She always had a key to get inside. She had access to the baby monitor on her phone. She knew when it was having connection issues, scheduled updates. My legs can no longer hold my weight and I let myself sink down to a seated position, still grasping one of the crib rungs.

"I trusted you, Amy. I trusted you with my baby." The words escape my raspy throat in sobs.

Amy rises from the chair. "I need you to calm down."

The kidnapping must have been her, too. She waited until I showered to get Addison. She knew the monitor wasn't working, and she took her, and left her in the park. She made me think that my daughter had been kidnapped. She made me sick with worry, and then pinned it on me, like I could ever leave Addison.

I could never hurt my own daughter.

"It's always been you, hasn't it? You kidnapped Addy. You made it look like I abandoned my own daughter at the park."

The car and the vandalism. I had called her the night of the karaoke bar and left a message about JP's infidelity. She must have keyed our car when she arrived that morning with the cake. I rub my fingers together and wiggle my toes to get the circulation back.

Don't do this now, Jo. You need to keep it together, for Addison.

The slides continue to click in my mind; one after another they appear.

The night she came over with soup, she let herself out while I slept on the couch. It would have been easy for her to move the stroller and my purse to the end of the driveway. All this time, she was the one I confided in the most. She had every opportunity, and she had my complete trust.

Amy closes the gap between us, clutching Addison like she never plans to let go

of her.

"Give her to me," I shout between cries.

"Jo, you're scaring me. You're scaring Addison. Just calm down. I'm going to put

Addy in her crib and then we are going to talk about this, calmly."

She places Addison in the crib, and Addy lets out sharp cries at the betrayal.

"I trusted you," I say as I back up, crab crawling towards the doorway. What is she planning to do now that I know? When will Meg be back?

"Jo, you're speaking nonsense. Take a breath." Amy inches toward me.

I pull myself to my feet with the help of Addison's dresser. "Why did you do it?" I ask, fearing the answer.

"I didn't do anything. Your mind isn't right. It was JP, remember? You told me JP was behind everything."

I back up, my bare feet stepping onto the smooth hardwood of the hallway. The pins and needles work their way up to my ankles.

"I think you should go back to your bed and lie down," she says.

"I'm not going to bed while you're here. What are you planning to do?" I swing open the linen closet and rise onto my tiptoes, stretching to reach the Maglite flashlight on the top shelf. I only expel my breath once I clutch the cold metal in my hands, my fingers turning white with my intense grip.

"What do you plan to do with that?" Amy asks, her hands splayed in front of her face. "Relax, okay? Your meds must not be right."

The medication—are they even painkillers? Did she put something in my water? Was she the one drugging me this whole time?

"Were the sleeping pills yours? Did you plant them in Margot's bag?" I ask, hoisting the flashlight up for protection.

"You're overreacting." Her eye twitches. "Put the flashlight down!" she yells. Then her voice softens, "Let's go to your room and sit down, okay?"

Addy's cries persist from the nursery, and I think about making a break for it. Amy catches my glance and shakes her head as a warning. "Leave Addison out of this, okay? Let's go talk this out."

"Tell me what's going on!"

She paces towards me, holding her hands out in front of her, and I shuffle backwards as if she holds the weapon. "Jo, it's clear you need help.

You haven't been well for quite some time. Maybe I should call Dr. Lui. Are you thinking of harming yourself?"

"What? No, I'm not. You're messing with me. You've been messing with me ever since that day."

"Jo, I need you to calm—"

"Amy!" I scream, the flashlight raised above my head. "I know!"

She freezes.

I drop the light to the ground and slide down the wall next to the stairs, my back against the door frame of my bedroom. "I know that it was you." I let out terrified whimpers that match Addison's.

Amy grabs the flashlight and rolls it down the hallway, so it is out of reach. She lets out a sigh and slumps down to my level. "Okay. I called Child Services. Someone needed to, Jo. You really aren't fit to be a mother to Addison, and I think you know that deep down."

"You don't get to decide that."

"I'm worried for Addy."

"So, you just fucked with me because you think you'd be a better mother?"

"That night you filled the bathtub with boiling water, you could have seriously injured her. You let her fall off the diaper table, Jo."

"People make mistakes."

"Mistakes? Is that what you think it is? You're showing signs. Signs that you'll end up like *her*."

I shake my head; she has no idea. She is comparing mistakes made from sleep deprivation to years of emotional abuse—which until today, she has never even acknowledged. "You're wrong. I will never be like Mother."

"You told me when Addy was born that you felt nothing. No joy, no overwhelming love. That's not normal, Jo."

"That's not fair. You're spinning my words. I confided in you when I was at my lowest. You're using that against me."

"Do you realize how many women want to be mothers but can't? How much people plan for it? You practically fell backwards into motherhood."

"It's not my fault. You can't punish me for that. You can't take her away."

"You said it yourself—you and JP rushed into this. You aren't meant to raise a child together."

"That's not what I meant. I've never regretted Addison."

Addy's cries subside until I can barely hear her at all. I try to crawl around Amy, but she raises her hand to stop me.

"It's okay to admit that being a mom isn't for you. It's better than pretending and ending up with a relationship like you and Mom."

"You have no idea what you're talking about. I would never treat Addison the way *she* treated me."

"Haven't you already?" She cocks her left eyebrow. "Or have you actually forgotten what you did? How you dropped Addison when she was two months old, like she was a sack of potatoes. You didn't think I saw that? You excused yourself to feed her. I realized you forgot your phone, so I came up to give it to you. You were rocking her on the chair, singing the lullaby and then you stood up and you just opened your arms."

The blood rushes to my head and I can hear my heart pounding in my ears. She's lying. She wants me to question everything. Maybe she's convinced herself, so it's easier to betray her own sister.

"I would never do that to Addy, and I would never do whatever the hell this is, to my sister."

She stands up and shrugs. "You're going to start to feel really dopey soon. The medication on the nightstand was valium, and I crushed some zolpidem into your water. Very soon, it will take effect, and you'll be unconscious. It will look like you couldn't handle the stress. Your husband in a coma, your diagnosed depression that Dr. Lui can attest to." She brushes my hair out of my face, tucking it behind my ear. It feels oddly maternal. "It won't hurt; don't worry. Addison will be more than fine. I will take care of her with every ounce of me."

I cover my face with my hands and look at Amy between splayed fingers. Who is this person in front of me? It's not my sister. "You can't steal my baby, Amy."

"The only other person standing in my way is now lying in a hospital bed in a coma."

It was Amy who messed with the tire. Loose lug nuts. Did she ask her mechanic husband how to make it look like an accident? "You messed with the tire?"

"I guess I was inspired by your teenage car crash. No one ever questioned whether you tried to kill Cody. Was it really an accident, Jo? My guess is that you couldn't handle that he didn't love you, just like you couldn't cope with Mom not loving you."

"It's not my fault." I look away from her. I don't want to think back to that day. I don't want to see Mother anymore and looking at Amy right now is like staring into Mother's eyes.

"I was there, Jo."

"Stop it." I stand up and move towards the stairs. I need to get out of here.

"I saw you. I know what you did."

"Amy, please."

She follows me to the landing. "I saw you push her down the stairs. You killed my mother."

It's too late. My hands are shaking again, the cold tingles enveloping my body. I can see Mother standing at the top of the stairs at the library, holding the stack of books.

"No, it was an accident."

"You ruined our family. You ruined everything for me." Amy hovers close by, like a bully taunting me. "I'm going to tell Meg, too. She deserves to know.

"It wasn't my fault!" I shout and I charge her.

She almost pulls me down with her, but I manage to grab hold of the brass railing, clinging to it as I watch her soar backwards. Her awestruck eyes meet mine seconds before her body is airborne. Her black tunic floats around her like a malfunctioning parachute.

Amy lands at the bottom of the marble stairs, unmoving.

I stare at her for a long moment then tiptoe down the stairs to get a closer look. When I reach the bottom, I nudge her with my foot. She lies still. Blood pools beneath her head. She's cracked her skull on the marble floor.

I kneel and take her hand into mine. I feel her wrist for a pulse. There is one.

Amy is alive.

With trembling fingers, I reach toward her and carefully take her head into my hands.

I close my eyes and with one swift movement, slam her skull against the floor.

Sitting on the landing, holding Addison in my arms, I wait for the cops to arrive. The shape of Amy's lifeless body looks less distinct, the longer I stare at it. Just a lump at the bottom of the marble stairs.

I didn't have a choice. I never wanted to hurt my sister, but Amy tried to kill JP. She might have hurt Addison. She told me how she had planned to murder me, to make it look like I had killed myself. I never did take the medication she left for me or drink the water. Maybe I knew, deep down, she was behind it all.

I rock with my daughter on the stairs, until Meg opens the front door, ready to relieve Amy of Joanna watch. Meg lets out a wild scream that I feel in my bones.

I tell her the truth—Amy tripped.

CHAPTER FORTY-THREE

Meg and Addison wait for me in the reception area at my therapy session. I make my way to the desk to book next week's appointment. After a couple of months, I'm finally getting used to my weekly sessions with Alice and it's comforting to know that Child Services has officially closed my case. I greet Meg, scooping Addison into my arms. Addy lets out a giggle and kisses me with an open mouth; her slobber smears across my cheek. She's been doing this lately, and it is the cutest thing I've ever experienced.

Addison will be seven months old in two days. I'm loving this age—she is sitting up now and starting to crawl. Her first tooth cut through last week and her peach fuzz is growing in thicker. She is still so fair—like Amy and Mother—but I'm starting to see more of me in her now. I think it's her nose and the shape of her face.

Outside, the snow is falling, floating like feathers that gather on the asphalt in clumps. I can't wait for Addy's first Christmas, but I'm disappointed JP isn't here to witness it. It's been six weeks since the accident, and he's showing minimal progress. He flutters in and out of consciousness, but isn't aware. Margot and Louis will make another trip to visit him for the holiday. I will time our visit so they can see Addison as well. I made two clay ornaments of Addison's handprint. I'll gift one to Margot for Christmas and reserve the other for the mini tree I bought for JP's room.

Margot calls me often, grasping for a relationship with her only granddaughter. I want Addison to have a relationship with her, too. I want her to have a grandmother who loves her unconditionally. Margot and Louis have been good to us. They'll ensure we are taken care of while JP recovers. I'm not ready to go back to work yet either. I'm still recovering from the concussion, but when the time is right, I'll be excited to reconnect with colleagues and flex my creative muscles.

Meg leads us out of the office to her parked car. "So, how'd it go today?"

I rub my cheek against Addy's and she reaches for a snowflake. "We talked more about Amy."

Meg opens the back door where Addison's car seat is secured. "And how was that?"

A lump forms in my throat. "Tough. I told her how I blame myself for her death. I never should have asked her to carry Addy's swing upstairs. Those stairs are so steep and slippery, it's no wonder she lost her balance."

I can still hear Meg's scream and Addison wailing in my arms. I shake my head to shoo it away.

310

Meg rubs my forearm. "It was just an accident. Okay? I don't want to hear you saying it was your fault again. Don't talk like that."

I buckle Addison into her car seat and then we take our seats in the front. Meg pulls out of the spot and coasts to the exit.

On the day of Amy's accident, Meg arrived at the house before the cops. I was still in a daze, processing what had transpired. Meg said we should get the story straight before they arrived—that the scene might look suspicious to an outside eye. We agreed to provide similar statements. Meg would tell a small, white lie that she had been there when it happened. That she too, had witnessed Amy's fall.

As I wipe my tears with the sleeve of my parka, I think about Mother. "Meg, do you believe in coincidences?"

Meg decreases the volume of the radio and shoots me a quick glance. "What do you mean?" The traffic light turns green and the person behind us honks for us to go through. Meg returns her gaze to the road and steps on the gas pedal.

"I don't know. Mother falling down a flight of stairs. The same thing happening to Amy."

"Jo, I don't want you thinking about this anymore, okay? Amy tripped. It was an accident. Accidents happen all the time, and we can't change them. We'll get through it. Just like we did with Mom."

She changes the subject to our upcoming Christmas dinner. Addison and I will spend it with her, Derek, and the boys. We invited Rich to join us, but he's been rather distant. He decided to move back to Australia indefinitely. It's sad to think of our family dwindling away.

When we arrive at my house, Meg helps me transfer Addison's car seat from her car to mine.

"I'm going to invest in one of these for my car. No point in us moving this one back and forth," she says.

"Sorry. Once I get clearance to drive, you won't have to do this any-more."

"That's not what I meant. I like helping. Okay?" She lifts Addison's carrier to the door, and I follow behind with the diaper bag.

"I know you do, Meg."

"I'll swing by tomorrow after my shift and we can have a coffee, sound good?"

Always Meg the caregiver, but I think that's what I need right now.

"Thanks, sis. See you tomorrow," I say, and I hug her goodbye, welcoming her familiar scent of hospital sanitizer and lavender lotion.

I unlock the door and watch as she pulls out of the driveway. Meg has always wanted me to be okay. After all those years with Mother, I think she hoped I'd be unaffected by it all, and that her sneaking me chocolate popsicles when I was sick could make up for Mother's abuse.

I lock the door behind me and release Addison from her carrier. We climb the stairs to the nursery, and I keep my focus raised on the light fixture above, away from the place where Amy took her last breath.

Addison will need a diaper change and then I'll make her lunch. I've started a few finger foods to help her develop her pincer grasp. Peas, small pieces of cheese. She's doing really well. Maybe she'll be a foodie like JP. Lunch will be followed by her afternoon nap, and I will do my best to rest so that I have energy for the remainder of the day on my own.

I lay Addison down on the changing pad and unbutton her onesie. She is wearing the next size up in diapers and I have half a box left of size twos. I can donate them somewhere. I'd hate to see them go to waste and I'm sure there's a mother who would appreciate them.

"Oh, Addy—that's a stinky one."

I blow on her belly, and a perfect laugh escapes her gaping smile.

"You're getting so big, baby girl."

After I clean her up, I carry Addison to the rocking chair to nurse. She suckles away, murmuring softly, while I stroke her head.

"My gosh, you look like her."

I doubt Addison will remember her aunt Amy. Six months old is too young for memories. Maybe she'll remember parts of her, like whenever she sees Elmo, she'll have a faint memory of Amy's impression.

That is what I'll choose to remember.

"Baby girl, I will never hurt you," I say. She looks at me as if she understands, and flashes me a knowing smile.

Mother Tripped

Sixteen years old

Jo reached down to retrieve *The Bell Jar*, which teetered on the edge of the upper step. She clutched the book to her chest, unable to move. Mother was a contorted mess on the cement floor eighteen steps below, the blood pooling beneath her head.

"What happened?" Amy yelled, and she ran down the steps to Mother.

Meg appeared on the step beside Jo. She looked at Mother's body for a long moment, then at Jo. She took Jo's head in both hands and turned Jo to face her. Meg's eyes were wide but assertive.

"Mother tripped," she said.

Jo shook her head in response.

"Mother tripped. It was an accident. Say it out loud."

"Mother tripped," Jo said.

THE END

Acknowledgments

For me, writing is a solitary endeavour—sneaking in sessions during naptimes or when the kiddies go to sleep for the night. Occasionally leveraging my insomnia for bursts of stream of consciousness, as I wildly scribble in my notebook. My path to publishing has been anything but solitary and I have so many to thank for bringing this idea, which began as a passion project on maternity leave with my firstborn, to the finished novel you've hopefully enjoyed.

To my family of five: my husband Sean Sommerville for being my champion and pushing me to finish the project I started five years ago; for your encouragement to keep going even when I had my doubts and for allowing me the time to step away and focus on this story; and to my kids Hannah, Ellie, and Calvin for making me a mother and providing me with first-hand experience to capture Jo's intense love for Addison.

To my original family of four: my mom Wendy Pickrell for being my very first reader and quite literally the opposite of Jo's mother in the story; for instilling in me a curiosity for the dark by introducing me to shows like "Unsolved Mysteries" and "Dateline" (perhaps a tad too young); my dad Bill Pickrell for showing me how to embrace literature; for encouraging our family to have reading nights together in the living room; and to my sister and childhood companion Jamie-Lee Warner for indulging in spooky stories of every medium with me.

To my first readers for your thoughtful insights and for putting up with my typos and contingency errors: my uncle and fellow author Randy Coates; dear friend Hilary Fender; my mother-in-law Beverley Barton Sommerville; good friends Melissa Howkins and Lindsay Caradonna; writing community friend and go-to editor Marion Lougheed; Flying Books writing mentor and Canadian author Amy Jones; and critique partner and creative writing classmate Nataly Shaheen.

To each member of my writing critique group "Let's Cross the Finish Line" for your attentive feedback on the manuscript, monthly virtual meetups, and for being my cheerleaders throughout every step of this process: Audrey D. Brashich; Jade Wright; Jody Gerbig; Katy Mayfair; Mary Taggart, Natalie Derrickson; and Robin Morris.

To the entire team at Rising Action Publishing Collective, which I am so proud to be a part of: the remarkable women co-founders Alexandria Brown and Tina Beier who are the biggest champions of our books and who I feel so lucky to be able to work with; the extended team at Blackstone Publishing; the editors, marketers, cover designers, publicists, film, foreign, and subsidiary rights agents and sales agents whom all contributed to bringing this story into the world; my pub-siblings and fellow Rising Action authors for creating a true community; and once again, Alex for taking a chance on me and this story.

Lastly, I want to thank the writing and reading community. My experience getting to know fellow writers and readers over the past few years has been incredibly positive. Special shoutout to the Toronto Area Women Authors community who welcomed me with open arms, the Off Topic Publishing community, and The Shit No One Tells You About Writing podcast community and hosts Bianca Marais, Cecilia Lyra and Carly Watters, whom I've had a chance to connect with and learn immensely from on social media.

ABOUT THE AUTHOR

Brianne Sommerville is a Canadian author of thrillers. She studied English literature and theatre before entering the world of public relations and marketing. She lives in Toronto with her partner and three littles under five and knows every episode of *Peppa Pig* by heart. If I Lose Her is her debut novel. Her second novel will be releasing October 2025 with Rising Action.